D0305630

'I'm on the train!'

AND OTHER STORIES

By the same author

Absinthe for Elevenses
Cuckoo
After Purple
Born of Woman
The Stillness The Dancing
Sin City
Devils, for a Change
Fifty-Minute Hour
Bird Inside
Michael, Michael
Breaking and Entering
Coupling
Second Skin
Lying
Dreams, Demons and Desire
Tread Softly
Virgin in the Gym and Other Stories
Laughter Class and Other Stories
The Biggest Female in the World and Other Stories
Little Marvel and Other Stories
The Queen's Margarine and Other Stories
Broken Places

'I'm on the train!'

AND OTHER STORIES

Wendy Perriam

ROBERT HALE · LONDON

First published in Great Britain 2012

ISBN 978-0-7090-9135-6

Robert Hale Limited
Clerkenwell House
Clerkenwell Green
London EC1R 0HT

www.halebooks.com

'Stellar' first appeared in the *Sunday Express's S Magazine*

2 4 6 8 10 9 7 5 3 1

Typeset in 10.75/14.5pt Sabon
Printed in the UK by the MPG Books Group

FOR MERYL JONES

In celebration of her lifetime's commitment to libraries:
inspiring people, enriching the community;
believing anything is possible, then actually making it happen.

'I'M ON THE TRAIN!'

'I'm on the train, Pete ... Yeah, I know it's an unearthly hour, but Jackie was mad keen to make an early start ... Yeah, 'course we're going to shop till we drop! Need you ask?'

Stephen winced at the loud, braying laugh. Mobiles should be banned, apart from strictly business calls. And ditzy shoppers should be barred from boarding rush-hour trains.

'What d'you mean, don't spend all my money? That's exactly what I intend to do!'

That laugh again – it grated. He hadn't laughed in weeks.

'Pardon...? Oh, I see. No, I don't expect I'll be back in time for that. You know what Jackie's like! But I can pop in this evening, if that's OK. Shall we say half-past eight?'

Did the wretched woman have to talk so loudly, when he was trying to concentrate? His natural instinct was to find a seat in another, quieter carriage, although it seemed unlikely in the extreme there would actually be a free one. Besides, he was more or less blockaded by a hugely overweight bloke – clearly in the running for the 'Britain's Biggest Beer-Gut Award' – wedged right-bang in front of him and all but treading on his feet. It had been standing-room only since Wadhurst and he was ashamed to admit that he'd fought an older guy for the last remaining seat. But, older or no, the guy probably didn't have an all-important job-interview and thus need to prepare his spiel one final time. Much easier to do that sitting with his papers on his lap, than clinging to a handrail and lurching to and fro. And also easier to do it in peace and quiet.

Welcome aboard this Southeastern train service to London, Charing Cross, calling at Tunbridge Wells, High Brooms, Tonbridge, Sevenoaks.....

'Pete, are you OK? You don't sound your normal self. I hope you haven't gone down with some bug. There's this sickness-and-diarrhoea thing doing the rounds at present and....'

He sighed in irritation, having no desire to hear more about the state of Pete's gut, nor to be alternately bullied and nannied by Southeastern Trains' announcements. *Please remember to take your personal belongings with you when alighting from* ... Waste of breath. Anyone careless enough to leave their bag or briefcase behind probably wouldn't be listening anyway. *If you see anything suspicious, please inform a member of staff.* Patently impossible to fight one's way through a throng and scrum of passengers to *find* a member of staff.

'If you want to go and lie down, Pete, I can always ring back later.'

Yes, please, Pete, he prayed.

'Well, if you're sure you're OK, I would actually like a word with you about this Christine thing....'

He gave a silent groan. 'A word' was bound to mean a torrent, and it was imperative that his interview went well. His whole future was at stake – even his children's future. Toby was a mere two years away from university entrance, which would mean crippling tuition fees. And Karen's ballet lessons were an increasing drain on the depleted family finances. Worst of all, Yvonne resented her new role as one-and-only breadwinner and was becoming distinctly tetchy. Just this morning, she'd observed, in a clipped and almost threatening tone, 'If you don't get this job, then....'

Then what? Divorce? The end of the marriage? He saw himself moving into a bedsit; his kids refusing to visit; harbouring a lifelong grudge against their failure of a father.

First-class accommodation is available at the front of this train. Any customers travelling first-class without a valid first-class ticket....

He had *never* travelled first-class, and never would, at this rate. He saw himself on the streets. Forget the bedsit – he'd be lucky to find a tattered sheet of cardboard.

'I mean, it really pisses me off, Pete, when she takes that high-and-mighty line. On the other hand, we can't afford a showdown. It's just not worth the aggro and she'll only win, in any case. Or do you think…?'

He made a supreme effort to tune out the woman's voice, although it was by no means the sole distraction. The young lad on his right was tapping his fingers on his knee in time to some maddening music leaking from his earphones, while the girl on his left was crunching her way through a giant-sized bag of crisps. She, too, was overweight and her fleshy hip was overlapping his and encroaching into his space. Worse, the smell of grease was beginning to turn his stomach and, if flakes of crisp landed on his lap, it would ruin the impression he'd spent so long creating, of a smart and well groomed candidate.

Ignoring both the phone-pest and the crisp-eater, he jotted down a few more points on his pad; trying, as he had done all week, to pinpoint the exact nature of the panel's likely questions. The thing he dreaded most was a searching enquiry into why he'd been made redundant. He'd already explained in his application that it was due merely to the takeover, but suppose they went on to ask: 'Yes, but after the merger, d'you think they let you go because you weren't as good as their existing Claims Manager?'

'Listen, *twenty* people lost their jobs. It wasn't only me.'

Useless. That sounded simply peevish and defensive, when it was imperative to keep his cool. In any case, they might start probing as to why *he* been one of those twenty, after almost two decades of presumably loyal service at Taylor, Braun and Phipps. He was stuck for an answer himself. Having expended so much effort – indeed, sweated blood on their behalf – the last thing he'd expected was to be handed his cards. Had he become self-satisfied, or stale – or was he just too old? Forty-five was over-the-hill as far as recruitment was concerned. He stole a quick glance at his reflection in the window. The train was passing through a tunnel, so he could see his blurry features in the dark glass of the pane. Blurry or no, his receding hair was obvious and, if the stress of being out of work continued, he'd probably end up as bald as a ping-pong ball, and with jowls and wrinkles thrown in for good measure.

Ladies and gentlemen, a buffet-service is available on this train, serving hot and cold beverages, sandwiches, crisps, confectionary....

'Save your breath,' he muttered. Even the slimmest trolley in the world couldn't manoeuvre its way along such a crowded train. And did they have to use such outmoded terminology? The kids talked about buying sweets, not purchasing 'confectionary'; Yvonne offered him a cup of tea, not a 'beverage'. In fact, *he* had made the tea this morning, while she rushed round in a panic, late for work and sounding off at Karen for borrowing her hair-drier. He had microwaved some Ready Brek for all of them, but she'd gone dashing off with barely a goodbye; calling out that she hadn't time to eat, before slamming the front door. He'd sat staring at the bowl of greyish sludge; the mere thought of food anathema, given the churning of his stomach. Finally, he'd pushed it away, untouched, only to be chided by the kids who said that *they* weren't allowed to leave their food, so why the hell should he? The pair had bickered and squabbled all through breakfast, behaving less like teens than toddlers, and even throwing toast-crusts at each other. His whole family seemed blithely unaware that, today of all days, he needed their support. Well, if he came a cropper at the interview, they'd know the difference soon enough – no more snazzy trainers or pricey ballet-shoes; no more holidays abroad.

'Look, this is how I see it, Pete – we have to avoid a dust-up, because *we* need her more than *she* needs us. So, if it only takes one phone-call, don't you think it's worth it? .... Yeah, I know that means more hassle, but....'

Didn't this windbag feel embarrassed that the entire carriage could overhear her private conversation? Not that anyone else seemed bothered, or even to be listening. Most people were oblivious; wired up to their iPods, busy with their BlackBerries, or deep in newspapers or magazines. And, normally, he, too, could block out such irritations. However, having lain awake all night, his nerves were at breaking-point – which would hardly help his chances, of course.

He glanced out of the window, in an attempt to calm himself. The countryside was flashing past in a glaze of burgeoning green; everything at a peak of June perfection, new and fresh and lush. He longed to be outside, inhaling blossomy smells rather than stale and over-breathed air. The air-conditioning on this Southeastern service was notoriously unreliable, as he knew from past experience, so it came as no surprise that the carriage was uncomfortably hot, even at 8.30 in the morning. He imagined strolling through a shady wood, with a refreshing breeze on his face and no restricting tie and collar like a noose around his neck. Did he really want to continue working in the City, with all its noise and grime? One of his former colleagues had recently gone deaf, due to the constant din from a pneumatic drill in road-works outside the office; another had developed asthma on account of the noxious fumes. If he carried on with this daily grind, he, too, would soon go down with some London-induced disorder. Besides, according to a recent piece in the *Telegraph*, commuting was as stressful as being a fighter pilot; causing rapid heartbeat, memory-loss and dangerously high blood pressure. And even fighter pilots weren't subjected to the additional stress of people with verbal diarrhoea endlessly jabbering on mobile phones.

'Listen, Pete, it's plain stupid just to shrug this off. You don't realize how obnoxious Christine is....'

Yes, 'obnoxious' summed it up: the long hours; the stroppy claimants and their unrealistic demands; the cramped and tedious journey. Indeed, the very word 'commuter' was a turn-off in itself – and 'insurance man' was worse, with its unpleasant connotations of conformity, pernickitiness and lack of original thought.

As a boy, he'd planned on being an astronaut; venturing far beyond the confines of normal time and space; walking on the moon – or even on Mars and Venus – watching in amazement as other planets spun and hurtled past. Yet, the minute he'd left school, his dad had sat him down and given him a lecture on the importance to a family-man of safety and security; punctiliously explaining that a steady job, with the prospect of a decent pension, was more or less essential if he didn't want to end up in the doss-house. But why the hell had he acquiesced – submitted so tamely to a father who had never spread his wings and who thought it perfectly normal to live in fear of penury when he was actually well paid? He should have put up some resistance; insisted on his *own* values, rather than adopting, second-hand, the paternal creed of meek subservience. But, in shaming truth, he had never taken a stand on anything whatever – not once in his whole life – never acted wildly or impulsively, or dared to throw over the traces. And, even more pathetic, he had never slept with any other woman but Yvonne. Who knew what he was missing; what delights he might have—?

The woman beside him suddenly scrunched up the empty crisp bag; the crackling noise making him jump. Next, she opened her newspaper – not a considerately compact one like *The Times* or *Daily Mail*, but a broadsheet so intrusive, it obscured his line of sight and forced him to read it, too.

Thirty million Africans still face the threat of famine....

Police hunt ex-con after fatal stabbing in Peckham....

Students on the march against increased tuition fees....

Well, at least such headlines had brought him down to earth; made him see that, in point of fact, his father was probably right. If he expended all his energies on amassing a harem, or zooming into outer space, how would he pay the mortgage, or keep his family in food and clothes? Returning to reality – and to the task in hand – he tried to anticipate the interviewers' line of fire.

'Right, Mr Dickson, what can you offer us that we wouldn't be getting with any other candidate?'

As he ran through the answers silently, he set his face into an expression of high seriousness, combined with unshakeable confidence. 'Well, eighteen years' experience, to start with, and for the last four of those I've been running a large department and dealing with every possible—'

We are now arriving at Tunbridge Wells. Customers are requested not to leave any unattended items either in the train or on the station....

That disembodied voice was like some new, imperious God

issuing His commandments from on high. If only He would command the garrulous woman never to speak another word in her life, or hurl a convenient thunderbolt at her poncy, puce-pink phone.

'I mean, what I really hate, Pete, is people who won't admit they're wrong – and that's Christine all over. She's so pig-headed, it makes me sick! When I rang her last week, she wouldn't budge an inch, even though....'

Her phone-bill must be truly astronomical, not that she appeared to be concerned. She would probably continue babbling all the way to Charing Cross, unless, by some miracle, she got off here, at Tunbridge Wells. She hadn't actually specified that she was shopping with her friend in London, rather than some town *en route*.

He held his breath as the train rumbled to a halt and the doors hissed slowly open. But, far from her – or anyone – alighting, yet more people struggled to climb aboard; causing the ten-ton fatso to press in even closer. The guy's enormous rear-end, clad, lamentably, in tartan trews, was now a mere six inches from his chest – hardly a sight to lift the spirits. In fact, all those standing were trying, vainly, to squeeze themselves to nothing, to make room for this new influx of harassed, sweaty bodies. He was sweating himself, from nerves, and, if the heat and crush increased much more, he'd arrive malodorous and sticky, with damp patches under his arms.

He studied the sea of faces; mostly male and mostly set in grim, unsmiling masks. Apart from the tartan maverick, the standard dress was sombrely conventional. He was just one of a whole army of Identikit businessmen – all neat, all correct – so why should *he* be given the job, rather than that suave guy by the door, or the successful-looking fellow in the corner, with his handsome profile and sleek designer briefcase?

Reproaching himself for negativity, he dragged his attention back to the inquisition.

'What would you consider, Mr Dickson, to be your particular strengths?'

Ah – that he'd rehearsed a good two dozen times: 'I never tolerate a job half-done ... I'm aware of team dynamics and aim to be cooperative and flexible in all team situations ... Should a customer have a grievance, I strive to remain cool and calm, whatever the—'

'Fine. And what about your weaknesses?'

Trickier by far. He would have to tread extremely carefully, so as not to make any damaging admissions. His weaknesses of character were all too woefully apparent: passivity and over-caution; lack of audacity and forcefulness.

'You haven't a clue, Pete, honestly! Christine doesn't give a shit about you or me or....'

Who *was* this idle Pete, who appeared to have all the time in the world to natter on till doomsday; who didn't have to leave for work, or cut the conversation short, in order to earn his living? Doubtless some scrounger on benefits, whom hard-working taxpayers were forced to subsidize. Not that *he* was a tax-payer, just at present, which made it all the more essential that he got the job and stopped relying on his wife. And, now he came to think of it, why should poor Yvonne have to slave away all hours, when this airhead of a woman could run up monstrous phone-bills and splurge obscene amounts of money in the shops?

'Pete, you don't know what you're talking about! How can you possibly defend the bitch? It's obvious she's out to do us down and....'

Welcome aboard this Southeastern train service to London, Charing Cross. Our next station-stop will be Orpington.

Both voices were drowned as a train roared past in the opposite direction. He fought an urge to leap aboard and travel right to the end of the line. Then, instead of facing an interrogation, he could laze on the beach at Hastings, cool his sweaty feet in a frill and froth of waves, even recapture his childhood pleasure in building sand-castles....

'Listen Pete, if you imagine you can trust her an inch, then you're utterly deluded! I know Christine of old, remember, and I can tell you straight she's a scheming little....'

He tried to focus on the brochure on his lap, although the very name – Alpha Insurance – only seeded further doubts. He had never been an alpha male – not at five-foot-eight, with no proficiency in any sport, no record as a Romeo and—

'What d'you mean, "give it a rest"? ... OK, keep your hair on! ... Yes, I *will* ring off, but only if you promise we can discuss it later on. I'm not letting that cow win! I insist we thrash it out this evening, so I'll phone you from the station and tell you when I'm on my way, all right?'

He dared to hope. Any moment, the maddening yakkety-yak would cease and he could concentrate, at last.

'What? But I thought you said ... No, I *can't* make it ten – that's ridiculously late! ... All right, let's compromise. How about nine-fifteen?'

'Yes, fine,' he hissed, replying on Pete's behalf. But the guy had clearly had his bellyful and must be seeking some sort of let-out.

'I'm sorry, Pete, but that just won't wash! How can you say you "won't be in", when you told me, half an hour ago, that half-past eight was fine?'

He leapt to his feet and, having heaved the tartan bottom to one side, pushed and shoved the other stolid bodies out of his way, until he was standing directly over the prattling pig of a woman.

One blow sufficed. He brought his fist down with such force, she crumpled in an instant. He could hardly believe his own strength – yes, an alpha male, who could annihilate any tittle-tattling fool and escape the consequences. No one had protested; no one rushed to the woman's aid. Not that he was surprised. Commuters were famed for minding their own business and never drawing unwelcome attention to themselves.

He strutted back to his seat. Of *course* he could act impulsively, take a stand, put up a fight, refuse to be ground down. And, of *course* he would get the job. Hadn't he just demonstrated the very qualities that Alpha Insurance sought: determination, assertiveness, confident conviction? And why settle for being just their new Claims Manager, when, given time, he could be their CEO?

He leaned back in his seat with a smile of anticipation, as he began working out the details of his enviable new lifestyle. A house-move, naturally. No alpha male would deign to live in the cramped and shabby bungalow he had called home up till now. He would need a large, impressive house, with extensive gardens, front and back, a conservatory, a three-car garage.... Once Toby had passed his driving-test, he would buy the lad a sports car, and Yvonne could have a BMW, a Jaguar, a Porsche – anything she liked, in fact, including a life of leisure. And he mustn't forget his daughter. He would gladly pay her fees at whatever swanky ballet-school she fancied and, as for ballet-shoes and tutus, she could stockpile them in shedloads and he wouldn't turn a hair.

He returned the jotter to his briefcase, along with the Alpha brochure; closed his eyes and let himself relax. There was no more need to prepare. Words would spring to his lips spontaneously – every answer spot-on. They'd immediately cancel all the other poor sods' interviews and he'd be swept into the chairman's office to celebrate with champagne; maybe even—

'Pete, I've told you ten times already, if you take that line with Christine, she'll simply walk all over us! Yes, I know I said I'd leave it, but no way will I ring off till you begin to see some sense.'

Startled, he looked up. The woman was unscathed; her whiney voice as shrill and intrusive as ever; no trace of blood or bruising on her face; no damage to her vocal cords. He glanced around the carriage. Nothing had changed at all. Those busy on their BlackBerries and laptops were still assiduously at work; the guy with the iPod still drumming his fingers in time to the vacuous music; the girl on his right now abandoning her newspaper to bite into a Mars bar, scattering chocolate crumbs dangerously close to his lap.

He froze. He was so cowed, so shocked, even his breathing seemed to have stopped, and he didn't dare to raise his eyes from the dirty blue of the floor until the train pulled in at Orpington. And there – abjectly, politely – with apologies to left and right, he squeezed his way through the crush of bodies and alighted on the platform. He stood a moment, motionless, feeling strangely chilled in the oppressive morning heat. Then, with a sigh of resignation, he crossed the footbridge to the other side and checked the times of the down-trains. According to the departure-board, there was over half an hour to wait for one that stopped at Wadhurst, which meant he wouldn't be home till mid-morning. Still, with the kids at school and Yvonne at work, at least he'd be alone in the house – the *bungalow*, he corrected himself; knowing how perilous it was to harbour ideas above one's station. So, once he had washed and changed, he would have plenty of time to work out what to tell them and just where to put the emphasis.

Pacing up and down the platform, he began rehearsing his lines right away; seeing in his mind the circle of expectant faces: his wife's, his son's, his daughter's; their hopes and dreams all resting on his heavy-burdened shoulders. It was essential that he retained their respect and didn't come across as a loser, so he must stress how well the interview had gone; how he'd actually been congratulated on a highly creditable performance, and hadn't, once, been lost for words, or failed to supply incisive answers. Nor had he forgotten the importance of judicious eye-contact and assertive body-posture. In short, he had done his absolute best.

But then had come the shocking revelation: he had discovered, later on, from another unsuccessful candidate, that the whole thing had been a stitch-up: they'd already decided to give the job to one of their own executives, and thus the interviews were just a sham; laid on simply for the sake of keeping up appearances by following empty protocol.

Yes, of course he was completely gutted and of course it was unfair – downright scandalous, in fact. But, now that he'd had more time to reflect, he had come to see it was self-defeating to allow himself to get worked up, or lose time and sleep on pointless recriminations. One just had to take the view that some companies were venal, some CEOs corrupt; put the matter down to experience and try again, elsewhere. His family would be proud of his maturity, his resilience and calm acceptance in the face of rank duplicity.

Wouldn't they?

CHARMED LIFE

'So tell me about yourself, Jo.'

She stared down at a breadcrumb on the tablecloth, unsure what to say. She was like that crumb – just an unimportant speck – so there was nothing much to tell. Anyway, she wasn't good at words and her voice might come out rude and loud, just because of nerves. The people at the nearby tables were speaking very softly, like you were meant to do in church. And they were all scary-grand and talked posh, so they might think she was common.

But her silence didn't seem to matter, because, after just a short while, the man went on talking himself. He seemed to like to talk; had been talking ever since they met.

'Remember I told you I was in Nigeria, working as a DO? Well, in 1955, I was transferred to Kenya and promoted to DC, which was how I came to....'

It was hard to understand him. What was a DO, or a DC?

'I was barely twenty-eight at the time, and although you may not realize, Jo, it's pretty rare for a chap to be DC before he's thirty, at the earliest. But then I've always been a high-flier. Even as a little lad, I wanted to be Prime Minister!'

He gave a big gaping laugh, which showed his three gold teeth. He must be very important, wanting to be Prime Minister and having real gold teeth.

'Of course, I was doing a damned good job as DO, so, when they needed someone tough to take charge of a large area in the very heart of the Mau Mau uprising, I was their obvious choice. They stationed me up-country in the White Highlands – a town called

Nyeri, which has grown much bigger recently. In those days, it was....'

He'd been all over the world; places that made her mind ache. Her own world was very small. There was Lockerley, where she lived, and Bournemouth, where they went by coach in summer, and now London, the big, frightening place, where she'd arrived very late last night. When he'd stopped her in the street, this morning, and asked what she was doing trailing round, with no proper coat, in the middle of November, she'd said nothing for a while. If she admitted that she'd run away from Sunnyhill, she knew he'd send her back, so, in the end, she'd told him the truth: that she was looking for her mother. She hadn't known how hard it would be to find just one special person, when there were such crowds of people everywhere; strangers bumping into you and not saying they were sorry. *He* was a stranger, too, although he'd been very kind and bought her tea – proper tea in a teapot, with a silver jug, for the milk, and something called a tea-strainer. And, afterwards, they'd come here to have dinner – except she mustn't call it dinner. He'd told her, twice, it was 'luncheon'.

'I took up my post in the very thick of the violence, and, of course, the White Highlands were the spark that set off all the trouble in the first place.'

She didn't know what trouble he was talking about, or where the White Highlands were. There were Highlands in Scotland, but they were grey, not white. Anyway, it wasn't easy to listen, because words always went too fast for her and left her miles behind. And she was distracted by the room: the biggest dining-room she had ever seen – even in a film – with huge windows and a painted ceiling and waiters wearing evening dress. The place was called a club – *his* club, he'd said, which meant he must be terribly rich, because it was enormous, like a palace, with loads of rooms, and several different staircases, and pictures in gold frames – even mirrors in gold frames; mirrors big enough for giants. When she'd first seen the great tall building, with two stone lions outside and a huge wooden door, like a church, she was sure they'd send her packing from such a fancy place. But he took her arm and led her up the steps and a man in a black uniform hurried forward to greet them and called them 'sir' and 'madam' and even gave her a little bow, like she was the Queen.

'I have to say it was a really hairy time, but, of course, there was bound to be conflict, sooner or later, since the Kikuyu were determined to grab the white settlers' farms – and to use any means to do so, however barbarous.'

He was eating while he spoke and sometimes little shreds of food sprayed onto the tablecloth, glistening with his spit. She didn't like the food here and most of it she'd never even heard of. The waiter had brought them both a menu – a big one, with stiff covers, like a Bible – but the words inside were weird: things like bisque and grouse and whitebait and ceviche. And, in any case, she was used to big black letters, not squiggly writing with lots of loops and curls. So she'd pretended to be thinking and just sat quietly for a while. He had chosen the whitebait, which were tiny dead brown fish, with their heads and tails still on, and coated in greasy crumby stuff, a bit like Kentucky Fried, but with a nasty fishy smell. After what seemed ages, she'd seen a word she *did* know – soup – so she'd said she'd have the soup, please. But it wasn't like the soup they had at Sunnyhill. They'd put a lot of cream on top, which turned it a funny colour, and also little bits of bread-stuff, hard, like leftover toast.

'But, d'you know, despite the dangers, I never received so much as a scratch. I reckon I live a charmed life, Jo – always have, probably always will. I remember, once, when we were driving over the Aberdares, on our way to Naivasha....'

She wished he'd go more slowly. A minute ago, he was in the Highlands; now he was somewhere else.

'This is quite a tale, Jo! You'll never believe what happened. And every detail's crystal-clear, even after all these years. We were rattling along this dirt-road and a bloody great ant-bear comes lurching towards us and charges straight into the Land-rover.'

You weren't meant to say words like 'bloody', but important people always broke the rules. She wondered what an ant-bear was. There were ants in the Sunnyhill kitchen and she'd seen a bear, once, in the zoo, but ants were black and tiny and scurried everywhere, while bears were big and brown and sat around doing nothing in particular, so how could the two be both at once?

'The driver was killed outright, poor devil, and Giles was badly bruised, but *I* escaped scot-free.'

His deep, booming laugh surprised her. If the driver was dead and Giles was badly bruised, shouldn't he be crying?

'Whenever there was danger, Jo, I was the one who was spared – illness as well as accidents. For instance, everyone I knew in Kenya went down with malaria, at one time or another, but I managed to avoid it the whole time I was there. The other poor chaps were falling like flies, but I stayed as fit as a fiddle. I must have brilliant blood, I reckon!'

'Your wine, sir.'

One of the waiters had come up – a tall, scary person, all in black, who looked even more important than the man, and spoke in the same posh voice. He was carrying a bottle, wrapped in a white bandage, and the bottle had a picture on it, of a building like a castle. But the waiter was very mean with the wine and poured just a tiny drop into the man's big glass. And the man took a sip and held it in his mouth and frowned and made a face. She was frightened he might spit it out but, all at once, he swallowed it and said, 'Yes, first-rate, Piers.'

Then the waiter poured some into her glass – a lot this time, not a tiny drop. She wasn't allowed to drink, on account of all the pills. And when she took a gulp, it tasted sour and horrid, so she was glad it was forbidden.

'Another time, when I was in the bush, I was bitten by a puff-adder. My boy kept me walking up and down all night, to stop the venom taking hold. I did feel a bit off-colour, but only for a matter of days. The following week, I was right as rain. I even played squash that weekend and beat my opponent hands-down. It was partly thanks to my boy's good sense, but even so....'

She wondered how old his boy was. Quite old, most like, if he was allowed to stay up all night. It was rude to ask people's ages, so she asked, instead, if he had a lot of children.

'Lord, no! None whatever. Sadly, my wife had problems in that department. We did employ a lot of staff, though, all waiting on us hand and foot. I never had to lift a finger until I came back here. Of course, I was up to my eyes with my own work – dispensing justice and all that sort of thing. I used to hold a daily court in Nyeri, to make sure the locals were kept in line. The *watu* were very fond of stealing each other's cattle, which often led to fights, so I'd have to put my foot down and order the culprits to be caned.'

At Sunnyhill, the staff weren't allowed to cane you, however naughty you were. In the old days, though, children were beaten black and blue, so Miss Batsby said.

'I was also personally responsible for the hospitals, the prisons, the state of the roads, and general law and order. Sometimes, I'd be called out in the dead of night, to deal with an emergency or....'

He was still eating the dead fish – even the heads and tails, which meant he was eating their eyes and teeth. Once, in Bournemouth, she had seen a fish's teeth, but that fish was dead, as well. She had never seen a live fish.

'I remember, during Mau Mau, there was a really nasty incident. An entire white family were hacked to death, in the early hours of the morning. I was fast asleep, of course, but the minute I was summoned, I leapt out of bed and we drove full-pelt to the house. We arrived too late, though – found the place full of mangled bodies. Even their new-born baby had been slaughtered, *and* the poor damned dog.'

He'd seen lots of people die – first, the man killed by the ant-bear, and now a whole family and a baby and a dog. Yet he didn't seem the slightest bit upset.

'The Kenyan house-staff managed to escape. They were warned in advance, you see, and got out before the butchery. And the perpetrators were never caught. They just disappeared back into the forest and....'

At last, he finished eating and wiped his mouth on something called a napkin, which was like a small piece of the tablecloth, very white and stiff. It left a lot of greasy marks, but no one told him off. Then, he leaned forward and inspected her, close-up. He probably thought her clothes weren't right for such a fancy club, or that she shouldn't have her hair loose. Edna said it was unhygienic to have it hanging round your shoulders and dangling onto your plate. But, all at once, he smiled – a big, wide smile that showed his three gold teeth.

'You're damned pretty, Jo, d'you know that? In fact, I'd go as far as to call you a real stunner. Which is why you need to be more careful, for God's sake, or someone will take advantage. I mean, a girl your age ought to be safe at home, not wandering the streets on your own.'

She should have added on two years and told him she was eighteen, instead of sixteen-and-a-half. But it was wicked to tell lies and, anyway, she wasn't even sixteen – or only on the outside. 'Sixteen in body,' Miss Batsby had told her, on her birthday, 'but a child of ten in mind'. She *wasn't* a child. She knew a lot of things that even grown-ups didn't know and, anyway, they called her 'madam' here and you wouldn't say that to a child. The man was eighty-four – he'd told her that as soon as they met, like he was proud of being old – but said he had the constitution of someone half his age. She didn't know what a constitution was, but probably something expensive, like the wine.

'And, if you don't mind me saying so, you have a quite sensational figure. I like women who are women and have a bit of flesh on them. Most girls these days are just skin and bone – and starving themselves half the time, to try to look like fashion-models. I hope *you're* not on a diet? You haven't touched your soup, I see, but perhaps it's not to your taste. We can change it for something else, you know – the game terrine, maybe?'

She'd never heard of game terrine and, in any case, she didn't want to eat. Her last meal had been dry Weetabix, yesterday, at Sunnyhill (Dave had nicked all the milk), but running away made you scared, not hungry. She ate a piece of roll, though, to stop the man being cross. The bread was sort of greyish-brown, with little seeds on top and, when she bit into the roll, the seeds fell off onto her plate and a few fiddly ones got stuck between her teeth.

'Well, if you don't want your soup, Jo, shall we move on to our main course, or would you prefer a little pause?'

She wasn't used to so many questions. At Sunnyhill, you were told, not asked. But he must have thought her rude, because, when she didn't answer, he pushed his big, red, flabby face almost into hers and peered at her again – even closer, this time.

'Are you *OK*, my dear? Not upset or worried or—?'

'I'm fine,' she said. Safer to pretend, or he might phone Sunnyhill and make them fetch her back.

'If there's anything I can do, Jo, you only have to ask. I have time on my hands at present and would be only too glad to help. To tell the truth, retirement doesn't suit me. I was extremely lucky in that I stayed on after Independence for almost thirty years. Of course, it wasn't only luck. I'd bloody well won my spurs by then! In fact, the president himself sent word that he wanted to appoint me a magistrate – a huge relief, I can tell you. You see, I assumed I'd have to leave the country, which would have really been a blow.'

He took another gulp of wine, then let out a great sigh. 'But it couldn't last for ever, alas. There comes a time when you're considered just too ancient and no one wants you around. Although it's damned difficult to take a back seat, when you're used to being kingpin.'

She knew all the kings and queens of England, because they were on the wall at school. There wasn't a King Pin.

'Still, old age comes to all of us, so we just have to accept it. But, listen, Jo, let's focus on you, for a change. I must admit I am a little concerned as to why you're alone in London. Please don't think I'm prying, dear, but perhaps you could enlighten me as to why you're looking for your mother. What exactly happened to her?'

She picked up a seed and swallowed it, wondering what to say. Miss Batsby had explained that some mothers couldn't cope if their babies were born with problems. It didn't mean Mother didn't love you; it just meant you were looked after in a home. She wasn't sure what kind of problems she had, but Dave had called her a halfwit, so maybe it was that.

'Well, if you'd rather not discuss it, I completely understand. Mothers are a tricky subject, aren't they? My own mother passed away when I was just a little sprog. Consumption, sad to say. There were no decent drugs in those days, more's the pity. And my dear wife died young, as well.'

He looked so sad, she thought he was going to cry, but, instead, he beckoned to another waiter, who came bustling over to take away their plates. The two seemed to know each other, because they chatted for a while and the waiter called him Mr Hornby-Phillips.

She wished *she* had two surnames, or at least a longer first name. Short names made you weak. Josie would be better and Joanna better still. But there was already a Josie at Sunnyhill *and* a Joseph, too. Sunnyhill was a lie. There was no hill anywhere and the house was so dark you hardly ever saw the sun.

'My wife was the most stunning woman I'd ever met – and I'd met quite a few, I can tell you! In fact, you remind me of her in some ways – the same fair hair and dark eyes, which I've always thought the perfect combination. And the same English-rose complexion. She was called Rose, actually – Rose Anastasia Louise.'

Lucky to have three names and one of them so long. *His* first name was Lionel. While they were having tea, in the teapot, he'd kept saying 'Call me Lionel'. But he was so old and rich she didn't feel she should, and she hadn't known his surname until now. He looked nothing like a lion, because he had just a few wisps of white, straggly hair, instead of a thick, brown mane. But he had seen real lions, he said – many times, and not in zoos. He had even shot a lion, although he didn't seem to mind about it dying. There'd been a lot of lions today: stone lions, real lions, dead lions....

The waiter had come back now, with their dinners on a silver tray. The man had ordered duck, but she fed them every Sunday, so she wouldn't want to eat one. She had found it very difficult to choose, so, in the end, he had ordered her a steak. It didn't look like steak, because it was covered with thick yellow sauce, like custard. She scraped off all the custard and cut into the meat, but a trickle of red blood oozed out. They must have forgotten to cook it, so she ate the chips instead. They weren't called chips, he said, which she couldn't understand, because they tasted just the same as the chips in McDonald's. She wished they'd gone to McDonald's, instead of to his club.

While he ate, he kept pulling at his nose, which was red and sort of squashed and had little, bristly hairs sticking out of the end of it. And he drank the rest of the wine, although he didn't pour it himself. The waiter did that for him and, every time he came over, he and the man had another little chat. She was glad about the little chats, because then she didn't have to talk. Even at Sunnyhill, she preferred to sit in silence, so that the others didn't laugh when she muddled up her words. Except there was never really silence. Everybody shouted and there were always fights and quarrels.

'But, to return to the subject of retirement, a chap like me is bound to feel a little spare when he's thrown on the scrapheap, so to speak. I've dealt with really weighty matters, in my time, and had people's actual lives in my hands, so it's something of a comedown to be reduced to deadheading roses and pottering round the garden.'

Roses were her favourite flowers. She even liked the thorns. It wasn't just plants that had thorns; people had them, too. She could feel her own thorns, sometimes, growing sharp inside her.

'Well, my dear, I can see you're not much of an eater! I've polished off my duck and all these delicious vegetables, yet you've barely eaten a mouthful of your steak. Never mind – just leave it, if you want, and we'll have a look at the puddings, shall we? Perhaps you have a sweet tooth?'

At Sunnyhill, you weren't allowed pudding unless you'd finished your meat, so he must be very kind. And the puddings were dished out, straight onto your plate, but here you had to choose one from a big silver trolley-thing. The waiter wheeled it over, like a pram.

'Anything there you fancy, Jo?' the man asked.

Her favourites were jam tart and Arctic Roll, but he said they didn't have those here and she didn't know the names of the puddings on the pram-thing, so she just stared down at her hands. He must have taken pity on her, because he asked the waiter what he'd recommend.

'Well, the sherry trifle always seems to be a favourite with the ladies.'

'Hear that, my dear? How about some trifle?'

Trifle was wet, with too much soggy sponge. The waiter was pointing to the trifle on the trolley, but she couldn't really see it, because of all the cream on top. She didn't want more cream. Her tummy felt frothy and runny, as if Edna was beating it up with a fork, like she did with scrambled eggs.

'And the mango sorbet is always very popular. In fact, it's one of the chef's specialities. The mangoes were flown in just this morning, madam, from Ecuador.'

'Yes, I think you'd like that,' the man said. 'It's rather like ice-cream.'

It would be rude to say no, when he was taking so much trouble, so she said 'Yes, please', instead. And the waiter passed her a small silver dish, with three round orange balls inside. There was even a silver saucer-thing, underneath the dish, and a silver spoon with a crown on the handle, like the ones the Queen must use. The orange stuff inside the dish looked nothing like ice-cream, but perhaps it was the Queen's ice-cream and queens ate different kinds. At Sunnyhill, ice-cream was white, not orange, and they put it out long before the meal (in plastic bowls, not silver), so it was always soft and squashy, never hard and round. She dug in the spoon, to try a bit, and it *was* cold, like ice-cream, but not as sweet or smooth, and there were little frozen splinters in it that made her back teeth jump.

'And what for you, sir?'

'I'll have the pannacotta, please – and another bottle of wine. The *Chateau Suduiraut* was exceptionally good last time.'

Pannacotta sounded weird but, when it came, it was small and pale and wobbly, like blancmange. He made her taste some, from his own spoon, which you weren't meant to do, because it gave you germs. It didn't taste of anything, just quiet and faint, like clouds. He also asked her to try the wine, which was yellowish, this time, instead of blackish-red. He said she'd love it, because it was sweet, but it *wasn't* sweet, so he drank it all himself, again. And, although he went on talking, his words sounded rather funny now, like they'd melted in a frying-pan.

'To tell the truth, Jo, when I came back to England, I felt totally adrift. I mean, I'd never so much as cleaned my own shoes or boiled a bloody egg – which is why I thank God for *this* place. But it's going downhill, I'm sorry to say, like everywhere else in the modern world. Once, you used to see a decent class of person here, but they tend to be more business types these days – so-called company directors, who think they own the world, but are really little more than brash young tykes. And they certainly wouldn't want to pass the time of day with a tedious old chap like me. When I first became a member in 1986, I could count on seeing my friends, but a lot of my former chums have fallen off the twig, poor devils. In fact, sometimes I can sit here all damned day – *and* all evening, too – and not speak to a single soul except the staff.'

She felt so tired, it was hard to listen. What she'd really like would be to lay her head on the tablecloth, shut her eyes and go to sleep. Last night, she hadn't slept at all. You couldn't sleep in London. It was too noisy and too scary and no one seemed to go to bed. But it would be rude to close her eyes while he was talking, so she left them open and thought about her mother. Perhaps tomorrow she'd bump into her, and her mother would take her home – a real home, with no rules, or pills, or punishments, or fights. And they could cuddle up together in a big, warm, comfy bed and have nice, quiet, peaceful meals. And her mother would say, 'I'm so glad you came to find me, Jo. I don't mind about the problems anymore, so why don't we live together, from now on?'

She had never known a dinner take so long. At Sunnyhill, meals were over in ten minutes, because everybody ate fast, so they could get down from the table. But this dinner had lasted hours and, just when she thought it was finished, the waiter had asked if they would like to take their coffee upstairs in the library. Usually, you weren't allowed to eat or drink in libraries, but this library was quite different from the one they used in Romsey. It was smaller than the other rooms, but every bit as grand, and there were no big desks with computers on, where kind ladies stamped your books. And the books were different, too – brown, boring ones with no pictures in and far too many words. And it had sofas, like a sitting-room; shiny-brown and made of the same stuff as shoes. And there was a wooden sort of ladder-thing, which the man told her people used to reach the highest shelves. But there were no people in the room – just the two of them, alone.

Even the waiter had gone, although first he'd brought them something called 'liqueurs', in two tiny, tiny glasses, as if he was being mean again. She had tried a sip, to please the man, but it tasted really horrid, so now he was drinking hers. All the drinks must have made him very hot, because there were little drops of sweat on his forehead; some rolling down his face and falling onto his shirt. He'd spilt pudding on his tie, but he didn't seem to notice either the pudding or the sweat. She hoped he'd soon go home, or even go to sleep. They were sitting on a sofa and people sometimes slept on sofas, if they didn't have a bed. But, suddenly, he leaned towards her and put his hand on her leg. The hand felt hot and damp and had fat veins on the top of it, like swollen, purple snakes.

'Have I told you, Jo, what a gorgeous girl you are?'

He'd told her four times – no, five. People never called her 'gorgeous'; only 'thick'. She took a gulp of coffee, which was bitter, like the liqueur, and very fierce and black. At Sunnyhill, coffee was made with just a dash of Nescafe and all the rest hot milk, but they didn't have hot milk here, only cream. She poured some in, but it went all sort of furry and made the coffee cold. Even the sugar was odd: brown and gritty and hardly sweet at all. When she found her mother, they'd eat sweet things all the time.

'Now, I hope you'll forgive me asking, Jo, but there's something I need to know.'

She felt very frightened, suddenly. He was going to ask her if she'd run away and then he'd phone the home and tell them. But his voice went furry, like the coffee, and he spoke right into her ear, so that no one else could hear. Except no one else was there.

'What I want to ask you, my little lamb, is whether anyone has ever made love to you? You know what I mean, Jo, don't you? Have you ever had ... sex?'

She shook her head. Dave had got his thing out, once, but she hadn't liked the look of it. It was red and sort of swollen, with a drop of spit at the end. And, another time, Joseph had shoved his hand down her front and tried to touch her breasts. But Miss Batsby had walked in and gone scarlet in the face with rage.

'If only I were younger, darling, I could give you a wonderful time – something you'd remember all your life. Sex is the greatest of all pleasures known to man – or woman, for that matter. But you must be absolutely sure, Jo, to save yourself for someone worthy of you; someone with a lifetime of experience who knows what the hell he's doing. The last thing you want is some fumbling young jackass, only intent on his own thrills.'

He was holding her hand now, so hard it hurt her fingers. And his hand was hot and sweaty and made her own hand wet.

'Although I say it myself, I'm an extremely tactile person, sweetheart. I know exactly how and where a woman likes to be touched.'

She ought to move away, but he was gripping her hand too tightly. And, when he let it go, he began stroking his fat finger round and round her palm, so, even then, it wasn't easy to get up. The finger felt tickly and horrid, like insects crawling over her skin.

'I remember one of my ex-girlfriends saying to me once, "Lionel, you old charmer, I'm convinced you were a female in another life. You're one of those rare men who completely understand what turns a woman on." She was a right little minx, Miranda. I used to take her to Hyde Park and we'd have it off *en plein air*. That's incredibly exciting, Jo – knowing any moment you could be discovered *en flagrante*.'

She wished he wouldn't use hard words. She wished he'd just be quiet. No one older than thirty had sex, and he was eighty-four. But perhaps he was like God the Father, who'd had a son when He was really, really old.

He was still talking in the whispery voice and still stroking with the finger. 'But you must have been kissed, Jo – I'm pretty sure of that. At least once in your young life?'

She shook her head again. Kissing was germy, like using the same spoon.

'Well, if you have no objection, *mon petit chou*, that's a deficit I intend to make good.'

Suddenly, his big, wet, flabby lips were pressing right against her own. She could smell wine and duck and coffee, all mixed up. And she could feel his tongue, like an angry little animal, trying to get inside her mouth. She closed her lips as tight as possible, but his tongue was so impatient, it was forcing them apart. She wanted to shout '*No!*', but she couldn't speak at all. There was no room for words in her mouth. His tongue had filled it up and was wiggling now inside it, all slimy, like a slug. His chin was scratchy against her face, and even his teeth were sort of banging into hers.

All at once, she pulled away – roughly, which was rude. But if you kissed a man, it meant you'd have a baby – Josie's gran had said. Josie and the others all told her that was crap, but she knew it must be true, because her mother had kissed a man and then had *her*.

She didn't want a baby. Edna said it was the worst pain in the world – worse than a broken leg, or an abscess on your tooth. And, as well as the baby, blood and poo came out. And her baby might be a halfwit, so they would send it off to a home, and it might never find her again, because of all the strangers in the way.

'I need the ... the toilet,' she shouted, jumping to her feet. Her voice came out very loud, not just because she was frightened, but because she *did* need it, desperately. But he grabbed her arm and tried to get up, too, so maybe he would stop her going and keep her here, a prisoner.

Then, all at once, he lost his balance and fell back into the chair, and made a funny sort of noise: half a laugh and half a groan.

'Promise you'll come straight back, darling. I just have to kiss you again. You're so utterly enchanting, I can't bear to let you out of my sight, even for a moment!'

She crept towards the door. It seemed a long way off; across miles of dark red carpet, the colour of dried blood. But, when she heard him following, she ran, instead of tiptoeing, and managed to get out. She dared to look behind her and saw him bumping into things and tripping over a rug, but then he reached the doorway and stood there, holding onto it.

'Don't get lost, Jo, will you?' he called after her, in his funny, furry voice. 'Ask someone to show you the way. The ladies' room is right down in the basement, so make sure they take you there in person and bring you safely back. Say you want the library. It'll be three floors up – they'll know. I'll be waiting for you, darling!'

She didn't need somebody to take her – she knew where basements were. There was one at Sunnyhill, where they stored mattresses and broken chairs. You were always safe in basements, because people didn't go there, only things.

She began walking down the stairs, which were very grand, with more pictures and tall mirrors, and even armchairs on the landings. But she didn't look at anything except her feet, going down each step. No one stopped her; no one told her off, so she just carried on, down and down and down. Then she reached a different sort of staircase – much narrower and smaller, without the fancy carpet. She was glad they'd run out of carpet, because it was covered with gold swirly things that made her tummy swirl.

At the bottom was a big black door, with a notice saying 'LADIES'. But, when she went inside, it was nothing like a ladies' room and she couldn't see a single toilet anywhere. It looked more like a sitting-room, mixed up with a bedroom. There were two sofas, like the ones in the library, but green instead of black, and a soft green carpet (with no swirls), and a round polished table, with lots of magazines on, and a vase of expensive flowers; the sort people sent if you were rich and went to hospital. But there was also a dressing-table – which were usually in bedrooms – with a silver hairbrush on it, and a matching silver comb, and three dark-green bottles: big, medium-sized and small, like the bowls in *The Three Bears*. And there were rows and rows of hangers in a kind of cupboard with no door, for people to hang their coats. Except all the hangers were empty and there were no people in the room, not even the lady who cleaned the toilets and gave you change if you didn't have 10p.

Without a toilet, she'd wet herself, which was the worst thing you could do. Last night, she'd had to pee in the street, and an old man had stood and watched, although he hadn't told her off. But she couldn't pee in the street now, because she'd been indoors so long she had forgotten where the streets were. Then, just when she was bursting, she saw another door and dashed through it to another room, and found seven toilets, side by side. She raced into the first one, only stopping when she saw the seat, which was made of shiny, polished wood, like the table in the first room. You were forbidden to sit on seats like that, so she squatted over the top and managed not to splash it with even one small drop.

When she came out, she washed her hands, because germs were everywhere: on your skin, in toilets and even in your bed. There were six basins, with gold taps, so she washed her hands six times, because she liked using posh gold taps. There was also a pile of fluffy towels – small, like flannels, although very thick and soft. But she was careful to use only one, because Edna said you had to save on washing.

Then she went back to the first room and sat down on the sofa. There were still no other ladies. In fact, she hadn't seen a single lady anywhere – not in the dining-room, or library, or in the big, grand hall. Perhaps ladies weren't allowed in the club, and this room was just a place for storing sofas. Which meant nobody could find her and send her back to the library, or back to Sunnyhill.

She looked slowly round the room. If no one ever came here, she could stay as long as she liked. And she would have everything she needed: toilets to pee in; basins to wash in; flowers to smell; a comb to comb her hair, and four lamps, with frilly lampshades, so she could see to read the magazines. She wasn't good at reading, but she liked looking at the pictures: photos of beautiful ladies and plates of fancy food. There wasn't any *real* food, but it didn't matter because she didn't want to eat. She just wanted to be quiet.

She sat listening to the silence, which was thick and soft and comfy, like the towels. This was the quietest place in London, because the traffic and the sirens and the buses and the aeroplanes had all been moved away to another far-off country, like the ones the man had talked about. Which meant she could sleep each night on the sofa and wouldn't be disturbed. She'd have a cushion for her pillow, and hangers for her clothes, so she could take them off before lying down and stop them getting creased.

She was even safe from the man, because men weren't allowed in ladies' rooms. But, if she was very lucky, her mother would come, instead. Miss Batsby said she lived in London, so she couldn't be that far away. London was a big place, yet the two of them might find each other, because her mother would keep on looking. Mothers always did.

In fact, if she waited long enough, it was bound to happen – one day. And she would start the waiting now, then the time would go much quicker. So she closed her eyes and sat very good and still, like Miss Batsby always told them. And, after quite a short while, she saw her mother, behind her lids, blurred and faint, but real. She was just coming through the door, wearing a white dress, like an angel, and walking right towards her. And she sat down on the sofa – kind and sweet and smiling – and whispered very softly, 'Josephine, I love you. And, I promise, this time, I shan't ever let you go.'

BAGGAGE

'This is completely ridiculous!' she said out loud, to no one. Would any sane person pack so much for a mere seven days in Cannes? Some women took clothes by the ton-weight, of course, but clothes were different – normal rather than shameful. If anyone saw what she was packing, they would label her either a raging hypochondriac or a chronic invalid.

OK, she'd *un*pack, starting with the herbal medicines. The bottles were too bulky and, anyway, the evil blackish mixture might spill all over the case. She removed them with a sense of triumph – lamentably short-lived: in less than twenty seconds, they were back. How could she control her hot flushes without that vital concoction of black cohosh and *agnus castus*, made up by her herbalist?

Damn the menopause, she thought, slumping onto the bed. It seemed to have turned her from a reasonably normal female to a mass of aches and pains, chills and sweats, moodiness and misery. Which is why she had packed her Litepod, a so-called compact light-box that took up half the case. Surely a further sign of madness to be lugging such an object to a Mediterranean country bathed in natural sunlight for fourteen hours each day. Although not, unfortunately, at 3 a.m., when the night-sweats usually woke her and she would switch on the consoling machine, to counteract the gloom. But surely she could manage for a week without it; soak up the sun all day, instead.

Her hand hovered over the case. Should it go or should it stay? Her former decisiveness had disappeared, along with her sense of humour and her once valuable ability to sleep through an alarm clock. And there were weightier decisions than the transportation of Litepods. Should she resign from her job, for instance, and strike out in a new direction, or settle for the old, safe routine and endure the tedium? Even more important, should she remain on her own in her neat but lonely flat, or move in with Richard and put up with his distinctly sluttish habits, in return for company? Admittedly, her libido was at an all-time low, but that didn't appear to bother him. Sex for Richard had always been low-key: more sluggish push-bike than high-speed Porsche.

Not that it was sensible to dwell either on the office, or on Richard's sexual deficiencies, until she had finished packing. Or should that be *un*packing? Did she really need a travel-iron and a set of travel-scales? Her gut instinct answered 'yes'. Creased clothes were hardly likely to attract a Richard-substitute and, since she'd hit the 'change', the pounds were piling on alarmingly. If she gorged in Cannes on cassoulets and croissants, brioches and bouillabaisse, she would return a good stone heavier, unless she kept a strict check on her weight.

Nor could she ditch the laxatives, as she had proved in Greece, last year. Any departure from her usual breakfast of All-Bran and stewed prunes resulted in a major stoppage. Perhaps the Eliminease could go, though, in favour of the Sennakot and Regulan? No. The stress of being away always seemed to necessitate a three-pronged remedy.

'Look, why not ditch the holiday instead?' she muttered, irritably. Not a bad idea, in fact. It would save both hassle and expense, and she would be freed from the chore of returning home to a pile of post, a tide of unanswered emails and a laundry-basket full of dirty clothes.

A little late for that, though. She had already paid in full, including travel insurance and airport-tax, and had even booked the taxi to Heathrow. Besides, what would Lesley have to say if she turned up for work tomorrow, having spent half of yesterday briefing the infuriating woman on how to deal with any problems in her absence?

'So Cannes, here I come!' she said, with determined cheerfulness, suddenly wondering whether Richard might break off the relationship if he realized quite how often she was talking to herself. If she did decide to move in with him, perhaps she could talk to his cat, instead – at least when he was out. Yet there was something about Tabitha's lofty disregard for any merely human problems that made the snooty feline decidedly unsuitable as confidante.

Having tucked the jar of Eliminease into a corner of the case, she tried to find room for the large box of Regulan. The main problem with a holiday was that you took yourself along – that self with all the ailments. Couldn't the Thomson Company introduce an innovative type of trip, in which, instead of going somewhere new and different, you *became* someone new and different – in her case, a radiantly healthy self, who could eat – and do – anything she liked.

'Concentrate!' she urged, returning to the task in hand. One thing she didn't need was her Dreamsack – the lightweight, pure silk sleeping-bag that allowed fastidious travellers to bypass hotel sheets and included a built-in pocket for the pillow, thus germ-proofing its occupant, head to toe. She always took it with her now, after her disastrous experience with bed-bugs, in Provence.

That was years ago, she reminded herself, and, anyway, she'd been staying in a small, antiquated guesthouse, where the very concept of hygiene was considered a modernity too far. A four-star hotel in Cannes was hardly likely to be bug-infested. She yanked the Dreamsack out, only to return it, as she recalled a recent report about even top-notch hotels re-using dirty sheets, to save on laundry costs. Suppose a guest with psoriasis had slept in those same sheets, or – worse – somebody with AIDS?

But, if the Dreamsack stayed, then the neck-pillow and back-support must go. Admittedly, her Back-Friend could transform a standard hotel-bedroom chair into something markedly kinder to her arthritis. Yet, if she wasn't careful, it would become her *only* friend. Why should anyone want an ailing, aching, constipated, indecisive, overweight depressive as their first-choice bosom pal?

Nonetheless, in another twenty seconds, both items were back in the suitcase. Pointless to spend her precious holiday in pain – although, all things considered, it might be better to change her destination and go to Dignitas, instead of Cannes. She was already past her sell-by date, so why not bow out gracefully at the age of forty-nine, rather than linger on for another three increasingly decrepit decades? Not that she could count on making it to seventy-nine, since both her parents had died in their early sixties, having suffered countless disorders throughout their unhappy lives. In fact, she could blame her mother for some of her own ailments, including the clearly genetic milk-allergy. If either of them imbibed a drop of cow's milk, by mistake, they would manifest exactly the same symptoms: itchy rashes, vomiting and stomach-cramps, and spectacular attacks of sneezing, snorting and wheezing. And her father, for his part, had bequeathed to her his early-onset arthritis, his migraines and his eczema. Indeed, considering their deleterious genetic legacy, perhaps they should have decided not to procreate.

Which reminded her – had she remembered to pack her Ibuprofen, her Migraleve and the new herbal ointment for eczema? On her way to fetch the latter from the bathroom, she paused to look at her parents' photo on the bureau. Both of them were smiling – a rare occurrence in reality. Although, to give them credit, at least they had stopped at one child. The fact she'd been born with jaundice and had suffered childhood eczema (her constant itching and scratching keeping them up most nights), had probably dulled their desire for any further offspring. She personally would have welcomed a sibling, so that the pair of them could have scratched and wheezed together, in mutual sympathy.

Returning to the bedroom, she sat contemplating the large, bulky carton of powdered soya milk, already sitting in the case. It would be even harder in France than at home to keep off milk, butter, yogurt, cheese, ice-cream. No Camembert or Brie, no vichyssoise or quiche Lorraine, no luscious creamy gateaux. Just as well she hadn't had any children of her own and passed on, once again, those distinctly dodgy genes. Not that she had avoided giving birth from any such noble motive, but because she had never met a man who wanted to start a family – and now it was too late.

'Cut out the self-pity!' she snapped, wishing *she* possessed a cat, so at least there would be the occasional answering mew. Instead of feeling sorry for herself, she should be counting her blessings: her well-paid job and comfortable flat, her circle of good friends – not to mention Richard, of course. OK, he might not be her ideal choice as partner, but if she disregarded his habit of peeing in the watering-can because he was too lazy to walk the few yards to the lavatory, they could probably reach some sort of compromise. She had to recognize the fact that relationships, for her, were very much a matter of balancing inadequacies: her allergies, depression, migraines and insomnia, set against Richard's untidiness and squalor, coupled with his own particular health problems. In short, each of them was forced to accept the other, because no one else was ever likely to do so.

Suddenly, decisively, she sprang to her feet, opened the case and threw in all the remaining clutter on the bed: the acupuncture-bands for headaches along with the Migralene and Ibuprofen, even the travel-kettle and its multi-voltage adaptor. French hotels rarely provided a kettle in one's room, but, with her handy little Easy-Boil, she could make hot drinks, even in the early hours. It didn't actually matter what she took or didn't take. She had booked a single room, so no one would see the kettle – or, indeed, the whole embarrassing cache of life-supports and health-aids.

Having closed the case with a bang, she strode into the kitchen to celebrate the miraculous fact that the packing was finished, at last. Booze aggravated hot flushes, but at least she could toast herself in a cup of innocuous tea – made with soya milk, of course.

'I'm sorry, Gillian, but the airline appears to have lost your case.'

She stared in horror at the Thompson rep: a big, strapping guy, bursting with youth and health and sporting a name-tag that declared, 'I'M SCOTT. I'M HERE TO HELP.'

And help he was valiantly offering – solicitous concern etched across his well-tanned face.

'Don't worry – we'll sort it out. You just need to fill in a form, describing the case and its contents. So if you could come with me to the Baggage Dispute desk....'

The very word 'dispute' made her spirits plummet further still.

Would there be arguments, unpleasantness, even a suspicion that she had failed to check in her luggage in the first place? She was already tired and tense, due partly to the flight's three-hour delay, and partly to the less-than-sparkling company of her fellow-travellers: a motley crew of mostly over-sixties, all booked into the same hotel, on the self-same package tour. Admittedly, Dora's moans about sub-standard airline catering and Trevor's rambling reminiscences about growing up in the War now faded into total insignificance compared with the trauma of being parted from her case. Scott's cheery smile was proof enough that he didn't – couldn't – comprehend how vulnerable she felt. And it wasn't just a matter of being prey to a myriad ailments without her drugs and prophylactics. Only now did she realize that those very things had become a sort of security-blanket and, deprived of its sheltering cocoon, she seemed fatally adrift.

Wretchedly, she followed Scott to the desk. The stylish female behind it looked every bit as hard as her varnished nails and stiffly lacquered hair – a female unlikely to waste sympathy on some neurotic traveller. Thank God for Scott, who was taking charge; even switching from English to impressively fluent French. In her present disorientated state, she could barely utter a word in either tongue, and merely stood dumbly, looking on.

Eventually, the woman passed a form across the desk, which Scott explained in simple words, as if addressing a retarded child – not far off the mark, in fact.

'Right, Gillian, see these pictures of cases? You just tick the one that most resembles yours. Then describe the make and colour in this column on the left. D'you understand?'

She nodded, still appalled by her own mental state. How could the loss of a mere suitcase induce such choking panic?

'Add any distinguishing features, like a special strap or luggage labels. Then list the contents in this large space here. Are you with me, Gillian?'

She was 'with him' in the sense of being one of his party, but he might have been a different species for all he was able to fathom the depth of her distress.

'OK, if you'd like to make a start....'

Nervously, she picked up the pen. Describing make and colour was easy enough, but the contents posed a problem. That supercilious female, waiting impatiently for the completed form, might raise her well-groomed eyebrows in derision once she saw the sorry list. Of course, many ailments *were* comic – so long as they were someone else's affliction. The menopause was hilarious; food-fads a total hoot.

The pen wavered to a halt. It might actually be feasible to catch the next flight back. Once safely home, she could order more herbal medicines; she wouldn't need the laxatives, and even the lost Back-Friend would be no inconvenience, since she would have her special orthopaedic chair.

Yet, one part of her was shamefully aware that she was overreacting to a ridiculous degree. Her case would probably turn up tomorrow and, if she couldn't cope without it for just a single night, then she was in need of professional help.

Watched by kindly Scott, she listed a heavily censored version of the contents and handed over the form.

'Don't worry,' he said, soothingly. 'I can lend you a comb and a toothbrush and a nice long t-shirt, to sleep in. I always carry a few spares, in case of emergencies like this.'

A comb, a toothbrush and something to sleep in were probably all most normal people needed overnight. For her they were so achingly inadequate, she all but howled aloud. Of course, if it was a matter of necessity, she could put up with sweats and flushes, migraines, back-pain, sluggish bowels and all the tedious rest of it. But what Scott had signally failed to grasp was that, without her crucial safety-nets, it was if she had lost her very skin and was now exposed to every savage wind.

'Right, that's all sorted,' Scott declared, giving her a thumbs-up sign.

If *only*, she thought, still disgusted by the way she was getting things so absurdly out of proportion. With soldiers dying in Afghanistan and children starving in Ethiopia, how could she possibly make such a ludicrous palaver about the loss of a few paltry items?

As Scott ushered her back to the group, all standing smugly by their *un*-lost, unscathed cases, she made a supreme effort to control herself; even forcing a nonchalant smile. Yet she knew deep down that the next seven days would be pretty much disastrous.

'Isn't this a fabulous beach?' Fiona remarked, leaning back on her recliner, with a sigh of satisfaction.

Gillian nodded in agreement, still surprised by the fact that the place actually resembled the pictures in the brochures, rather than being a pale approximation. Shading her eyes, she gazed out at the far horizon. Both sky and sea were so emphatically blue, one merged into the other; the only difference between them the latter's shimmer and sparkle, as if it were made of ground-up sapphires. And the beach itself more than surpassed her expectations; not a speck of litter in sight, and the sand so fine and smooth it might have been primped and preened in the local beauty-salon. This particular stretch was owned privately by their hotel, and was dotted with colour-matched recliners and umbrellas, all in stylish olive-green and bearing the hotel crest. She herself had spurned a recliner, preferring to stretch her limbs luxuriously on that well-groomed, sun-warmed sand. The traffic on the boulevard had faded to a lazy drone and she was aware only of holiday sounds: the slap of a speedboat as it skimmed across the waves; the enticing clink of glasses from the hotel's own beach-café, a few yards up the strand. And foodie smells were wafting in the air: sizzling butter, garlicky fish-soup....

'More cheese?' Fiona offered, leaning down to pass her the Camembert.

She helped herself to another sizeable chunk, then broke off more baguette, plastered it with butter and added a thick layer of cheese. 'This picnic was a great idea. I was feeling really peckish.'

'Me, too. The others may be able to last from breakfast through to dinner, but I have to say I do like my three meals a day.'

'We bought far too much, though,' Gillian observed, surveying the mini-banquet, set out on a beach-towel. 'Enough for a whole tribe.'

'Mm, but it wasn't easy to resist, let loose in that fantastic market.'

'I only hope it'll keep.'

'It won't – not in this sun! The quiche is already going runny. Why don't we finish it up?'

'OK.' Gillian divided the remaining quiche in two. 'But if we pig ourselves on all this savoury stuff, we won't have room for the desserts.'

'Speak for yourself! I intend to be a total glutton. We can always work it off when we swim. Talking of which, what bliss to swim in a nice, warm sea in the middle of October!'

'Yes, they say it's unseasonably warm this week, yet it's freezing back in England, so I heard.'

'Don't mention England or I'll start worrying about work. My PA's new to the job and she's probably made a major balls-up already.'

Gillian realized with a distinct sense of glee that she didn't care a jot if Lesley had made a million major balls-ups. Let the maddening woman rot!

'Anyway,' Fiona added, scooping a gloop of cheese from her lap. 'I want to hear about this man of yours.'

'He's hardly "mine". All we've done so far is have a quick coffee together.'

'But how on earth did you meet him? The men in our party are all pretty dire, don't you think? Trevor must be pushing ninety; Norman's stone-deaf, and even Alistair seems old before his time, although he can't be more than forty. Did you hear him at dinner last night droning on about his stamp-collection?'

'No, I was sitting next to Gregory. Who's not that bad, in fact.'

'A bit dreary, wouldn't you say? And I'm always suspicious of blokes who wear their glasses on a chain. But, listen, you still haven't told me where you met Jean-Pierre.'

'Well, I went out first thing this morning to do a spot of shopping …' Gillian paused, to take a bite of quiche. No way would she add that she had been heading for the pharmacy to buy replacement drugs and laxatives, and to see if she could purchase a milk-substitute. 'And he literally bumped into me. He wasn't looking where he was going, so we collided almost head-on. It was quite painful, actually, but he apologized at least a dozen times and insisted on buying me a coffee, to make up. Anyway, it turns out he owns a yacht here. Actually, I've never been sailing in my life, but, of course, I showed an interest and – would you believe, he's offered to take me for a cruise? It's fixed for this coming Saturday – we're sailing down the coast to Saint-Tropez.'

'God, I'm green with envy! And I suppose he's drop-dead gorgeous, as well?'

'No, just average, I'd say, but very well turned out. Thank heavens you lent me that sundress! I'd have felt a total disaster if I'd been wearing the clothes I'd travelled in. You know what Frenchmen are like.'

'Actually, I don't. And my French is decidedly ropy, so even if Nicolas Sarkozy were to leap out of his limo and try and chat me up, all I could say would be "*oui, oui, oui, oui, oui.*"'

'Well, *he* speaks perfect English, so I reckon you'd be in with a chance! I find most French people have a pretty good grasp of the language and Jean-Pierre, in particular, seems keen to improve his linguistic skills. In fact, that's probably the only reason he suggested the sailing trip.'

'Don't put yourself down, my love. And for God's sake don't settle for being his English tutor, when he may have more exciting things in mind!'

Gillian deliberated, pretending she needed to concentrate on eating. Probably better not to let on that she was also meeting Jean-Pierre this evening, for dinner at *Chez Victoire*. The last thing she wanted was to alienate Fiona by seeming to boast, or gloat, or engage in one-upmanship. She was extremely lucky, as it was, in having made a friend so soon – and one roughly her own size and shape, who'd been generous enough to share her plentiful supply of clothes, when most women would have been grudgingly possessive. As yet, all she'd had to buy, whilst waiting for her case, was underwear and cosmetics. Even Fiona's spare bikini fitted to a T. Her own lost swimsuit – a prim, one-piece affair – bore little relation to the skimpy riot of polka-dots now adorning her ample limbs. No – 'voluptuous', not 'ample'. Fiona's terminology was so much kinder than her own.

However, she would certainly have to dream up some excuse as to why she'd be missing dinner at the hotel, especially as she and Fiona had already arranged to sit together, to avoid Dora's incessant complaining and Alistair's philatelic obsession. When she needed such excuses at home, there was rarely any problem – indeed, sadly, they were often all too true: she had ingested some hidden allergen, such as casein or lactic acid, and suffered a bad reaction; she was stricken by a migraine, or a particularly troublesome series of hot flushes. But all that was in the past. In fact, she could barely remember the dreary old hag, once martyr to such afflictions. She didn't even have a twinge of backache, despite the fact she was now squatting on the sand, in a position that would normally result in atrocious pain. Nor had the dazzling sun brought on the slightest headache, let alone a flush or sweat. She was just sensuously warm, with the beginnings of a tan, instead of lobster-red and drenched with perspiration. And, far from waking in the early hours, this morning she had actually overslept.

'Oh, look!' she said, deciding to distract Fiona from the subject of Jean-Pierre by pointing out a passer-by. The woman in question was a riot of pink: pink, sculpted curls, pink halter-top, ultra-short, pink spangly shorts, pink high-heeled sandals – patently unsuited for walking across the sand – and, to cap it all, a miniature French poodle, dyed pink to match its owner's hair.

'Jeez, she sure loves pink!' Fiona whispered. 'All the women here seem to like to go to extremes. I saw a girl this morning, dolled up in gold lamé, literally from head to toe – and that was just at breakfast-time. God knows what she puts on in the evening!'

Gillian laughed, although it was hard to keep her mind on fashion, when she was so preoccupied with this morning's kiss. *Why* had Jean-Pierre kissed her – yes, right there in the coffee-shop, in full view of everyone? And not the sort of casual peck suited to an English tutor, but a real exuberant smacker of a kiss. She was decidedly older than he was and, in any case, could hardly compete with the sophisticated Frenchwomen she'd seen strolling along the

Croisette. Yet, if he didn't find her attractive, why had he asked her out? And why *shouldn't* he fancy her – a woman in her prime, with a clear skin and a Junoesque figure; possessed of robust health and a decidedly perky libido? Indeed, she could barely wait for tonight and the sheer thrill of being kissed by a guy who knew exactly how to make a female turn liquid with desire.

She reached out for the gateau and cut two generous slices; smiling as it oozed a whoosh of cream. She mustn't spoil her appetite for this evening's splendid dinner, but the way she felt at present, she could eat for France – and still some – all without suffering the slightest reaction, or putting on an ounce.

'*Au revoir*,' Jean-Pierre whispered, giving her a last, lingering kiss. And, once he had finally released her, she stood looking back at his lithe, athletic figure as it was swallowed up in shadow. Until this very evening, she had tended to assume that Frenchmen's reputation for being superior lovers was just another instance of crowing by *le coq gaulois*; deliberately inflated, as a matter of mere national pride. However, if Jean-Pierre's skilful overtures were anything to go by – the way he'd driven her half-wild before they'd even left the restaurant – she would be forced to reconsider that assumption. They were meeting again tomorrow, and this time not just for dinner, so she would find out soon enough. Fiona was still a problem, but if they spent a girly day together, shopping, swimming, sightseeing, surely her friend would understand that the evening must be sacred to *l'amour*.

As she turned into her hotel, she all but tripped on the edge of a flower-bed; aware she was gloriously tipsy on champagne. It was decades since she had drunk so much and she had triumphantly chosen dishes awash with milk and cream: *oeufs en cocotte au parmesan*, with lobster Thermidor, to follow, and *île flottant*, for dessert. Her usual sojourns to the Pizza Hut with Richard simply couldn't compare. And as for his perfunctory kisses, they were in the remedial class. In fact, only now did she realize how totally unsuited she and Richard were, not just in sexual matters but in every other way. Why aim low, when you could reach for the stars?

Reluctant to go inside on such a balmy evening, she gazed up at the sky. Yes, there were the stars – brilliant and unfathomable and barely dimmed by the bright lights of the town. The air was as warm and musky as Jean-Pierre's breath; the night as dark as his eyes. She was tempted to race after him and invite him up to her room. But she had only to wait a mere twenty hours and they would be together again. Already, his highly seductive repertoire had whetted her appetite for more. Closing her eyes, she replayed the last half-hour: the thrilling way he had fluttered his long, dark lashes against her own, then kissed the inside of her elbow, with a slow and sensuous brushing of his lips. Even then, he wasn't finished, but took her hand and clasped it and caressed it, before running his tongue languorously up and down each finger, and finally circled her palm with the tongue-tip. Those lazy, teasing circles had made her palm a new erogenous zone and the sensations seemed to spread through every cell in her body and even to galvanize her bloodstream. Foreplay was an unknown concept for Richard, as, indeed, was after-play. On the few occasions he did gear himself for action, the earth certainly never moved. Rather, the bedsprings gave a timid squeak, while he laboured for a scant five minutes, then, collapsing with a self-satisfied grunt, soon fell fast asleep.

Sleep? No way! She was too elated to do anything but just lie and think of her French lover: the scent of his skin; his headstrong thatch of hair – different altogether from Richard's thinning locks – his throaty, sexy voice; inventive hands....

In a joyous daze, she entered the hotel, seeming to float across the gleaming marble floor.

'*Bonsoir, madam*,' the receptionist smiled, handing over the key. '*Vous sera très contente d'apprendre que votre valise est arrivé a l'hôtel et elle est maintenant dans votre chambre*.'

Her missing case – now waiting in her room. So what? The last thing she wanted was to douse her enchanted memories by unpacking at this time of night. Besides, she would hardly need a nightdress if she didn't intend to sleep. More exciting to lie naked and just indulge in steamy fantasies about tomorrow night.

Key in hand, she sauntered up the stairs, but her blissful smile morphed into a frown on entering the room. The case had been plonked in the middle of the carpet: a definite blot on its cream perfection – indeed, an insult to the elegant suite as a whole. How scuffed and shabby the hulking object looked, and how ludicrously over-sized – out of all proportion to what she actually required for these all-too-short few days. Lugging it into the wardrobe, she closed the door with a bang. The clothes she had packed with such care in England now seemed completely wrong. Tomorrow, with Fiona's help, she could buy replacement gear on their shopping expedition: maybe a zanily coloured outfit, to express her new upbeat mood, or a slinky, backless little number, like the one she was wearing now, on loan from her warm-hearted friend, for the all-important date.

Draping herself over the edge of the bed, she unzipped the exquisite dress, imagining Jean-Pierre's deft fingers slowly easing it down. Yes, his lips were on her naked skin, kissing every inch of her back, as the zip crept lower, lower. And now the dress had rustled to the floor and he was slipping his seductive hand inside her silky knickers and that hand, too, was gliding lower, lower, and....

She woke with a start, burning hot and soaked with sweat; lay for a moment, wincing, as the flush engulfed her in waves of breathless, clammy heat. Why in heaven's name was she sleeping naked, when her sensible, all-cotton nightdress would have absorbed at least some of the perspiration?

Snapping on the bedside light, she peered at her watch. Three o'clock, for pity's sake! Last night, she hadn't thought to draw the curtains and the windowpanes looked menacingly black. Black as her mood. Wearily, she eased herself out of bed, dragged the suitcase from the wardrobe and heaved it up onto the luggage-stand. Having struggled with the straps and locks, she found her nightdress lying on the top and immediately put it on. It was totally inappropriate for a woman of her age and size to be wandering round in her birthday-suit. Next, she unpacked her medicines. She already had a raging headache, and would need a double dose of Ibuprofen to ease the now savage pain of her arthritis.

As she limped into the bathroom to fetch a glass of water, she stared, aghast, at her reflection in the mirror. Her allergic rash was worse than ever: lumpy, red pustules had erupted all over her face and spread even down her neck and chest. She turned away, unable to endure the sight, and swallowed each medicament in turn, including the herbal potions, of course. And she had better take her laxatives, as well, since she could hardly count on All-Bran and stewed prunes for breakfast in a French hotel. The bulk laxatives required at least a pint-and-a-half of liquid, some of which she would drink in the form of tea – less unpleasant than gulping down more tap-water. Thank God for the travel-kettle and soya milk, both of which she now dug out of the case; also extricating the light-box. She knew already that she would never get back to sleep, so best to switch it on and sit in front of it, to help lift her jaded mood.

Having made the tea, she set the Litepod on the writing-desk and placed her Back-Friend ready on the chair, while she went to fetch the neck-support. She would need them both, judging by the way her joints were aching. However, before beginning her light-box session, she unpacked her clothes and put them all on hangers. They were already badly creased and she would have to iron the whole damned lot, as soon as it was light. While that murky night was pressing against the windows, she just didn't have the energy for so onerous a chore.

Once her things were in the wardrobe and she had choked down all the laxatives, with the help of three large cups of tea, she positioned herself at the desk, in front of the Litepod screen. However, hardly had five minutes gone by, when she was overtaken by another flush, which galloped through her body, leaving her breathless and disoriented. One of the worst features of the menopause was the way it plunged the sufferer into uncontrollable states. She couldn't choose *not* to flush or sweat – her hormones simply overruled her and went their own pernicious way.

On impulse, she rushed over to the window and flung it open, breathing in the cool night air, to counteract the surge of heat, still throbbing through her limbs. As the flush gradually subsided, she remained leaning on the sill, drenched with perspiration and exhausted from lack of sleep. Tomorrow, she must have an early night. The minute dinner was over, she would sneak up here on the quiet and leave the others drinking in the bar.

Oh, my God, she thought, only now recalling that tomorrow she had arranged to meet Jean-Pierre. Out of the question! How could an overweight, rash-infested, arthritic, menopausal wreck even entertain the prospect of allowing a virile young lover to lure her into bed? First thing in the morning, she must ring his mobile and say she was unwell – all too miserably true. She now felt shivery and nauseous, as she often did following a flush. In fact, if she didn't lie down, she might actually faint, as had happened twice before. The sheets would be disgustingly sweaty, so she had better resort to her Dreamsack. The smell of her unwashed body was odious, but she felt too defeated even to shower. All she wanted was to crawl into the Dreamsack, close her eyes and imagine being safely home; back in her steady job and regular routine.

Holidays were lethal – the uncertainty, the change of diet, the risk of illness and accident; the way you were thrown together with completely unsuitable people, who just happened to be members of your group. Fiona might be younger than the rest, but she was far too much of a hedonist to be counted as a friend. Tomorrow's shopping trip must certainly be cancelled, otherwise the frivolous woman would only persuade her to lash out on absurdly unsuitable clothes: blatantly backless numbers, or outfits in some flagrant shade of puce. Besides, being out of doors in the glaring sun was bound to bring on another migraine – or worse. What her body actually needed was to lie down all day in a darkened room.

She mooched over to the writing-desk and switched off her trusty light-box. Whatever its merits, it could hardly alleviate her aching sense of isolation, as if she had travelled not just to France, but to the far reaches of the universe, where no other human being lived. She longed for company and comfort; for someone to confide in, someone who could understand. Illness cut you off from normal, healthy people, who either shunned you as a bore, or tried to jolly you along. Only fellow-sufferers could empathize – people like dear, faithful Richard, with his haemorrhoids and sinusitis, his tendency to athlete's foot, his need to rest after any heavy meal.

In fact, once she had rung Fiona and Jean-Pierre, she would phone him, too, tomorrow, and tell him she was missing him. More than that, she would give him the news he had been waiting months to hear: that she had made her decision, at last and, yes, she *would* move in with him, and on a permanent basis. Putting up with fungal feet and constant sniffles, day and night; with indigestion, stomach pains, messy cupboards and cluttered rooms; indeed, even with pee-filled watering cans, was an incredibly small price to pay for being accepted as she was: a fast-disintegrating crone.

Dispiritedly, she slumped down at the desk, hands outstretched, as if surrendering. But, as she stared down at her open palms, the exquisite sensations experienced last night suddenly came stealing back: the subtly insistent pressure of Jean-Pierre's tongue, as he traced those ingenious circles; his tongue-tip like a touch-paper that set off deeper feelings; exploding her whole body into life.

All at once, she strode over to her case and began collecting up the things she had just unpacked: kettle, light-box, medicines and laxatives, Dreamsack, Back-Friend, neck-support, rail of dreary clothes. The travel-iron and weighing-scales were still lying in the case, so, having crammed the rest of the stuff on top, she hauled the thing off the luggage-stand and lugged it to the open window. The whole of Cannes was spread below: the beach, the shops, the restaurants, the enticements, possibilities....

Without a moment's thought, she hurled the case from the window; heard its satisfying crash as it hit the flagstones below.

Only then did she freeze; appalled by such an unpardonable offence. Not only had she disturbed the whole hotel, she might have caused some fatal injury. And it was totally out of character, as if someone else had acted; someone dangerously irresponsible, completely cavalier. She must ring down to reception and grovel her apologies; even pretend it was an accident – except that no one would believe her.

She rushed over to the phone and snatched up the receiver. But, instead of dialling reception, her fingers started stabbing out a different number entirely, as if they had acquired a will of their own. The phone-lead was coiling and snaking from the tremor in her hand – no wonder she was nervous at making such a blatant call. Heinous to wake a man from sleep – and a man she barely knew – yet, if it awakened her, as well, to passion and romance, her whole life might be transformed.

Or was that just an insubstantial dream; a mere holiday illusion?

As the muffled, husky voice suddenly pulsated in her ear, she realized, with a curdled blend of hope and trepidation, that, in a scant five seconds, her fate would be determined.

SECOND SEX

'Shut your trap, you sleaze-ball – or you won't have a trap to shut!'

The gangster moved the muzzle of the sawn-off shotgun even closer to his victim's mouth, threatening to ram it between his teeth. 'Another word and you'll be cats' meat!'

But, as if involuntarily, the cowering Latino gave a yell of fear and, all at once, a shattering explosion reverberated through the hushed and darkened cinema. More swarthy-faced figures came darting from the shadows, in a bid to protect their leader, but the rest of the gang closed in on them and a hail of bullets ricocheted in all directions, amplified by the Dolby Digital sound.

'I'm sitting this bit out,' Alice whispered. 'There's been so much violence already, I'm feeling a bit queasy!'

Josh gave her a distracted nod, clearly riveted by the carnage.

She squeezed past him, with some difficulty, stepping over his coat, which he'd left bundled up on the floor. Fortunately, they were positioned on the aisle, so there was no need to disturb a whole row of peevish strangers.

'Back in a few minutes,' she hissed, although her voice was drowned in the continuing bombardment. In any case, Josh was deaf to everything except the on-screen drama.

As she crept towards the door and pushed it open, the relentless gunfire echoed in pursuit. It was a relief to emerge into the basement foyer, which, in contrast, was mercifully quiet and deserted, save for the tall young guy who had taken their tickets, earlier. He was still perched on his high stool, but now deep in some book or other.

She sank into the squashy chair beside him. 'Mind if I sit here?'

''Course not. But I see you've left the film. Are you OK – I mean, not feeling ill or anything?'

'No, I'm fine. I just hate blood and guts!'

'Well, in that case, you shouldn't have chosen a film like *My Name is Vengeance*.'

'My boyfriend chose it, actually and we don't have the same taste. Though, to be honest, I'm surprised they should be screening such a shocker at the Curzon.'

'Well, we're not exclusively art-house,' he explained. 'We do show other stuff, and this particular film was selected on account of the director. But why did you let your boyfriend overrule you?'

She flushed. 'I didn't. We take it in turns to choose and, to give him credit, he did sit through a distinctly sloppy rom-com last week, for *my* sake.'

'Nevertheless' – he fixed her with his dark, reproving eyes – 'it means half of the movies you watch you don't enjoy. Compromise is a big mistake, you know. Why not see something you actually like and see it on your own?'

Incensed, she looked away. This guy was barely twenty and, as a total stranger, was hardly qualified to advise on her and Josh's lifestyle. 'Some of it's quite gripping,' she said, in her defence. 'In fact, I'd better go back in now. The shootout should be over.'

'No.' He checked his watch. 'It lasts at least ten minutes longer. The police turn up in force and there's a vicious three-way gun-battle with the mobsters and the rival gang of drug-dealers. Then another gang moves in and all hell breaks loose and—'

'In that case, I'll stay put. But, if you want to read, don't let me distract you.'

'I'm glad of some distraction, to be honest. This book's a bit hard-going – fascinating but best digested in small doses.'

'What is it?'

'*The World as Will and Idea*. You know, Schopenhauer.'

She suppressed a smile. Typical of a Curzon employee to be reading Schopenhauer, rather than some mindless pap. 'I have to confess I've never read it, but I did get interested in Schopenhauer at university – only via Samuel Beckett, though. Beckett seemed quite taken with him and absorbed a lot of his ideas.'

'So you were reading English, I assume?'

'Yes, at Bristol.'

'What a weird coincidence! I was there, as well.'

At least ten years after *my* time, she refrained from pointing out. 'Reading English, too, you mean?'

'No, Philosophy. But I dropped out halfway through. I hated the way the course was structured – all in rigid modules that had to be covered in a certain order. I needed much more thinking-time and the freedom to study what I chose, instead of sticking to a syllabus.'

He had probably chickened out of his degree, she thought, with wry amusement, which is why he was taking tickets at the Curzon, instead of working at a proper job. And, if his shabby clothes were anything to go by, he was clearly underpaid. The blue-denim jeans had faded to a murky grey, and the battered black suede boots were worn down at the heels. Even his 'Curzon' T-shirt looked shrunken and ill-fitting. He was strikingly attractive, though: lean and rangy with longish, wavy hair as dark as dark molasses, and equally dark stubble accenting his strong chin and sensual mouth. Josh had sandy hair and less emphatic bone-structure and, if anything, his lips were rather thin. Horrified to be making such comparisons, she quickly resumed the conversation.

'I never really got to grips with Schopenhauer. Apart from anything else, he's such a thorough-going misogynist. In his view, all women are, without exception, superficial, trivial, subservient and second-rate.'

'Yes, but that wasn't quite so shocking in his time. Women were often regarded, then, as essentially unequal and definitely the second sex. Besides, he had such a bad experience with his mother, that probably coloured all his views.'

'Come off it! If you're meant to be a philosopher, you can't base a whole system of thought on what happened to you personally.' She broke off, as a doddery old lady made her halting way towards them and handed over her ticket.

'Your film's in Screen Two, over there' – the guy pointed to the right – 'but I'm afraid you've missed the first half-hour.'

'That's OK, I've seen it twice before. I just want to see the end again.'

Barely waiting for the customer to shamble off across the foyer, he returned to his defence of Schopenhauer. 'Look, forget about his mother and concentrate on his good points – his interest in Buddhism, for instance. He believed the best way of dealing with life's traumas was to cultivate an attitude of acceptance, even resignation, combined with deep compassion for suffering humanity, and I don't see how you can argue with that. He was also fervently anti-slavery and cared passionately about the rights of animals, which was quite unusual in his day. And I really like the way he said we should address each other not as "*Herr*" or "sir" or "*monsieur*" or whatever, but as "*Leidensgefährte*" – "my fellow sufferer".'

'That's typical!' she exclaimed. 'He's such a fearful pessimist. In fact, the only two things I remember about him was his dismissal of the entire female sex and his view that we live in the worst of all possible worlds.'

'We probably do.'

'Speak for yourself. *My* life's pretty good.'

'We can't just speak for ourselves. That's no basis for morality. We need to consider all our fellow humans, especially those who find life intolerable – you know, people living in war-zones, or in crippling poverty, or those imprisoned for their political beliefs, or tortured by—'

She fought a surge of irritation. So immature a guy had no right to adopt this moralizing air of superiority. Had he attained a ripe old age, he could at least claim the wisdom of experience, but hardly at his early stage of life. Nonetheless, she did feel abashed by his mention of 'crippling poverty' and just hoped he hadn't noticed her watch: a Rolex, worth a good three grand; made of eighteen-carat gold and set with diamonds. Her punishingly long hours of work surely justified a few rewards, although *he* would disagree, of course.

'I think I'd better go back in,' she said, unwilling to prolong the conversation, 'or Josh will be wondering where I've got to.'

'Please yourself.' With a shrug, he returned to his book.

She stole back into the fuggy darkness. Josh had moved over, leaving his aisle seat free for her. 'All right, darling?' he whispered.

She squeezed his hand. 'Fine. Have I missed anything important?'

'Only another bloodbath!'

'Sssh!' reproved a man in front, turning round to glare.

They both subsided into silence and she tried her best to concentrate. The plot was so convoluted, however, she had long since lost all track of it. And the young dropout in the foyer had triggered emotive memories of Bristol University: the intense, in-depth discussions; the burning concern for global justice, which she had shared, once, long ago; the lack of any real pressures beyond handing in one's essays on time. Her present job allowed little scope for reading or philosophizing. In fact, the only things she'd read in the last twelve months had been client profiles and company reports – or women's magazines when she was too exhausted by her ten-hour days to tackle any book at all, let alone Schopenhauer or Beckett. Yet she could still recall her excitement at discovering both writers, and encountering new philosophies of life. In those days, even pessimism and nihilism had been bracing, and often the subject of heated debates in the wee small hours, over coffee and cheap plonk. Nowadays, staying up too late at night was something of a risk – she might be late for work next morning, or find herself too tired to concentrate.

All at once, shrilling sirens assaulted her ears, as a car-chase and more gunfire erupted on the screen; the sounds of screeching tyres and whining bullets resounding through the auditorium. The baddies were shooting indiscriminately through the windows of their Cadillac, not just at the cop-cars hurtling in hot pursuit, but also at innocent bystanders. Blood was gushing forth in lurid Technicolor, and shrieks from the wounded and dying only added to the uproar.

'Josh ...' She jogged his arm, spoke right into his ear to avoid annoying other patrons. 'This is really not my sort of thing. In fact,

I'm beginning to get a headache. Mind if I go upstairs for a minute, to get a bit of air?'

Engrossed, he shook his head; his entire focus on the screen.

'Is that OK with you?'

'Yeah, fine.'

Having grabbed her coat and bag, she emerged into the foyer again, where the tall young guy was now busy with a pencil, underscoring passages in his book.

'Sorry – shan't disturb you. I just hate the racket in there!'

He flashed her a disarming smile. 'In that case, Schopenhauer would have approved of you. He said the amount of noise anyone can bear stands in inverse proportion to their mental capacity.'

'Really?' she said, uneasily aware that Josh always turned his music up full-volume.

'I'm Daniel, by the way,' he added. 'And you're *not* disturbing me. As I said, my brain needs a rest every now and then, in order to absorb this stuff. So sit down, relax and tell me about yourself.'

'Well, I planned to go outside for—'

'It's noisy out there, too, with all the junketings for Chinese New Year.'

She nodded. Before the film, Josh had taken her to lunch at an upmarket Chinese restaurant, so jammed with native revellers, they could hardly hear themselves speak. 'OK,' she said, subsiding into the chair again. 'I'll opt for peace and quiet! And it's as quiet as the grave down here.'

'It's either one thing or the other,' he explained. 'Manic when a film ends or one's just about to begin, but otherwise completely calm.' He swivelled round on his chair to give her his full attention. 'So, what's your name?' he asked.

'Alice,' she said, wondering how Josh would view this extended tête-à-tête with a young, attractive stranger.

'And what do you do?'

'I work for Roebuck-Rayner – a big PR firm in Belgravia. My main client at the moment is a luxury car-boutique and—'

'A *what*?' He looked aghast.

'Well, that's what they like to call themselves, although I suppose it's a sort of dealership. They sell specialist sports cars – top-of-the-range ones, mostly: Ferraris, Aston Martins, Maseratis, Alfa Romeos, all that sort of thing – and my job is to get them into the media spotlight in any way I can.'

'But that's immoral. Cars are seriously bad for the environment.'

'We can hardly do without them,' she retorted, bristling at his rudeness, not to mention his *naïveté*. 'Or would you prefer us to go back to the horse and cart?'

'Sports cars are particularly evil. They use too much fuel and they're extremely dangerous.'

She forbore to tell him that it was Josh's dream to own a Lamborghini – not yet, of course; no way could he afford it, but, having just been made an associate director, the prospects looked more promising. In truth, she had only got her own job on account of Josh's influence. In the PR world, personal contacts were crucial and string-pulling a fact of life. 'How about you?' she asked, keen to steer the conversation away from poverty, the environment, or his narrow view of morality. 'Do you work here full-time?'

'No, twenty-one hours a week – long days on Sunday and Wednesday and a shorter one on Thursday. We get lots of breaks, though, and we're often not that busy, so I manage to wangle quite a bit of reading time. Actually, I've only been here since Christmas. Before that, I used to help out at an arts complex and I also did a spell at the British Museum. I may move on yet again – to a gallery in Bethnal Green, but not unless it's very much part-time. I consider it unreasonable to give away the whole of your life to work, even work you enjoy.'

His views really were exasperating and she felt duty-bound to put him right. 'Unreasonable or no, most of us need to earn a living, so that we can pay the rent and keep ourselves in food and clothes.' Not to mention handbags, she thought, glancing down at her latest acquisition: a mulberry-coloured Mulberry, which, even in a sample sale, had been something of an extravagance.

'We own far too many clothes,' was his rejoinder. 'And eat excessive amounts of food. And, as for rent, I don't pay it. I'm sleeping on someone's sofa at the moment and I have an option to join a squat. A guy I know called Boyd is squatting in what used to be a Museum of Antiquities in Shoreditch. It closed down in 2007 and it's been empty ever since, so Boyd moved in to prevent the local council nabbing it for some nefarious purpose, and he wants me to give him moral support.'

'But squatting's *wrong*,' she objected. 'In fact, you could say it was theft – taking over property you're not entitled to.'

'What do you mean by "entitled"? There's not just one morality, you know. In my opinion, it's infinitely more immoral that buildings should stand empty and unused, when hundreds of people have nowhere to live, often through no fault of their own. In any case, once squatters move in, they usually improve the place – do repairs and suchlike and make it habitable. Squatting isn't easy, though. You have to be prepared to live like a speculative nomad, with an ever-changing tribe, and be able to stand your ground and cite the law, in order to get the heavies off your back. That needs dedication and a good deal of hard graft. But, look, apart from any principle involved, the arrangement with Boyd will benefit me personally. The fewer outgoings I'm saddled with, the more time I'll have to think. In fact, if I didn't need cash at all, not even for absolute basics, I'd spend my entire life brooding.'

'Brooding?' she echoed, sarcastically. This guy really was bizarre.

'In the best sense, yes – thinking out who I am and what my purpose in life is. It amazes me how other people accept the status quo. Most of my contemporaries have gone into jobs they hate, just because the current view is that high income and high status are desirable in themselves. In my opinion, that's selling out. In fact, it's outright slavery. I mean, just last week, one of my friends was seriously reprimanded for – wait for it! – wearing red socks. His boss told him, and I quote, the socks were "inappropriate, if not disrespectful to the client". Well, as far as I'm concerned, he's sacrificed his autonomy to a company with pretty ludicrous values.'

'You can't generalize like that,' she said, feeling increasingly annoyed. 'I mean, *I'm* well paid, but I love my job and the firm I work for *does* have proper values.'

'How can it, Alice, for heaven's sake? Any PR firm must be severely compromised, on the grounds it's willing to push anything and everything in return for filthy lucre. OK, lots of people don't see the harm in that, but only because they swallow what society keeps telling them about the importance of a so-called good career. My parents are the same – always on my back and nagging me to get a "proper job". They think I'm wasting my life, because I'm not an adman or accountant. They just can't grasp the fact that I need time and space to work out who I am and what my role in the world should be.'

It was obvious he was still a student in terms of his whole mindset. As a greenhorn of eighteen, she, too, had agonized about the meaning of existence, but her priorities had changed since then, as had those of all her friends. 'Look,' she countered, tetchily, 'some of us want *other* things – things that only money can buy. Holidays, for instance. Surely you agree we need to travel, if only to make us less insular, but if you're penniless you can't go anywhere.'

''Course you can, if you're willing to hitchhike or backpack, and doss down with friends or strangers. I've been to quite a few places – although I refuse to fly, because that's immoral, too. But I'm quite prepared to be destitute in Delhi or Djibouti or wherever, so long as I can get there. A year ago, I spent two months in Gaza, supporting the Palestinian resistance movement, and I've even been overland to Siberia, to help the Russian environmentalists clear up the pollution in Lake Baikal.'

She shifted in her seat. She and Josh preferred to visit more congenial spots. Last July, for instance, they'd enjoyed a relaxing fortnight in a villa in the Seychelles and, the year before, booked a boutique-hotel in Barcelona.

'It made me livid, Alice. I mean, there's Baikal, the oldest lake in the world – three hundred million years old, at least – yet it's polluted by this factory, standing directly on its shore, belching steam and pumping dangerous chemicals into what was once the cleanest water anywhere on earth.' His legs were twisted round the chair-rung; one hand tightly clenched, as if even his body attested to his vehemence.

His sincerity was patent – that she had to concede – yet all this philanthropic talk made her feel discomfited. If she were brutally honest, she probably cared more about the size of her next pay-rise than saving some lake from pollution. 'Siberia's a hell of a way to go,' she muttered, at last; aware it sounded distinctly lame. But, with her scanty knowledge of environmental issues, she was hardly qualified to start holding forth about saving the blue whale. In truth, she was keen to change the subject again, before he suggested she joined Friends of the Earth, so she asked him what his parents did.

'My dad's a management consultant and a complete organization freak. Even when we were little, he treated us like his employees, rather than his kids – gave us printed rotas for the household chores; even promised us an incentive bonus if we did them well, and on time.'

So, she mused, sanctimonious Daniel was merely reacting against his personal circumstances, in the same way as Schopenhauer; setting up a system of philosophy that was really little more than a way of getting back at Dad. 'Your father sounds quite sensible to me. At least he gave you a useful training for later life.'

She and Josh hadn't yet discussed the controversial issue of whether or not to have children. They'd been together three whole years now, but she had to accept that his career came first – as indeed did hers. In truth, she was in his debt. As an alpha male, par excellence, he had not only got her the job and taught her almost all she knew, he'd also invited her to share his elegantly spacious garden flat in Islington; a far cry from her former flat-share in an insalubrious part of Holloway.

'In fact, I reckon your father would get on well with my boyfriend. Josh is a whiz at time-management. He's produced this six-stage system that helps you take control of your life and get on top of your workload. Before I met him, I was all over the place, yet I didn't even realize. I'd allow things to pile up, or just fritter away my time, without thinking out my personal goals, or setting up a timetable.'

'That sounds healthier to me than Josh's system, if you don't mind me being frank. It's a *good* thing to waste time. Otherwise it becomes a sort of tyranny that demands your total servitude. Besides,' he asked, 'where will it ever end, as time gets more and more precise? It used to be measured in a rough and ready way – sunrise, sunset, time to milk the cows, or get up, or go to bed – but now we have nanoseconds, for God's sake! Forget nanoseconds – I prefer not to wear a watch at all. OK, I need one for work, but at home, I don't keep track of time, unless I absolutely have to. I regard it as an artificial concept, imposed on us by employers and bureaucracies, or other glutting cretins who want to tell us how to live.' He tapped his fingers sharply on the book, to express his disapproval. 'I also feel strongly about the evil of possessions. I've cut mine down to just the bare essentials, but you should see some of my friends! They own so many things, they move around like spiders in their webs, clinging to the honey-trap of swanky consumer goods.'

Josh would fit that description, she thought, disloyally. Wasn't he overly attached to his BlackBerry, his home cinema and home exercise machine, his Sony Surround-Sound system and all his other executive toys? Yet who was she to talk, with her expensive cache of shoes and bags, her state-of-the-art mobile and self-important watch?

'Why are they even called "goods",' he demanded, 'when all they do is perpetuate desire? I detest the very idea of being a "consumer". That word for me is just a term for meaninglessness and greed.'

She tried to put up a defence; riled that this romanticizing zealot should keep laying down the law. 'Josh believes there's nothing wrong with being rewarded for hard work and, since we live in a technological world, why not take advantage of it and buy stuff that makes life easier?'

'Because it doesn't, Alice – it makes things much more complicated. And, anyway, we soon become slaves to our possessions, or start craving bigger and better ones. What your boyfriend fails to understand is that *being* is more important than doing. That's obvious from his attitude to time. If every single minute of his existence is so rigidly controlled, when can he simply sit and think, or follow up some random idea that might flit into his mind? And what about those transcendental moments triggered by a song, or sunset, or by some sudden new perspective, that frees you from your normal narrow confines? They're impossible unless you have some leisure time. Besides, if he's tied to a job, nine till five – or eight till seven, or whatever hours he works – there's no scope for spontaneity. Let's say he felt the urge to take himself to Mongolia, or Bhutan, or any damned place, for that matter, just because he felt a need to see them, or could experience a different way of life there, how could he just drop everything and go?'

She tried to imagine Josh popping off to Bhutan, simply on a whim, and with a bedroll on his back, rather than leaving for the office on the dot of seven each morning, immaculately attired and armed with his laptop in its special designer case. This self-righteous beanpole really didn't have a clue. Yet, for some inexplicable reason, she found him disconcertingly sexy – all the more bizarre when she was never normally turned on by scruffy clothes and stubble. And, although he wasn't sporting red socks, even his grubby white ones were somehow strangely appealing, and she found her eyes returning to the small stretch of naked flesh exposed between his boots and tattered jeans.

Fortunately, his attention was now claimed by a middle-aged couple, who had come downstairs to the foyer and were asking about a film that wasn't actually showing at the Curzon. A good chance, she thought, to cut short their encounter before she made a fool of herself.

'I think I'll go and get a drink,' she said, once he had redirected the couple to the Empire, Leicester Square. 'I'm feeling rather dry.'

'You can get one here,' he told her, indicating the kiosk opposite.

'No, I want a coffee, and they only serve that in the bar upstairs.'

'OK.' Instantly, he returned to his book, now refreshed, presumably, by his 'brain-rest'.

The spacious upstairs lounge was unusually crowded and buzzing with conversation on all sides. She suspected many people used it as a home-from-home, sprawling on the comfy sofas and reading the free newspapers. It was still below ground-level and therefore windowless, so she couldn't check on the weather, but the forecast had been dire – rain on and off all day – so best to stay inside, in the dry.

Having ordered a latte from the bar at the far end, she found a free armchair, draped her coat across her lap and settled back with a frustrated sigh. It did seem a waste of a Sunday to be sitting here on her own, when Sundays were her one day off. Saturdays seemed to disappear in a blitz of chores and shopping, or catching up with emails and work-related reading. And, since Josh's recent promotion, even their sex seemed confined to Sunday mornings. She hadn't dared discuss it; simply concluded that the demands of his job must have doused his sex-drive, since he was apparently too tired now for their once regular nightly sessions. But why make an issue of it? Things would return to normal, if she didn't pressure him – or at least so she fervently hoped.

She took a sip of her coffee, looking with interest at the couple opposite; he with a tattoo and one green dangly earring; she in stripy purple leggings and shiny red Doc Martens, and both of them wearing crazy hats. She imagined the horror on her boss's face if she breezed into Roebuck-Rayner clad in such eccentric gear. Yet she did sometimes find her 'uniform' of elegant dark suit and crisp white shirt constrained and over-formal; often longed to kick off her high heels and simply go barefoot. Even today, she felt over-dressed. Josh liked her to look glamorous when he took her to expensive restaurants, but her low-cut, slinky dress made her distinctly conspicuous amidst all the jeans and sweatshirts.

Her eyes returned to the couple, who were talking in an animated fashion; the man gesturing extravagantly; the woman throwing back her head in a bray of hilarious laughter. She and Josh rarely laughed, these days. In truth, he seemed so tense and drained, it was as if the job had sucked him dry. Here, the atmosphere was relaxed and almost studenty and, again, brought back happy memories of her days at university and being surrounded by the sort of people who had the time and interest to engage deeply with each other and exchange ideas on life and art. A group of bohemian types in the corner were vociferously debating the relative merits of Visconti and De Sica, while the two men on her right were arguing about the new film, *Crazy Heart*. It was months since she and Josh had discussed anything save work and – frankly – she was tired of him obsessing about clients' needs and problems, even in the evenings and at weekends.

A few people did appear to be actually studying. One girl, sitting cross-legged on the floor, was making notes on an A4 jotter-pad; another was surrounded by a pile of books on astrophysics. Yet, the more she thought about her time at Bristol, the more guiltily aware she was that her old student self had, in Daniel's parlance, undoubtedly sold out. Once, she had felt aghast at the prospect of selling her soul in what Daniel's father called 'a proper job'. Instead, she'd indulged, as a nineteen-year-old, in airy-fairy notions of seeing the world, saving the planet, or 'doing good' – the latter always vague and probably quite unfeasible. Only when she had graduated and so lost the crutch and cushioning of her student-grant and student-hostel, did brute realities force her into work. And doubtless Daniel, too, would be compelled to compromise, once he was a few years older and no longer willing to live on baked beans in a squat.

Or would he? He had clearly thought out his position in surprising depth and detail and she was impressed, despite herself. When it came to the crunch, she and Josh were basically too selfish to spend their precious time in Gaza, helping beleaguered Palestinians, or clearing up pollution in Siberia. They might express polite regret about such problems, but it would be purely superficial, whereas Daniel's idealism seemed steely and determined, as if it went through to his very bones. She found herself mentally undressing him, seeing not his bones but his lithe, strong, naked body; a springy tangle of dark-as-dark-molasses hair accenting his determined, steel-hard cock.

She rammed her cup down on its saucer, appalled to be indulging in such erotic fantasies about another man. In fact, the minute she'd finished her coffee, she would go straight back to the cinema and sit through the rest of the film, however vile the second half might be. In her haste, she all but burned her mouth, then catapulted down the stairs, where she found the steely idealist deep in his book, of course. However, this time she strode past him with just a casual wave, and made her way into the darkened auditorium.

Dark maybe, but no way hushed. Shrieks of 'Cunt!' and

'Motherfucker!' stopped her in her tracks. The mobsters were hurling insults at each other, accompanied by savage kicks and blows. Too bad. She owed it to Josh to put up with all the violence, verbal, physical or lethal.

Having crept into her seat, she reached out for his hand and gave it a loving squeeze. But irritably he shook it free, turned on her and hissed, 'Do you *have* to keep disturbing the whole cinema? You've been up and down like a yoyo and it's driving people mad.'

'What people?' she retorted, cut to the quick.

'Me, to start with! And everybody sitting near. It's impossible to concentrate, with you continually—'

'Sssh!' The man in front swung round in angry protest, as if confirming Josh's words. 'Some of us are here to watch the film, not listen to you arguing!'

She sat stock-still, wounded by the accusation, but still more deeply hurt by Josh's attitude, which seemed totally unreasonable. She had got up only twice and, both times made an effort to be as quiet as possible. In any case, *he* had yawned and fidgeted throughout last Sunday's movie; made it all too obvious that he hated every minute. His bad temper had increased, of late – that was beyond dispute – despite the fact she did everything she could to make his life less pressured. How ever would he cope if they did get round to having kids, when he was already so frazzled with only himself to think about? Over the past few months, she had taken on all the housework, shopping and laundry, and even ran his errands. But why *should* she, for God's sake, when her own schedule was equally stressful? Was he beginning to share Schopenhauer's belief that women were lesser beings and should be essentially subservient?

No, that wasn't fair. He did have many good points, so the least she could do was try her best to concentrate on what was happening in the film – except she could hardly bear to watch. The gang members had drawn knives now and were slashing at each other's faces, which made her feel physically sick. Yet Josh appeared to relish the brutality; his eyes riveted to the screen, as if barbarity and bloodshed were mere harmless entertainment. Daniel's disapproving voice seemed to echo in her head: 'If your tastes are so vastly different, should you even be living together, let alone considering marriage and a family?'

On an impulse, she jumped to her feet and seized her coat and bag again. 'See you back in the flat,' she barked at Josh, striding to the door without waiting for his reply and deliberately banging it behind her. He had accused her of disturbing the whole cinema – right, she would do just that.

She erupted into the foyer, stopping dead when she saw Daniel had gone. His seat was empty; even his book had disappeared. Ridiculous to feel so disappointed. Surely she hadn't intended confiding in him; pouring out her intimate troubles to a stranger, and one completely unrealistic about relationships and life?

She walked slowly up the stairs, pausing in the lounge and again envying the couples eating, drinking, conversing – and all wearing casual clothes. Her skin-tight dress felt almost like a straitjacket and her new Kurt Geiger shoes were pinching at the toes. Why should Josh control her wardrobe, as well as everything else? Did he regard her as just another possession: his well-groomed girlfriend, whose designer clothes and ostentatious watch bore witness to his own wealth and status?

Angrily, she stomped up the next flight of stairs, to ground-level, and marched straight out into the street, almost surprised to see broad daylight. Not only had the rain stopped, there were even a few half-hearted rays of pale, weak, winter sunshine, as if in honour of the Chinese New Year. The celebrations were still in full swing, and Shaftesbury Avenue had been closed to traffic to allow space for the throngs of revellers.

She stood irresolute; reluctant to return to the lonely flat, yet unsure where to go or what to do. Then, with a shrug, she joined the crowd, deciding she might as well enjoy the festive scene. And festive it undoubtedly was. Jaunty music was pouring from loudspeakers and a huge video-screen had been suspended overhead, showing dancers in elaborate costumes twirling and cavorting; their heavy make-up and richly embroidered headdresses lending them an exotic air. Rows of paper lanterns were looped high above the shop-fronts, in vivid fruit-drop colours: lime-green, acid-yellow, flame-orange, vibrant red. The whole atmosphere was one of jubilation – a babble of different nationalities jostling in the street; some sporting tiger-tail-hats, in honour of this new Year of the Tiger. And the stalls set up along the pavement were also selling tiger-wares – tiger hats, tiger masks, toy tigers in every shape and form – as well as painted fans and dragon-shaped balloons.

The cold, crisp air and diverting sights and sounds were beginning to lift her mood and her feet were moving of their own accord to the rhythmic beat of the music. She took a diversion down Wardour Street, where more lanterns adorned the lamp-posts and were strung across the road to form a canopy of colour. Peering in at the crowded restaurants, she admired the rows of Peking ducks hanging in the windows, then stopped at one of the stalls to buy some Chinese candies. She hadn't failed to recognize that she was following Daniel's maxim and deliberately wasting time. Perhaps he wasn't so wrong-headed, after all. Why have a goal in mind, or a purpose, when she could simply *be*, for a change?

It did feel a little odd, though, to be celebrating New Year on 21 February. But her English New Year had been distinctly disappointing. Josh had gone down with a chesty cold, which had made him snappy and unsociable, and having cancelled their ritzy dinner, he had retired to bed at half-past nine, only to complain vociferously when the fireworks woke him up. Well, she would celebrate *this* New Year, instead, and who cared if she was on her own? Better that than being slighted by an irascible partner.

Humming to herself, she turned left into Gerrard Street, which was a riot of red lanterns and gold-and-scarlet flags. And many of the restaurants had 'gold' in their names: the Golden Dragon, Golden Harvest, Golden Pagoda, Golden Palace; the last decorated with green-and-crimson scrolls. Only now did it strike her how starved of colour she had been. Josh's flat was starkly black and white, and most of her possessions he had vetoed as too garish. Her turquoise sequinned cushions had been unceremoniously dumped; her patchwork quilt donated to a charity shop; her brilliant purple beanbags offloaded to a friend. Anything too gaudy seemed to offend his sensibilities. Indeed, earlier today, he had even damned these lanterns, stalls and decorations as so much 'oriental tat'. Did she really want to continue living in so black-and-white a mode? She *needed* sequins and colour; needed glitter and sparkle – emotionally, as much as in her home.

She stopped so abruptly, a Chinese couple bumped into her and began to stutter out apologies, although the fault was entirely hers. But an idea had just occurred to her: she could return to her old flat-share in Holloway – just for tonight, of course – to give Josh a salutary shock; make him realize she simply wouldn't stand for being insulted and controlled. Her former flatmate, Charlotte, had stayed on in the flat, and they were still in frequent contact. She was also friendly with Veronica, the girl who'd been co-opted to take over her old room. Neither would object if she turned up unannounced and she could easily sleep on their sofa, so as not to be a nuisance. In fact, they could all have a good natter, let their hair down, open a bottle of wine or two.

Automatically, she reached for her mobile, only to remember she'd deliberately left it behind. It had suddenly struck her, this morning, that her phone had become a sort of body-part, as essential as an arm or leg, and tied to her by an umbilical cord. So, in a calculated act of rebellion, she had sauntered out without it, just for once, feeling weirdly free and unencumbered. Now, however, she cursed herself. But did it really matter? Charlotte was usually in on a Sunday, so she would simply take a chance.

'Yes, but what about tomorrow?' the voice of duty reproved. 'That crucial Monday-morning meeting? If you stay overnight in Holloway, you won't have your cuttings-book with you, or your all-important contact report, or any proper office clothes.'

'Well, ring from Charlotte's and say you're sick,' another voice suggested – an irresponsible, student voice that failed to understand how imperative it was, in career terms, to be regarded as reliable, and never to take sickies unless they were strictly unavoidable.

She stood, indecisive, an obstruction to the revellers, who had better things to do than agonize about tomorrow. They were living for the day – the moment – and, if this was her New Year, wasn't it time for her to learn from them? She could even make a complete new start; rethink her priorities and embark, maybe, on a different kind of life. But did she have the courage to withstand the social pressures to be successful and high-status, or do without those things that people in her circle considered indispensable?

Her gut-instinct knew the answer and, instantly, she headed for the underground. Leicester Square was on the Piccadilly Line, which would take her direct to Holloway Road tube station. However, just as she approached the entrance, she suddenly darted back the way she'd come, taking short cuts via Newport Place and Gerrard Place, until she was opposite the Soho Curzon once more. She dashed across the road, burst in through the door and went straight up to the box office.

'Could you give me a piece of paper, please?' she asked the man selling tickets. 'I want to leave a note for one of your employees. Oh, and I'll need an envelope, as well – a largish one, if possible.'

'Hold on a sec.' He got up from his seat and disappeared.

She waited in a fever of impatience, it might take him an age. The film would be ending shortly and the last thing she wanted was to run into Josh as he left the cinema. However, the guy was back in a couple of minutes, with a sheet of paper and a strong Manila envelope.

'There you go,' he said. 'Just write their name clearly and I'll make sure that it's passed on.'

'Thanks a lot.' She found a quiet corner in the foyer and unfastened her Rolex watch, pausing a moment, for one last look at the gleaming gold bracelet, shimmering mother-of-pearl dial, and sparkling, round-cut diamonds. Then she took a wad of Kleenex from her bag, wrapped the watch in several layers and put it in the envelope. Next, she scrawled a hasty note:

Daniel, I know you hate possessions, and watches most of all. But I want you to sell this, to buy yourself more thinking-time. Don't try to give it back, or even try to thank me.

I don't need it any more.

Should she add her name, she wondered, or make some jokey reference to Schopenhauer? No. Schopenhauer concerned her, right now, on a highly serious level, not a facetious one. But that was a private matter, to be privately resolved. Just give her time – thinking-time – and she would show the old misogynist that not all women were subservient or should be classed as the second sex.

And, unless Josh learned that, too – and learned it pretty sharp – there would have to be a parting of the ways.

THE 'LITTLE WAY'

Helen glanced around the piazza with a grimace of distaste. Could this really be October 2009? That long, snaking line of credulous 'pilgrims', queuing to view the dismembered relics of St Thérèse of Lisieux, was more suggestive of the Middle Ages, and of a devoutly Catholic country, than of nominally Protestant England, in the increasingly secular twenty-first century.

Suddenly, she tensed, aware of a black-cassocked figure striding towards her, across the square: Father Thomas Mortimer, a fellow guest at her mother's recent lunch party. Her immediate reaction – mingled apprehension and annoyance – was hardly appropriate for such an eminent priest, so she forced her features into an expression of polite respect.

'Helen!' he enthused. 'How nice to see you again! You've come to view the relics, I presume? The response has been phenomenal, you know.'

'Yes, I read about it, Father.' The word 'Father' stuck in her throat of late; although she was so conditioned to using it, no way would she address this tall, distinguished, elderly prelate as just informal 'Tom'.

'Huge crowds have turned out everywhere – seventeen thousand in Liverpool, and that was in only twenty-four hours. And eleven thousand in Birmingham. Oh, and an exceptional attendance in Manchester and Newcastle. And we're expecting over a hundred thousand during the four days that they're here. I take it as a sign that God is at work in the world.'

Or perhaps a sign of desperation, Helen refrained from pointing out. One had only to think of Lourdes to realize that, if all else failed, people were compelled to rely on miracles, however vain the hope.

'Non-Catholics, too, have been flocking in their thousands – even non-believers. And when the relics were taken to Wormwood Scrubs, it resulted in several conversions, so the governor said.'

Given the failure of deterrence or rehabilitation to reduce the prison population, if a gruesome box of bones could help, good luck to it, she thought. In fact, according to an article in her mother's *Catholic Herald*, only a third of the remains had been transported to the British Isles; namely a thighbone and various pieces of the foot. The other two parts remained permanently in France; one in Thérèse's home town of Lisieux and the other on continual tour; both attracting the same pious hordes.

'Two of the prisoners served on the altar at Mass – a lovely idea, don't you think?'

She nodded, wondering if the two cons in question had been tempted to nick the altar-plate.

'Mind you, although we're extremely gratified, it's been a huge responsibility, as I'm sure you can imagine. Just the organization involved was something of a headache and, of course, there's always a risk to life and limb when such big crowds gather in one place. We've done our best, here at the cathedral, to ensure that things run smoothly, but we can't rule out some sort of hitch. For instance, we issued printed instructions to those queuing – suggested they wear warm clothes and waterproofs, and bring food and drinking water and maybe a portable seat. But you only have to look, Helen' – he gestured towards the queue – 'and you'll see that not everyone heeds our advice.'

Following his gaze, she realized that the recent downpour had left many people wet, bedraggled and obviously uncomfortable. However, she was struck less by the lack of waterproofs, than by the contrast between the pilgrims' shambling shabbiness and the richness of the cathedral itself, with its soaring bell-tower and intricate brick-and-stone façade. It never failed to rile her how flagrantly the Catholic Church had ignored its founder's plea to sell all one possessed and give the proceeds to the poor. Rather, it had accumulated extensive lands and properties; portfolios of shares; a mass of gold and silver plate; sumptuous vestments and precious works of art. Yet the featherbedded hierarchy were hardly likely to renounce their splendid residences, or give up the convenience of housekeepers and gardeners and other servile flunkeys, let alone pour their vintage claret down the sink. As for the Vatican itself, its treasures and resources seemed woefully out of kilter with the teachings of the God of Poverty.

'Still, the technical side of things has been a great success' – the priest flashed her a smile, revealing expensive dentistry – 'the video-screen, in particular. It's easier for people to be patient while they queue, if they can watch what's going on inside the cathedral.'

'Yes, it's a really good idea,' she murmured, peering up at the gigantic screen, erected in the piazza, which showed the actual reliquary and those who had finally reached it, after their long wait in the cold – a beacon of hope, presumably, to those still waiting their turn. Indeed, any form of diversion must be welcome, when the average time spent queuing was said to be four-and-a-quarter hours.

'We're all been struck by people's devotion. It's obvious how much it means to them to have St Thérèse's relics here at the cathedral.'

Again, she nodded in agreement, aware that bones and other body-parts (blood, teeth, fingernails and hair) were classed as first-class relics, as against a saint's mere clothes, or an object they had touched. And Signs and Wonders were already being reported: a barren rosebush in a pilgrim's Sussex garden had miraculously burst into flower; sprouting 150 lush, deep crimson blooms. Roses were very much in evidence today: on sale in the piazza, as St Thérèse's symbolical flower. Even those pilgrims who looked distinctly down-at-heel had been buying them with profligate enthusiasm, and she only hoped their families weren't going short of food on account of such extravagance. She also reckoned privately that many poor French peasants could have been lifted out of poverty, had the cash squandered on the reliquary been devoted to them, instead. That elaborate construction, made from jacaranda wood and lavishly encrusted with gold, must have cost a fortune.

Again, she watched it on the screen; the faithful filing past, or stopping to press their hands or lips against the protective Perspex case. Most were holding roses, which they also touched against the case, perhaps believing that the essence of the relics could emanate through wood and acrylic.

'Well, I mustn't keep you, Helen. Remember me to your mother, won't you?'

'Yes, of course.'

Once he'd bustled off, she continued to watch the screen; her eye caught by an elderly gentleman, who pressed his handkerchief against the case, then held it to each leg in turn; obviously hoping that his pain or disability would be cured by St Thérèse's intercession. She was reminded of her mother, who shared the same simplistic faith and who would be deeply shocked, even scandalized, if she could see into her daughter's mind. Indeed, she would find it all the more distressing that her beloved only child should harbour such rebellious thoughts on so special an occasion and in so hallowed a spot.

Mooching on across the square, she felt her usual guilt and sadness that the person she loved most in the world – her patient, gentle, unselfish, pious mother – had not the slightest notion that she'd long since given up her faith and now viewed the Church as reactionary, intolerant and profoundly hypocritical. Yet how could she admit her doubts, when that Church was so important to her mother, who'd even moved to a flat in Vincent Square, to be nearer to the cathedral? It had become her second home; offered her great comfort and support. She knew all the priests by name – and often entertained her favourites, including Father Thomas – attended daily Mass and was a fervent member of the Legion of Mary, the Prayer Group and the Guild of the Blessed Sacrament.

Although there were advantages for *her*, as well, in knowing that, if her mother fell ill or needed help at home, a whole bevy of parishioners, all living close at hand, would offer immediate aid. It would have been considerably more worrying had such local support been lacking, since she herself lived seventy miles away. Today,

Bernadette and Ruth, fellow members of the Prayer Group, had promised to act as nurse and chef, respectively, and to hold the fort until four or five, when *she* would visit, to give her mother a full account of the afternoon's proceedings. Which reminded her – she'd better buy some sort of souvenir, rather than turn up empty-handed.

She made her way to the gift-shop, skirting the long, zigzag queue, which was being strictly marshalled by church officials; the latter determined to chastise any stragglers, shovers, or – God forbid – pushers-in. Once in the shop, she was appalled by the tat on sale – tinny medals, hideous statues, cutesy angel candle-holders, and a whole range of St Thérèse-imprinted merchandise: key-rings, prayer-cards, Biros, tumblers, fridge magnets. Having inspected the shelves with increasing distaste, she eventually chose a 'Shower of Roses' rosary, sold complete with a gift-box, rose-embossed and velvet-lined. Since her mother said a daily rosary – and had done so every day since childhood – at least the present wouldn't languish in a drawer.

Then, with a sigh of resignation, she retraced her steps across the square, wrinkling her nose against the smells of grease and onions. Needless to say, commercial interests had been cashing in on the presence of the relics. A hamburger-bar, a coffee-stall and a mobile fish-and-chip van were all doing a lively trade, although looking distinctly incongruous against the imposing cathedral façade. Relics had always been big business and she remembered reading somewhere that a few unscrupulous medieval churches had even stolen body-parts from other, rival establishments, to swell their coffers by attracting flocks of pilgrims. Could profits still be made, she wondered, by modernizing the cult? People would probably queue for hours to view David Beckham's foreskin or Keira Knightley's fingernail.

As she cut round the side of the building to the entrance on Ambrosden Avenue, she saw another queue snailing the length of the street. Wearily, she tagged on to the end, cursing her swollen arm – throbbing badly now – and the uncomfortable compression-sleeve swathing it from armpit to wrist. She had come to accept that the swelling would probably be permanent, since it was a symptom of the lymphedema that had set in just a couple of months after the removal of her lymph-nodes, and been aggravated further by her radiation treatment. In her pious mother's view, though, it made her a natural candidate for today's Sacrament of the Sick – as did the cancer itself, of course. And because of her contacts in High Places, her mother had managed to secure two tickets for the service, blithely hoping for a miracle. Impossible for *her* to share such naive optimism. It seemed unlikely in the extreme that the lymphedema would vanish overnight, let alone that her mutilated breasts, shorn off in the mastectomy, would be restored to their former prominence. Besides, she felt a strong aversion to the prospect of being herded into the church with a mass of other invalids, for an anointing and a long and tedious service, although she was guiltily aware that most good Catholics would envy her good fortune, since tickets were like gold-dust.

'Hey, *you*! Move back!'

Helen jumped at the imperious tone. An overweening official had pounced on some poor old woman, who had tried to sneak her way into the queue.

'Will you kindly join the *end* of the queue?' he barked. 'But, first, may I see your ticket?'

'I ... I don't have a ticket,' the woman stuttered – an ashen-pale, emaciated creature, walking with great difficulty on two gnarled and mismatched sticks.

'Well, this service is for ticket-holders only, so I suggest you go back home.'

Would Jesus have taken such a draconian line, Helen was tempted to retort? But she held her peace and, only once he had moved on, out of sight, did she rummage in her bag for her spare ticket and press it into the frail and bony hand. 'You're welcome to this one,' she smiled. 'It's actually my mother's, but she went down with bronchitis this morning, so she wasn't able to come.'

'God bless you, dear,' the woman exclaimed, her face alight with joy.

It seemed doubtful, Helen mused, that the Almighty would oblige, not only because of her lost faith, but because divine blessings had been noticeably thin on the ground in the last traumatic decade. After the initial blow of the cancer and the loss of both her breasts, had come a second shock: the desertion of her husband, who clearly couldn't live with a scarred and breastless wife, and had recently found comfort with a girl twenty years her junior, who boasted impressive mammaries of double-D proportions.

'Don't go to the end of the queue,' she whispered to the woman. 'You'll only tire yourself. Slip in here with me and we'll pass you off as my mother.... No, don't thank me. You're welcome. I'm Helen, by the way.'

'And I'm Vera – Vera Thérèse. I'm so lucky in my second name. My father chose it on account of his deep love of the Little Flower.'

'That's lovely! My mother's a devotee, too. And, though I wasn't called Thérèse, I took it as my Confirmation name.'

Suddenly she was twelve again, a pious Catholic child, desperate to emulate her Confirmation saint by becoming a Carmelite, the minute she left school. To be worthy of Thérèse, she had put pebbles in her shoes; refused all food on Fridays and given away her sweet-supply to the one girl in the class she loathed. Since Thérèse had said, 'all suffering is sweet to me', she, too, must practise self-denial, especially as her life was easy, in contrast to the saint's. Thérèse had suffered constant childhood illnesses, whereas her own health had been robust as a girl, so her duty was to compensate by daily acts of penance. What she had found the hardest, though, was following the 'Little Way', which meant being simple, humble, artless and meek and pursuing the path of sanctity through tiny, unseen, sacrificial acts, as Thérèse herself had done. Born feisty and ambitious, her natural inclination was to be famous and acclaimed; not settle for obscurity. It went against the grain to strive to be a 'Little Flower', when, secretly and sinfully, she yearned to be the tallest, brightest, most bee-attracting bloom.

She was helped by her best friend, however, who shared her urge to be a Carmelite. Virtuous little Daphne had even once reported that the Blessed Virgin had smiled at her; thus mimicking Thérèse, who had claimed the self-same thing as a precocious child of ten. Determined not to be outdone, she herself had prayed fervently for the Moors murderer, Ian Brady, again in imitation of Thérèse, who, in 1887, had secured a deathbed conversion for a brutal criminal, thus saving him from hellfire and damnation.

Only now did she realize, with a certain wry amusement, that, far from following the 'Little Way' and seeking self-effacement, she and Daphne had been guilty of the sin of pride, in expecting to be canonized themselves and to join Thérèse in the highest rank of Heaven. Indeed, they'd spent earnest hours, whilst still on earth, discussing the major miracles they'd work; hoping to rival the saint's achievement in curing the seven-year-old Edith Piaf, no less, of blindness.

'Do you know, not a single day goes by when I don't call on St Thérèse for help.'

Helen jumped at the voice – not Daphne's piping treble, but Vera's asthmatic drone. Hastily, she dragged her mind back from the past.

'In fact, I've come to see her as almost a close personal friend.'

Helen gave a murmur of assent, although her own view of the saint had changed markedly since childhood. Now she abhorred Thérèse as a sentimental, simplistic goody-two-shoes, not to mention seriously neurotic.

'All those blessings she sends from above, I've experienced them myself, my dear – whole showers of heavenly roses bringing comfort to my life. So now I have total confidence that, if I ask her for a favour, she'll never fail to grant it.'

As Helen surveyed Vera's missing teeth, sparse, lank hair and arthritic finger-joints, she entertained grave doubts about such 'favours'. And, despite her two sticks, the poor woman had been limping badly, as they inched their stop-start way towards the entrance. So couldn't her 'close personal friend' have done a better job?

'What I love about her is the way she cares about every single soul, however unimportant they may seem. I don't know whether you realize, dear, but her relics have toured over fifty different countries? And, wherever they've gone, people have been healed, spiritually as well as physically. Even hardened sinners, who've neglected the holy sacraments for years, have been brought back to the faith and started going to confession and Communion.'

Helen swallowed. Confession had been bad enough in childhood; admitting to the priest that she'd been mean to Anne-Marie; told fibs to Miss MacDonald about skimped hockey practice or uncompleted homework, or committed the sin of greed by asking for second helpings of steamed jam roll. But confession now would be totally horrendous – not just her utter godlessness, but her unspoken desire that a grisly death should befall her ex-husband's second wife, just as the pair were in the throes of making love. And that would destroy their unborn child, of course, whom she loathed even more than its mother, despite its total innocence. No way could she be granted absolution when guilty of such irredeemable wickedness.

Again, her thoughts were interrupted by Vera's enthusing about the saint.

'Apparently, a fragment of her bone was even sent into outer space. So, if extra-terrestrial life exists, maybe aliens will come to God, through the power of St Thérèse.'

Helen racked her brains for a suitable reply, although the prospect of extra-terrestrials becoming ardent Catholics didn't exactly convince.

'Ladies, may I see your tickets, please?'

At last, they'd reached the side-entrance to the cathedral – but whether they would be welcomed in was a different matter entirely, since yet another official was scrutinizing both them and their tickets with a high degree of suspicion. Perhaps he judged them not infirm enough for the Sacrament of the Sick. Did you need to be a double amputee to gain admittance here? However, he finally relented – even gave a grudging smile – almost a miracle in itself.

As they stepped inside, she lent Vera a supportive arm – making sure it was her *good* arm, since the other one was extremely sore when touched. They both paused a second, impressed by the atmospheric gloom of the interior and its thrilling sense of space. She had come to know the place through accompanying her mother to the occasional Mass or Benediction, and never failed to respond to its awe-inspiring majesty. Cost apart, she had nothing against ecclesiastical splendour. It was the irrational beliefs that riled her; the popery and superstition; the authoritarian patriarchy. Still, in an hour or so, the service would be over and her only remaining duty would be to gratify her mother with an enthusiastic account of the beauty of the hymns, the ardour of the faithful, and whatever else she could justifiably praise.

'I want to sit right at the front,' Vera whispered, once she had hobbled across the north transept, still clutching Helen's arm.

Having found her a good seat just behind the rows of wheelchairs, which had been given pride of place, Helen settled her down carefully. 'I hope you don't mind, Vera, but I'd prefer a seat near the back myself.'

'Well, that shows true humility, my dear, just like St Thérèse! You're a truly lovely person – I can see that.'

Helen flushed in embarrassment. Her motive in sitting at the back was certainly not humility, but a wish to distance herself from the sanctuary, the altar and the whole panoply of priests.

Having said her goodbyes to Vera, she tiptoed back down the aisle, trying not to disturb the congregation, all expectantly waiting for the proceedings to begin. Only part of the cathedral was being used for the service; the area nearest the main entrance having been reserved for the throng of pilgrims. A rope-barrier had been set up across the central section of the nave, closing off all access to the reliquary. But, as she settled into the very last pew, adjacent to the barrier, all she had to do to see the casket was turn round in her seat. A few more church officials were policing this sensitive spot, to ensure that no one ducked under the rope, or behaved in an unseemly fashion. However, surely it couldn't be an offence to simply *look*. Fascinated, she kept her eyes on the stream of people filing reverently past – not just the blind, the lame, the halt, but also the young and vigorous – in fact, every conceivable age and type. And their faith and hope were palpable, as they pressed their hands or rosaries against the Perspex case. Many made the Sign of the Cross; some fell to their knees on the hard wooden floor, as if overcome by their proximity to St Thérèse's actual bones.

Whatever her own misgivings about credulity and superstition, she accepted the fact that people were bound to crave relief from the bleakness and injustice of this world. Irrational or no, it was clearly more consoling to believe in a benevolent God, who could compensate for the sufferings in this life by the promise of a better one to come. And, although relics, in her opinion, could be dismissed as religious placebos, many serious drug-trials had shown that even placebos could be surprisingly effective.

However, she winced in mingled horror and compassion as a pathetic specimen of humanity dragged his painful way towards the reliquary. Half his face was missing – presumably lost to some form of cancer far more terrible than hers – and his back was hunched and distorted by osteoporosis. If Thérèse had any power, or God had any mercy, surely this poor soul deserved a miracle. No miracle was forthcoming, though, and, having devoutly kissed the casket, he shuffled on; his place taken by the next in line: a Downs Syndrome child and its patient, prayerful mother.

Was there anyone who *hadn't* suffered, she wondered? Certainly not St Thérèse, who had lost her battle against TB and gone to her grave at the age of only twenty-four. And Thérèse's mother, Zelie, had lost five of her nine children and also died tragically young – ironically, of breast cancer – while her father, Louis, had ended his days in a state of mental paralysis, as the result of several strokes. Even her own mother had suffered three late miscarriages, before giving birth to *her*, only to be widowed the following year. Nor had she herself escaped. Long before the cancer and the divorce, she had experienced both grief and loss. Not only had she lacked a father, but the whole of her twenties and thirties had been taken up with a struggle to conceive. Her failure to have a child had been a devastating blow and made Felicia's effortless pregnancy all the more insufferable. The woman's very name was hateful. Of *course* she was felicitous, now that she had Simon, as well as a baby on the way. Yet, confronted with the horrendous plight of some of those around her here, self-pity seemed inappropriate, if not downright indulgent.

She noticed that the Downs Syndrome child had left her roses by the shrine, as indeed had many other pilgrims. A church official was busy gathering them up and it crossed her mind that perhaps they were recycled; secreted back into the shop, to be repurchased by the unsuspecting faithful. Such thoughts were quite improper, though, in a cathedral, of all places and, again, she felt a surge of guilt, posing as a pious Catholic when it was so far from the reality. But love brought real dilemmas. To spare her mother pain, she was forced to live out a charade, but surely that was less unkind than causing deep distress by revealing the stark truth.

The organ, which had been playing softly, suddenly swelled in scale and resonance to a deeply sonorous boom. Aware the service was about to start, she quickly turned to face the altar. Her mother would want a full report on the elaborate flower-arrangements and the large portrait of Thérèse, set up outside the altar-rail. Having noted first the details of the flowers, she focused on the picture; peering through the serried mass of heads, to make out a flowing habit; a shower of roses cascading from the saint's uplifted hands; shifty eyes, a sanctimonious face. Some words would need adjusting for her mother: 'angelic', not 'sanctimonious'; 'beseeching', rather than 'shifty'.

At three o'clock precisely, an impressive band of clergy processed slowly up the aisle: at least twelve priests, as far as she could see, along with altar-servers and acolytes, some carrying lighted candles or gold crosses, and – bringing up the rear – a balding, bespectacled figure, clad in bishop's purple. According to the service-sheet, the celebrant was the Right Reverend Hopes – surely an auspicious name – Auxiliary Bishop of Westminster, and maybe even a friend of her mother.

The congregation had risen to their feet (those, at least, who had the use of their legs, which, in fact, ruled out quite a number) and she, too, stood up, to join in the opening hymn. A Catholic education was designed to stay imprinted on one's mind till death, so she knew the words by heart, of course, and those of every hymn and prayer featured in the service-sheet. Indeed, as she sang the line, *Help me to mortify the flesh*, she was reminded again of Daphne and how the pair of them had jabbed their palms with sharp scissor-blades and happily drawn blood, as their somewhat ghoulish way of sharing in Christ's Passion.

Everyone around her looked reverent, focused, prayerful; only she distracted and dissenting. The swarthy man on her left might be mispronouncing words; the woman on her right singing out of tune, yet they weren't wishing they were back at home – as she did.

Once the hymn had ended, the bishop greeted the congregation, before launching into the Penitential Rite, calling on all present to acknowledge their faults and failings.

No problem for her there: blasphemy, hypocrisy, apostasy, irreverence – not to mention lethal fury towards Felicia and her unborn child, and an intense wish for revenge. Her mother, in contrast, actually prayed for the detestable woman, but then her mother was a Christian in all senses of the word.

After the prayers for forgiveness – clearly impossible in her case – everyone remained standing for the Gospel. Her arm was aching so much, she barely heard a word of it and preferred, anyway, to savour the attractions of the building. Her eyes travelled from the honey-coloured marble of the towering baldachino, to the mosaic, above it, in shimmering green and blue, then up to the large crucifix, suspended over the sanctuary, and from there to the highest of the domes. The Gospel was a short one, so she was still gazing up at all the gorgeous grandeur when the congregation was requested to be seated, in readiness for Bishop Hopes's sermon.

With a sigh of mingled pain and irritation, she subsided onto the pew; inwardly prepared for a long-winded, leaden homily. However, the bishop seemed a kindly man; his voice gentle and benevolent; not the hectoring tone she had somehow been expecting.

'We must become like little children,' he urged. 'Follow St Thérèse's "Little Way" and rediscover our littleness....'

'Little', 'little', 'little' – even now it irked her. Why not greatness and renown? Not that *she* had achieved anything even approaching greatness in her fifty-five inconsequential years. Her lofty childhood ambitions had long since shrivelled to dust and, after an early marriage and the protracted efforts to conceive, she had eventually settled for a steady, unexciting job as PA to a local solicitor. And even that had been forfeited, as a direct result of her cancer, making her present life very much a 'little way': a petty round of charity work, visits to her mother and various volunteering duties in the village.

'We must trust God, as little children trust their fathers,' the bishop continued, gesturing towards the assembled throng, 'and expect everything from that father, in a spirit of total dependence.'

Nice, she thought, with a shrug of resignation, to have *had* a father to trust. Hers had been mown down by a drunken driver when she was barely six months old. God the Father had provided a certain compensation, but He hadn't exactly been available to teach her chess or cricket, nor had He made His presence felt at school sports days, plays, or prize-givings.

Her neighbour's fit of coughing drowned the next part of the homily, but, once it had subsided, she realized that the theme remained unchanged: the 'Little Way', the 'Little Way'.

'Following that "Way" will prevent us worrying about the future, or indulging in irrational fears of what might happen tomorrow....'

She shook her head in annoyance. Most people's concern about the future was far from being irrational, as was obvious in her own case. The cancer might well return, or she might develop chronic cellulitis, having had two bouts already, both accompanied by fever and unpleasant, flu-like symptoms. And money was a continual worry: would she find the wherewithal to finance her old age – if she ever *reached* old age? She also fretted about her mother, who, valuing her independence, had declined to come and live with her in Kintbury. The obvious solution would be to sell the cottage and move to Vincent Square, yet the prospect of being so far removed from her local friends and contacts was itself a source of dismay. There were emotional worries, too. When Felicia gave birth, how would she cope with the burning jealousy the baby would induce? She'd already contemplated murdering the fecund, bosomy female, but, once a new-born infant was suckling from those bosoms, a double murder might be more in order.

'The "Little Way" will make our pain easier to bear and, if we unite our sufferings with those of Christ on the Cross, we'll come to realize how deeply in love with us He is.'

In love. If only! Forget God's love; it was Simon's love she craved – yes, even now, when the relationship was long since over. His desertion had hurt profoundly; the implication that he valued only her breasts and not her deeper self. And she still missed acutely the whole sense of being a couple; the quiet contentment and confidence it brought, which one simply took for granted until it was removed. Simon had even shared her religious doubts, but been compelled, like her, to dissimulate, to avoid scandalizing his equally pious mother. Their joint anxiety in colluding in deception had forged a special bond, yet, once he met Felicia, he was blithely prepared to offend both mothers deeply, by suing for divorce and remarrying in a Register Office.

All at once, she was aware of tears streaming down her cheeks. Horrified, embarrassed, she hid her face in her hands and pretended to be praying. Yet her shoulders shook with sobs and she was tempted to leave the church – except that would mean drawing unwelcome attention to herself. Her hands were wet; the tears dripping onto her lap and making damp splodges on her coat. She had barely cried at all these last few years, despite the loss of Simon and the loss of her health and breasts. Yet that traumatic time of grief and loss had come surging back, prompted by the service. How much easier things would be if she could only share the bishop's belief in a kindly, loving God, or share her mother's confidence that she would be reunited in the life to come with her dear, departed father. Indeed, once she got to Heaven, even her breasts would be restored, according to her mother's simple faith.

But it wasn't just those certainties – or fantasies – she missed, but some fundamental meaning to existence. The beauty of the choirboys' voices reminded her of all she'd lost: the whole spiritual dimension, once so precious and fulfilling, and those very treasures of the Church she now affected to despise. Just sitting here, surrounded by this splendour, this sense of the sublime, only served to emphasize the shallow mediocrity of her present paltry life; its lack of point and purpose.

'Excuse me, madam, please.'

The man beside her was trying to squeeze past. Hastily jerking up to her feet, she realized that the rest of the sermon had completely passed her by, and even part of the service, since the anointing of the sick was now about to start. A whole bevy of priests was moving from the altar; some remaining at the front of the cathedral, while others proceeded along the aisle and transepts, and took up their positions further down. The congregation, too, were rising from their seats and forming orderly queues behind each priest. Stewards in red tabards had also made an appearance, and were marshalling the crowds or offering assistance to the priests.

Conscious of her tear-stained face, her first instinct was to bolt, yet she remained standing where she was, whilst the other people in the pew struggled past her and made their way towards the nearest priest. The organ was playing; the choirboys still singing with that pure, ethereal radiance, yet all she could do was agonize; torn three ways between a sense of duty, a fear of sacrilege and a strong wish to escape. This anointing was a sacrament, which meant she had no right to receive it in what the Church would call a persistent state of sin. Yet her mother was bound to question her about it: which priest had she approached; had he spoken to her personally, and had the experience affected her, either spiritually or physically? Had she felt more ease of movement in her arm, or some lessening of discomfort, or even a marked reduction in the swelling?

'I felt nothing!' she knew she'd want to shout – nothing but a sense of sham. Such brute honesty would be callous, though, so if her anointing would give pleasure to her mother, then clearly she had to overcome her scruples.

Venturing out of the pew, she dithered again about which queue to join. The nearest was also the longest, but she had no wish to go parading around the cathedral, so she took her place at the end. The priest looked far too young to have had any real experience of life. What did *any* celibate priest, for that matter, know of love, sex, coupledom, divorce?

Distracted by such thoughts, she almost bumped into the person in front of her; a thin, anxious looking woman, pushing a child in a buggy. Having stuttered her apologies, she stole a glance at the child, which seemed more dead than alive, with its drooling mouth, sunken eyes and greyish, waxen skin. It made no sense, of course, to blame a non-existent God for the sufferings of humanity, yet she still felt highly indignant at the concept of an omnipotent, all-merciful deity being responsible for such a flawed creation. It also riled her that all these stricken people should be so pathetically grateful for a mere dab of holy oil. Indeed, from what she could see by peering towards the front of the queue, the process smacked of a production-line; each person speedily dispatched, with no time for any personal exchange or individual counsel.

As she waited for her turn, her mind reverted to childhood again, when this rite was known as Extreme Unction and normally administered only to patients *in extremis*. She and Daphne had both hoped to die as young as their tubercular role-model, since the sooner they reached Heaven, the sooner they could work their mega-miracles. Thus, they'd assumed they hadn't long to wait before they received this final sacrament. As for any fear of death, it never crossed their minds; they simply took it for granted that the anointing itself would give them the grace to endure their terminal sufferings. The word 'grace' had meant so much, then: that mysterious gift of God that descended on your soul, especially in the sacraments, and which she had always pictured like golden candyfloss: a sweet and special treat – gold, not pink, because it was sent direct from Heaven.

How smug they'd been, in those days, yet how enviably serene. And, of course, another good thing about Catholic schooling was that it extended one's vocabulary. Phrases such as Extreme Unction and Viaticum tripped lightly off their tongues, and they hadn't had the slightest trouble spelling tricky words like longanimity or transubstantiation.

She was suddenly aware that the woman with the sickly child had reached the head of the queue, which meant it was *her* turn next. She could now see the priest quite clearly: a stripling of a fellow, with limp brown hair and watery blue eyes, who didn't exactly inspire great confidence. Yet she watched in surprise as he bent towards the pushchair with such reverence and respect, the child might have been Jesus Himself. Then taking each of its hands in turn, with the deepest of compassion, he anointed them with dignity and deference, as if imbuing the poor suffering scrap with a sense of the utmost worth. The toddler made no sound, perhaps already too far gone for help, yet the mother gave a radiant smile, as she, too, was anointed.

Once the woman had wheeled the pushchair away, she herself came face to face with the priest, who gazed into her eyes with a look of such sheer kindness and concern, she felt an uneasy mix of gratitude, misgiving and embarrassment.

'My child ...' he said.

How could two short words have so profound an effect; stirring a fierce longing for her simple childhood faith; for that uncomplicated time when God had been as close as Daphne; an intimate friend who would listen, care, respond, at any hour of the day or night?

'Do you remember what St Thérèse said when she entered the cloister?' he asked, still looking at her with the same intense solemnity.

Flustered, she shook her head.

'She said, "I will be love",' he continued, supplying the answer himself.

She flushed. Was he aware of her decidedly unloving feelings, not just towards the Church, but towards the obnoxious Felicia and her equally loathsome foetus? And why was he addressing her at all, when he hadn't spoken personally to anybody else, not even that afflicted mother, with her shadow of a child? Merely because she was the last one in the queue? Or was he about to tell her that his conscience would prevent him from anointing her, because he could see into her mind and knew it would be sacrilege for him to go ahead with the ritual?

But, without the slightest hesitation, he dipped his thumb into the cup of holy oil and applied it to her forehead, and did so with great humility, as if, extraordinarily, the honour was all his. He was bringing to this rite a sense of genuine love – a true Christian love, like her mother's, that extended to all humanity and that she could feel in his very touch.

'May the Lord in His mercy help, through with the grace of....'

Grace. For a disorienting moment, a stream of celestial sweetness seemed to envelop her whole being; the sensation deepening as he proceeded to anoint her hands. She must be imagining things, or – appalling prospect – totally losing her grip. Perhaps she had finally cracked, as a result of too much stress, because all solidity and boundaries appeared to be shifting and dissolving, as if she were no longer tied to a bodily form but floating and adrift. Somewhere, vaguely, she heard the words of the rite being solemnly recited and knew she ought to say 'Amen', but she had lost the power of speech. All sense of time and space was also disappearing, and she seemed to move into a different plane entirely, as gleaming marble and glittering mosaics became one with her and part of her, and seconds passed with the slow, majestic rhythm of eternity. Even bronze and alabaster were molten and ablaze now, and she, too, was only fire and light; suffused with radiant grace.

'Madam, are you all right?'

With difficulty, she opened her eyes. The priest had gone – but where? A steward was standing over her; the shriek of his scarlet tabard slowly returning her to consciousness.

'Madam, did you hear? I asked if you were all right.'

Uncertainly, she nodded; let him guide her back to her seat – a cautious, halting process, as she still felt strangely faint. Her arm was every bit as painful; her body still as weak; her doubts and disbelief just as deeply ingrained. Nothing had outwardly changed; no miraculous cure, or even reconversion; no Falling to her Knees and Seeing the Light. Yet, as she slumped into the pew, she was conscious of the fact that some inexplicable form of grace had indeed descended, together with a sense of peace – all the more extraordinary in light of her former anger and resentment. And it was a grace that would allow her to endure; to embrace her 'little way' and even see the worth in it, however unfathomable the whole thing seemed. All she knew was that the phrase, 'I will be love', had somehow elicited that dramatically transformative grace. Her mother's own example of loving everyone, without exception – even those who had harmed her or betrayed her – had proved, of late, an impossible ideal. Not now. For some reason way beyond her grasp, she could now love Felicia – even love her child.

The congregation was rising for the final hymn, *Lord of all Hopefulness, Lord of all Joy*. This morning, she would have found the words ironic; mocked them with her usual bitter cynicism, since no gleam of joy or hopefulness had touched her life for months. But as she stumbled to her feet and, haltingly, began to sing, the first, weak stirrings of them both took flimsy, foetal root.

WORLD'S YOUR OYSTER

'Is that Buckingham Palace?' the big, blubbery American asked, in her lazy Southern drawl.

'Er, no,' Hayley muttered, trying to shift away from the mass of sweaty flesh pressing against her own thin thighs.

'It's the Foreign Office,' her father, Kenneth, put in, swivelling round from the seat in front to deliver one of his lectures. 'The building was begun in 1861 and originally housed four separate government departments: the Foreign Office, the India Office, the Colonial Office and—'

'But where's Buckingham Palace?' the woman interrupted.

Hayley winced at the pronunciation. Emphasizing '*ham*', like that, made the place sound like a pork factory.

'If you want to see the Palace, I suggest you get off at the next stop – that's Trafalgar Square. Walk through Admiralty Arch and go all along the Mall, which will bring you into....'

Her dad had moved from history to geography, but the woman had switched off the minute she heard the word 'walk'.

'Oh, no. I couldn't walk. Not in this heat. I packed all the wrong things for the trip – raincoats and rubber boots. They told us it was always raining in London.'

'That's a myth,' Kenneth stated pompously. 'If you study the rainfall statistics, you'll see that....'

Hayley suppressed a groan – although she should actually be grateful to the Yank for monopolizing her dad's attention. Otherwise *she* would be the recipient of all this useless knowledge. The family usually sat together, on the two pairs of front seats on the upper deck; her parents side by side and she next to her brother. But, today, they'd been forced to split up, having lost their prime position when they got off the bus at Westminster – her father's fault, as usual, since he'd insisted on yet another tour of the Abbey, with him as guide and lecturer. She found the place depressing, with all those gloomy tombs, and dead marble people lying on their backs, reminding you that nothing lasted long. And, of course, her father always gave his spiel about the different styles of architecture, which she had heard ad infinitum. Anyway, it meant they'd had to wait for another bus, along with scores of tourists, all pushing, jostling, fighting to get on, so, in fact, they were lucky to get seats at all. Her brother was standing actually – not that he objected. She envied Tim his easy-going temperament. He didn't mind the Abbey; didn't even mind this ludicrous idea of taking their annual holiday on a *bus*. Other people went abroad, or at least on proper holidays in England; hired caravans or canal boats, or even booked into hotels. She would bet her life they were the only family in the entire western world that spent the last week of August travelling the same boring route each year, then returning home every night to sleep in their own beds.

'The 24 is the oldest bus route in London,' her father informed his audience of one. 'Dating back to 1910. Originally, it terminated in Victoria, but, two years later, they extended the run to Pimlico. That's where we live,' he added, 'right near the start of the route – very handy, in fact, because it means we board the bus when it's empty. And it really is the perfect way to see London, since it goes directly south to north, and passes many important landmarks on its way.'

Except you get sick and tired of those landmarks, Hayley reflected, especially after five whole summers repeating the same journey. And what made it worse was that she was forbidden to use her mobile – a totally pathetic rule, but typical of her schoolmaster dad, who was dead keen on self-improvement and couldn't understand why she should want to text her friends, rather than listen to his words of wisdom.

'Well, I'm heading for the end of the line,' the woman volunteered. 'My English aunt used to own a house in Hampstead, and I want to find exactly where she lived.'

'In that case, do make sure you see the Heath. It's one of the jewels of London – eight hundred acres of open woodland, with outstanding views over the city, especially from the higher ground by Jack Straw's Castle.'

'There's a castle?' the woman asked, now displaying genuine interest.

'No, it's actually an old coaching-inn, named after one of the leaders of the Peasants' Revolt – Jack Straw. He commanded a rebel band in 1381 and is best known for....'

Hayley sneaked a look at her magazine, as her dad embarked on yet another history lesson. Although it wasn't easy to concentrate, especially when her mother, Maureen, joined in the conversation, having found an empty seat close by and moved up from four rows back.

'The weather's so glorious today,' she told the fat American, 'we thought we'd picnic on the Heath.'

More sweltering than glorious, Hayley thought. This top deck was like a sweat-box; the sun pounding through the glass and making her feel sticky-damp all over. The picnic food would probably have turned rancid by the time they got off – *if* they ever got off. The bus always took an eternity, crawling along at the pace of a hearse; diverted by road-works; held up in traffic; delayed by bumbling old ladies, who started pouring out their troubles to the driver, or by bolshie kids who had lost their Oyster-cards and refused to pay the fare. Oyster-card – weird name. According to her father, it was a variation on Octopus – the original travel-cards introduced in Hong Kong in 1997 – but it made her think of the phrase 'the world's your oyster'. If only. Unfortunately, the tatty piece of plastic was limited to London Transport, rather than being an open sesame to any destination on the globe.

She closed her eyes and, in less than twenty seconds, was winging her way to fantastic ports of call – Timbuktu, Antarctica, the Himalayas, Tristan da Cunha – and flying in her own private plane, with no member of her family in sight; no drunken louts, or doddery old ladies. Yes, she was zooming high, high up, above the traffic jams, the trees, the tallest of tall buildings; zipping along at supersonic speed. Any minute, the plane would land and she would step out into a rainforest, or onto shining snowfields, fringed with glaciers, or desert sands stretching to infinity and criss-crossed by camel-trains.

Only a violent lurch of the bus brought her down to earth again, as it resumed its jerky, stop-start motion, and she was back with a bump in suffocating London.

'And, after lunch, we plan to swim in one of the Hampstead ponds,' Maureen continued, clearly keen to share the family plans with anyone who'd listen. 'We feel so close to nature there, although I must admit the ponds are terribly muddy. You can't even see your feet! And in this sort of weather, you do get a lot of algae, which can sometimes make you itch.'

The American was looking deeply shocked. 'But isn't that unhygienic?' she asked, shrinking back from Maureen, as if scared she might catch some bug.

Yes, utterly, Hayley didn't say. Apart from mud and algae, the ponds were full of weed and slime, dead leaves, dead beetles, people's sweat (and worse) and even rats' piss, so she'd heard. She hadn't brought her swimsuit – never did.

'Well, you can always go to a proper indoor pool. We're lucky here in London, with so many places to swim. Where we used to live, the nearest pool was twenty miles away.'

'Yes, we moved five years ago,' Kenneth said, taking up the story from his wife.

Hayley felt embarrassed for her parents, neither of whom had grasped the fact that they were no longer living in a friendly Yorkshire village, and that it wasn't done in London to discuss your personal life-history with strangers. On every single bus trip, they would strike up conversations with whoever was in earshot; her father never missing a chance to enlighten the ignorant.

'That's the National Gallery,' he was busy explaining now, as the bus panted its slow way around Trafalgar Square. 'It was founded in 1824 and it may interest you to know that at first it was just a private house in Pall Mall, with only fifty-odd paintings on show. Then, in 1838, this larger, grander gallery was built, and the collection was moved here. The original frontage was extremely narrow, but it's been enlarged since then, of course, and now holds over two thousand works of art.'

About a thousand of which we were forced to look at yesterday, Hayley refrained from saying. She didn't really get art; couldn't understand why people wasted time dawdling from painting to painting, and from room to endless room, when all the pictures looked much the same, give or take a few haloes, wigs and whiskers. After half a tedious hour of Madonnas, saints and pompous old gents, she had actually sneaked off and taken herself to Top Shop; rejoining her family later, in the gallery. The respite was short-lived. Under orders from her father, they had caught another 24 and got off again at Warren Street, for a detour to the British Library. Old books were just as boring as old paintings, although her dad could have an orgasm over some tatty, yellowed document, or so-called priceless manuscript.

Best not to think of orgasms, which only reminded her of Luke and the hideous way he'd dropped her: just texted to say sorry, it was off. Now she was the only one of her group without a boyfriend – and hardly likely to meet one on a bus. Lisa was in Alicante, and Melissa – lucky thing – had gone abroad for the whole of the summer, and was staying with her Italian uncle, who ran a restaurant in Rome. At this very moment, she was probably being chatted up by foreign dishy waiters, or even dating some gorgeous hunk. Whereas *she* was sharing a seat with a gross American called Sydney-Sue, of all things. Yes, prompted by her mother, they had all introduced themselves, and even Tim – who had also found a seat nearby and joined the little circle – didn't seem to mind being described as 'cute' by the Yank.

'So, Kenneth, you teach school.' Sydney-Sue mopped her sweaty forehead in a flurry of pink tissues. 'And what subject might that be?'

'Maths. In fact, that's why we decided to relocate to London. They had a vacancy for a Maths teacher in a really up-and-coming school, with an inspired headmaster and brilliant Ofsted results, and I felt it was just too good a chance to miss.'

Except you didn't bother consulting *me*, Hayley accused him silently. She much preferred the North – what she could remember of it. It seemed more like a dream now: their peaceful cottage, the sweep of lonely hills beyond, the small, safe school she had left behind, along with all her friends. OK, she'd made new friends, but they weren't special like the old ones and, in any case, she loathed the fact that London was so overcrowded; everyone fighting for their tiny inch of space. Even here on the bus, they were all jam-packed together, and the constant noise was driving her mental: sirens screaming past, police helicopters stuttering overhead and the maddening whine of the automatic doors. Couldn't they design a bus with ten decks instead of two, so there would be seats for everyone and she could get away from irritating tourists and read her magazine in peace? Or why not one with an air-balloon on the top, so it would float free of the traffic and pick up speed, for once? Or perhaps a special model with built-in guns along one side, to shoot down any yobs, before they could get on.

'Of course, we were worried sick about the financial side,' Maureen was confiding, as if Sydney-Sue was already a close friend. What would it be next? The state of her bowels? The stuff she did in bed with Dad?

'I mean, living in London costs an arm and a leg – everyone knows that! But teachers are classed as key workers, which gave us a head-start. It means we qualified for affordable housing, well below the market rent. And, once my husband had registered, the agency went out of its way to find us a decent flat.'

Hayley cleared her throat impatiently. Her mother made it sound as if they were living in a palace as flash as Buckingham, instead of in a cramped and noisy basement. Her bedroom was so small, they could hardly fit the bed in, despite it being a child's bed and thus shorter than the average. If she grew an inch or two taller, they'd have to chop her feet off, or else drill a hole in the wall. And, anyway, the flat wasn't all that cheap. In fact, if they didn't spend so much on rent, they might be able to afford to go on proper holidays abroad.

Her parents pretended they actually *preferred* settling for seven day-trips every year, but that was just a matter of pride. They were always delivering dreary lectures about how much there was to do in London, and how people came in droves from every country in the world to see the sights and soak up all the history, so she and Tim were exceptionally lucky to be living here full-time. Tim was such a nerd, he swallowed all such guff and invariably took their side, not hers. Her insufferable brother even claimed to like history; he also liked dragging round museums, so it would never even occur to him that sunbathing in Zanté, or clubbing in Ibiza might be marginally more exciting than yet another visit to the Abbey.

'Oh, look!' he cried, peering through the window at someone's balcony. 'There's a real live parrot perching on that woman's shoulder.'

'Yes, an African Grey. Well spotted, Tim!' Kenneth turned to Sydney-Sue, who was trying to doze – fat chance. 'That's the advantage of being on the upper deck. You see lots of things you'd simply miss at street-level – the details of a pub-sign or a statue, a carved stone balustrade, maybe, or just a stretch of fancy brickwork or unusual Victorian tiling....'

Brickwork, tiling – the excitement was unbearable! But Tim, of course, was trying to earn triple Brownie points by reeling off more 'upper-level' sights. It was depressing, really, the way her father favoured him – not just for being a boy, but for being such a boffin. He'd obviously inherited the maths gene, because he was already a whiz at algebra and, although he'd only just turned twelve, he could beat everyone at chess. He was also what her parents called 'sweet-natured', whereas *she* had a reputation for being moody, prickly and prone to sulks. Genes were totally unfair. It was just a matter of blind chance whether you inherited the good ones or the bad, so no credit to the lucky few who happened to be sweet and placid, as well as budding Einsteins.

'We're coming up to Camden now,' her father was explaining to his pupil. She was beginning to look distinctly bored, but since she could hardly move away, he was making the most of his captive audience.

'It was a peaceful rural area until 1820, when the Regent's Canal was extended eastwards and brought quite a bit of industry here – coal-wharves and the like. Camden Town itself is full of history. Charles Dickens used to live here, when he was a boy, and the last fatal duel was fought near the Brecknock Arms in 1843.'

Who cared? Not Sydney-Sue, for one, judging by the glazed look in her eyes. She probably didn't even know who Dickens *was*. The best thing about Camden wasn't duels or coal-wharves, but the market and the shops, which sold everything from herbal skunk and Jimi Hendrix T-shirts to eyebrow studs and belly-button rings. In fact, once the bus had nosed into the High Street, she was tempted to get off and browse the stalls. Except it would only lead to arguments and, anyway, she could just about endure one more lousy picnic on the Heath, because she had secretly decided that this was her last bus-holiday – last *ever*, in point of fact. Next year she would be eighteen, which meant officially an adult, so she had every right to go off on her own, for once, to some exotic foreign hot-spot. Apart from anything else, she would need an escape from the gloom and disappointment bound to follow in the wake of her A-level results. It was actually quite pointless to be doing them at all, when she knew she would fail the lot, but her father had laid down the law – couldn't bear the thought of any child of his not getting four straight A's. And he kept arguing the toss about her refusal even to try for university, despite the fact she hadn't the slightest wish to study any longer, let alone sit any more exams. Let *Tim* be the star, win an Oxbridge scholarship, fulfil her parents' dreams. She had other plans. In fact, she might stay abroad for good; find a job in Italy or Spain; fall in love with some tall, dark, hunky guy and refuse to come home even for the wedding. If her father wanted to lead her up the aisle, then he and Mum would have to take a plane, stretch themselves, for once. Even the amazing, brilliant, culture-brimming number 24 didn't go quite as far as Italy and Spain.

'Goodbye, darling.'

'Bye, Mum.' She'd said goodbye three times already, but her mother seemed unable to tear herself away. Her parents had insisted on seeing her off, which really was a pain. With them in tow, she couldn't explore the concourse – all those shops and cafés just begging her to step inside: order a drink, buy a top, try on trendy shoes. In any case, she needed time and space to relish the sheer excitement of being in an airport for the first time in her life. Seeing all the destinations flashing on the departure-boards not only gave her a buzz; it was a valuable reminder that the world stretched slightly further than from Pimlico to Hampstead Heath. Besides, her mum was spoiling everything by continually fussing and fretting, and had been issuing dire warnings about every sort of danger, the entire way to Heathrow.

'Promise me you'll be careful. I can't help worrying.'

'Mum, I'm only going to *Rome*, not Iraq or Afghanistan. Europe's pretty tame, you know. Lisa's backpacking in India, and Christie's trekking right across the Australian outback.'

'It doesn't matter. There's danger everywhere. And don't forget to phone us the minute you arrive.'

'I've said I will, OK?'

Her mother peered at her hand-luggage, as if convinced a terrorist had already slipped a bomb inside. 'Are you sure you've got everything you need?'

'Well, if I haven't, it's too late now.'

Her father had been uncharacteristically quiet, refraining from any lectures on the history of aviation, or the design of the terminal, although he had taken charge, of course: carried her cases, breathed down her neck at check-in, warned her (twice) not to lose her boarding pass. All at once, he unpeeled a £20-note from his wallet and pushed it into her hand. 'Here's a little extra, to buy yourself a drink.'

'I don't want her going to bars, Kenneth. Not with all those scares about people spiking drinks.'

'I'll buy an ice-cream, OK, Mum? *They're* not laced with drugs. And thanks a lot for the cash.'

'I just wish it could be more.' Her father dodged a bruiser of a bloke, who, loaded down with baggage, had all but cannoned into him. 'Now listen, Hayley, dear, make sure you see those churches I mentioned – St Balbina, and Saints Neruus and Achilleus. They may be off the beaten track, but you'll find they're well worth the effort.'

'Yes, Dad.' If her father really thought she intended wandering round fusty old churches, with her nose glued to a guide-book, he was seriously deluded. Still, wiser to say nothing about her actual plans: to find some hot Italian footballer and spend her free time groin to groin with him, flashing about in his sports car. She was getting sick of Jason. OK, he was faithful, unlike Luke, last year, but he sometimes seemed like a soppy spaniel puppy, racing off to retrieve the sticks she threw and dropping them adoringly at her feet. A macho type would be much more up her street – some feisty, hardcore sort of guy, who wouldn't fawn or slobber, or crawl submissively to heel if she so much as raised her voice.

'Oh, Lord! They're calling your flight.' Her mother sounded close to tears. 'You'd better hurry, darling. Give me one last hug.'

The hug was horribly embarrassing, especially in a public place. All those people watching must imagine she was about to start a life-sentence in some sleazy foreign gaol, rather than simply going on a jaunt. Even her father clung to her for ages, like he believed he'd never see her again. Her parents meant well, of course. They were just fussed about her going off on her own, as if they thought she was five, instead of eighteen-and-a-half. Anyway, once she got to Rome, she wouldn't *be* on her own, but surrounded by the buzzy crowd at Melissa's uncle's restaurant. It was a real stroke of luck, in fact, that things had panned out so well. Federico wanted extra help for the summer, and *she* wanted a job and somewhere to stay. The only disappointment was that Melissa had already left for her gap-year in Bangkok, so wouldn't be there herself. But at least her friend had provided her with a respectable Italian family, who would help her learn the language – indeed, who had made the trip possible at all. Her parents would have gone berserk if she'd just buzzed off on spec, with no proper base or forwarding address.

'*Ciao, Mamma, ciao, Papa*,' she carolled, showing off the Italian she had learned from phrase-books and CDs. '*Non ti preoccupare. Ti chiamo sta sera*.'

And, with a last determined wave, she strode ahead through security, refusing to turn round; refusing to listen to any more warnings about food poisoning, contaminated water, dangerous drivers, handbag-snatchers, or mad Italian bottom-pinchers. In just an hour, she would be flying at 30,000 feet, above France, above the clouds; free, at last; unchaperoned, at last, and never – repeat never – having to clamber up the stairs of another 24 bus.

'I thought you said you weren't coming with us again.'

'People are entitled to change their minds, Tim.'

'Sorry – I don't get it. I mean, you still haven't told us why you came back from Rome so soon, when you'd planned to stay a year.'

Hayley didn't answer. Since she'd arrived in England, two days ago, everyone had asked her the same question, and she'd been forced to resort to lies: Federico already had too many staff and couldn't really use her, and it was impossible to live in Rome without a proper wage. And she'd been unwell, with a nasty case of sunburn, after a seaside trip to Anzio. Oh, and she'd had cystitis, too, and an infected mosquito-bite.

Thank God she was sitting next to Tim. Being grilled by her brother was marginally better than being grilled by her parents, who were a good six rows in front on this more-than-usually-crowded number 24. Yet, despite the crowds, despite the constant cross-questioning, she had to admit she felt overwhelming relief – yes, even with a bunch of kids squalling right behind her and aiming vicious kicks at the back of her seat. In fact, more than just relief – she felt very nearly happy, without a trace of her normal grouchiness. The weather was fantastic: breezy, bright and not too hot for August – nothing like the blistering heat of Rome – and they were heading for Camden Lock, for a walk along the canal, followed by a guided tour of Lords. Nothing wrong with that. OK, she wasn't a wild cricket fan, but her father said you could see the players' dressing-rooms and even the urn that held the Ashes.

Tim was jogging her arm. 'Why can't you tell me more about the trip? Or is it top-secret or something?'

'What do you want to know?'

'Well, that Italian geezer – what was he like?'

'Which Italian geezer?' she asked, warily. There had been a few too many, and she was still reeling from the experience.

'The one you stayed with, of course – Frederico, or whatever he's called.'

'*Frederico*. He's big and fat and and hairy, and angry all the time.'

'And what about his wife?'

'Big and fat and hairy, too! Better-natured, but talks non-stop.'

'Did she teach you much Italian, then?'

'A bit.' She fished *Grazia* from her bag and pretended to be reading it, but, undeterred, Tim returned to the fray.

'Know what *I* think?'

'No.'

'That Federico fired you, but you're too scared to tell Mum and Dad, which is why you're being so edgy.'

'Shut up, Tim! I wasn't fired – no way. I just decided to come back because ...' Her voice tailed off. There were so many different reasons, most of which she would never admit to anyone. She'd been homesick, for God's sake – she, the intrepid traveller, pining for her mum and dad; even missing her usual goodnight kiss. How pathetic was that? And she'd hated flying, which wasn't fun at all, just terrifying at the start, then boring and uncomfortable – and even more cramped than the bus. And she'd proved hopeless as a waitress; muddled all the orders because her Italian was so sketchy and, once Federico twigged, he had demoted her to skivvy, after just three days. Even then, she couldn't seem to please him. He was always going mental and yelling the place down in great scary sort of rages. In fact, it made her realize how good-tempered her own father was. He never swore or shouted, or broke cups and plates on purpose, just to vent his temper on everybody else.

And the younger guys she'd met had all been nasty. One had all but raped her, and another thrust his tongue so far down her throat, she very nearly threw up. And, although most of them spoke English, they liked to pretend they didn't, so that when she said, 'Look, I barely even know you. Can we take this a bit slower?', they translated it as 'Go full steam ahead'. Jason was an angel in comparison; a decent sort of bloke who never forced the pace and understood if she was feeling a bit off. She'd text him again this evening; tell him she loved him, again. She *did* love him – madly – even loved her geeky brother; loved everyone in London, just because she was home and safe and no longer exiled in an alien land. She wouldn't say a word, of course, about such shameful feelings, for fear of being thought a total wimp. Yet, mixed in with the shame was a sense of celebration, because the experience was over now and she was back where she belonged.

As the bus swerved round a corner, her father came swaying down the aisle towards them, clutching at the rail, to keep his balance. 'Two seats have just come free, kids, so do join us at the front. I want to point out a couple of things in Whitehall.'

Having grabbed the empty seats just across from their parents, she and Tim – along with the Indian couple in front – listened to him explaining how King Charles I was executed on the exact spot they were passing. And she actually felt proud of him for being so clued-up on history (and art and books and architecture), and not an uncultured yob like Federico, who wouldn't know King Charles from Charlie Brown. In fact, she had come back just in time. There were five more bus-trips left and, for the first time ever, she was really looking forward to them. Tomorrow they were getting off at the stop for Kentish Town, for a visit to St Martin's church – famous for some reason – then to three old staging inns and a flat where George Orwell had lived. Also, her dad was going to show them the course of the River Fleet, when it used to flow freely from Hampstead down to Blackfriars Bridge, before being caged up underground. And the day after that, they were going to the National Gallery, to see an exhibition, chosen in her honour, because it was all Italian artists – people called Divisionists, whatever that might mean. Perhaps she'd listen, for a change; learn a bit about them, and, even if she didn't, every painting would give her a real kick just because she was here in England, and not in Italy.

Weird as it might sound, since returning from her month in Rome, it actually seemed a good idea to take holidays on a bus. No lost luggage, to start with. Hers had gone missing for a whole five days, and the only clothes the airline had dished out, to make do with while she waited, were a gruesome T-shirt, printed front and back with *Alitalia*, and a pair of passion-killer knickers that came down beyond her knees. And, on a bus, you didn't get mosquito-bites or sunstroke; didn't have to queue for hours at check-in and, best of all, there wasn't that hideous feeling of being completely alone in the world, because you were miles away from everyone you loved. In fact, she didn't really care if they did this same bus-trip every year – for ever. And if she got married and moved away, she might even take her own kids; choose a different bus-route, but follow the same basic plan of setting out seven days in a row. Perhaps she could make it a family tradition – something a bit crazy, but original and fun, which should be carried on right down the generations by her children's children's children.

'Are you listening, Hayley, dear?' her father asked, pausing a moment in his account of King Charles's death: the clothes he wore; the inspiring words he spoke....

'Yes,' she said. 'I am.' And, all at once, she felt stupid tears pricking at her eyelids just because he *was* her dad – a clever, decent, kindly dad, who had cancelled an engagement to come to meet her at the airport, brought her a sandwich made by Mum, in case she was hungry after the flight (ham and cheese – her favourite), and lugged her heavy cases all the way to the car-park, despite his dodgy back. And he hadn't nagged the slightest bit about her change of plan; simply said he'd missed her and gave her a big hug. Before, she'd been so clueless, in completely failing to realize that things like that were desperately important; that parents cared about you, cherished you, kept you safe and rooted, when other people wouldn't dream of bothering. OK, she wasn't one for sentiment and she'd rather *die* than admit it to her cool, globe-trotting friends, but she knew – deep-down and secretly – that being back in the haven of her family was ... well, almost ... precious.

STELLAR

The break-in had been meticulously planned. She'd deliberately waited till it was dark, chosen a dank December evening, with most people safe indoors, and made sure it was a night when Mark would be out till late. And, of course, she had avoided parking in his street, but left her car outside the Swan, a pub he never frequented.

Nonetheless, as she slunk along St Mary's Road, the contents of her stomach seemed to be turning curdled somersaults and, despite the weather, she was sweating from sheer nerves. Each familiar landmark only increased her agitation: the spiky railings, stunted tree, the pair of scarlet phone-boxes, disfigured by graffiti. On impulse, she darted into one and, having fumbled for some coins, dialled his number and stood listening to it ring. Phoning from her mobile was no longer really an option, because he either cut her off, or, should he fail to pick up, traced the calls and sent her angry texts to stop 'bothering' him. In fact, when his answerphone clicked in, his warm, friendly tone of voice seemed profoundly hypocritical, being so at variance with those cold, uncaring texts.

Please leave a message after the....

She slammed down the receiver. Her 'message' would be rather different from a disembodied voice on a machine. Besides, now she had done the necessary – double-checked he wasn't at home – she could turn into his apartment-block with slightly less unease.

The structure seemed to dwarf her, though; its glass and steel oppressive; even the Christmas trees in the landscaped gardens mocking her unfestive mood, with their strings of glittering lights.

Yet she tried to assume an air of confidence as she walked into the building; nodding at the porter, who knew her as Mark's girlfriend. Dead right – she was. She *was*.

As the lift purred open, she stepped inside, recoiling at her reflection in its smugly mirrored walls; her wan complexion and dark-ringed eyes the result of sleepless nights. She transferred her gaze to her shoes while the lift glided up to the seventh floor. Mark had loved those shoes, yet now she was tempted to trample him with their sharp stiletto heels.

Having emerged into the corridor, she stole cautiously along, relieved to see no residents in view. Yet, despite the fact she was unobserved, her hand was literally shaking as she approached Mark's actual door and slid the stolen key into the lock.

Memories came flooding back the instant she walked in: cruel flashbacks to her last time here: the horror and humiliation of discovering she'd been traded in for another, younger woman. At first, he'd cravenly pretended there was no one else involved and that he simply wasn't ready for commitment, but, by dint of pestering, she'd managed to extract the whole unedifying story. Basically, he'd picked up some piece of trash at a conference in Las Vegas – a city every bit as trashy as the uncouth bimbo he'd hooked. And he had even had the nerve to claim he was genuinely in love, rather than admitting to a brief and tacky affair.

It was then she had decided to make off with his key; realizing how vital it was to retain the means of entry to what had been their love-nest. Besides, the key seemed almost symbolic, as if it might possess the power to unlock the portcullis of his heart.

Again, she winced at her reflection as she passed the circular mirror in the hall: no more flattering than the mirrors in the lift. All the time that she and Mark had been together, she had felt no need to apologize for the slate-grey of her eyes, or the unexuberant mid-brown of her hair. But the pictures of her rival, continually swarming in her mind, always showed the Vegas bitch as a flaunting redhead or spectacular ash-blonde, with the sort of dramatic violet eyes normally found in romantic fiction. And, no doubt, the vulgar woman had already put her imprint on the flat; made it resemble some bordello.

Fearful of such outrage, she steeled herself to creep into the living-room, which, to her great relief, looked totally unchanged: elegant white walls, contrasting with the two black leather sofas; distinctive marble floor; huge abstract painting in dramatic bluey-black. Just months ago, she had lain on one of those sofas, while slowly Mark unpeeled her dress, then knelt to....

No! This was not the time for reminiscing, let alone for tears. She had to be safely out of here before the pair of them returned, which meant getting down to business right away. Unzipping her large shoulder-bag, she removed the bundle of letters – sixty-three in total – most of which she knew by heart. Extracting each from its envelope, she began spreading the sheets of notepaper on the table, chairs and sofas, then right across the floor, so that Mark's energetic handwriting seemed to be imprinted on the room itself.

She saved some twenty letters for the bedroom, gazing with disgust at the preening double bed, now the lair of odious Barbara. Well, tonight that brazen female wouldn't be lying there with Mark – not once she'd cast her eye over this cache of rapturous outpourings. She arranged them in a row across the counterpane, then placed a few on the dressing-table, where a cluster of garish-looking pots and jars, with gold lids and fancy labels, now supplanted her own self-effacing toiletries. Mark had acted out of character in opting for a type like Barbara; favouring frippery and empty show above any sterling qualities. But although she despised his lack of taste, she preferred to regard this recent fling as just an aberration; something he would come to view as a mortifying lapse and soon bitterly regret. Far from feeling she was well rid of him, her whole purpose was to win him back – back not only to his senses, but back to her embrace.

Which is why it was imperative to force the Yankee numbskull to understand that Mark was deeply serious; a knowledgeable and cultured man who craved intellectual companionship. Their own, two-year relationship had never been confined to sex but involved mind and spirit, too, so how could a crass and clueless type like Barbara possibly compete?

'There's the proof,' she muttered, propping the last missive against a bottle of cheap scent. 'Read these letters and you'll see.'

The very fact she was talking to herself – worse, talking to an absent woman she hadn't even met – only proved how disturbed she was. Indeed, Barbara seemed to have turned her from a coping, capable PA to an insomniac, neurotic wreck now permanently off work. Yet she felt compelled to formulate what she'd *like* to say, at least, to show the ignoramus exactly how unworthy she was of Mark's rhapsodic sentiments.

'Look at what he called me: "beloved Stella", "bewitching Stella", "sublime and special Stella". Stella's the Latin word for "star" – although I don't suppose you'd know that. And I *was* his star, he told me – a radiant Cassiopeia who lit up his whole universe. He wrote me these amazing verses in almost all the letters, describing me as his midnight sun, his eye of heaven, his meteor. He promised me the Pleiades, to wear as diamonds in my ears; said he'd buy me the whole Milky Way – I only had to ask. I've never met another man so incredibly romantic – a poet, through and through, not scared of expressing feelings most other guys would avoid as over-the-top. Of course, to *you* he's probably nothing more than a cash-cow. You just saw this successful City bloke and used your wiles to....'

She tensed in shock, as the sound of footsteps broke into her imaginary tirade. Was it coming from outside, or from another floor? Or had he and Barbara left the function early and were now entering the building, about to burst in and discover her? Paralysed by indecision, she stood stock-still and listened; unable to locate the sound. The acoustics in the flat were strange and, several times when here with Mark, she had mistaken a noise below for one outside. Yet the risk of being seen was so unthinkable, she bolted in a panic straight out through the door and headed for the emergency stairs. The lift was just too risky. What in God's name would she do if *they* stepped out as *she* stepped in?

She dashed headlong down the seven flights of stairs, yet, even in her haste, she was aware of their grubby concrete and of the bare, unpainted walls. Everything in Marlborough Court was outwardly luxurious, but here was its grungy underside, concealed from common view. And, doubtless, that was true of Barbara: a seductive face and figure disguising a base core.

As she juddered to a stop at the bottom of the stairs, she paused to catch her breath; experiencing a sense of triumph, mingled with the fear – she had wreaked a truly gratifying revenge. That interloper wouldn't last, not when she saw the passion steaming from Mark's letters and knew he would never address a slut like her in so high-flown a fashion. Indeed, once her tinsel coating had rubbed off and he came face to face with the dross beneath, he would realize just how badly he had been duped. Even her name was inferior. Barbara, meaning 'foreigner' or 'stranger', was utterly appropriate for some barbarous little upstart he had met on alien soil. 'Stella', on the other hand, suggested celestial spheres.

She emerged into reception, exchanged a brief word with the porter, then quickly left the building; darting past the plashing fountain and shimmering Christmas trees. Once in the street, she broke into a run, trying to conceal herself in the shadow of the fence until she had turned the corner and was almost at the car. She was about to drive straight home, when, suddenly, she changed her mind and strode into the pub. The deed was done, so she deserved a drink, to celebrate.

Stumbling out of the Swan, having lost all track of time, she walked over to the river and stood shivering on the bridge, reluctant to return to her lonely, empty flat. How black the water looked; fathomless and sinister, with the threat of dangerous currents churning underneath. And the sky was equally dark; entirely overcast; no glint of moon or stars; just lowering banks of cloud, pressing down remorselessly, as if to suffocate the earth.

All at once, she slumped against the parapet; hands gripping its rough edge. Only at that moment did recognition dawn; a surge of horror shuddering through her body as she realized what she had done. How could she have been so utterly obtuse, in casting away a source of genuine treasure: the lasting proof and record of Mark's love? He could easily destroy those letters – and destroy her in the process. Maybe, even now, he was consigning them to the shredder; blitzing them to paper-dust. Perhaps Barbara hadn't even read them – he might have lured her into the kitchen, or delayed her in the hall, while he annihilated every shred of evidence. Which meant this act of revenge was not only completely pointless, but had left *her* the ultimate loser.

She paced up and down the bridge, still unable to believe her folly in actually relinquishing a poet's homage. She might know those letters off by heart, but that was little comfort. If only she possessed them still, in authenticating black and white, she could have re-read his praises constantly, as a source of pride and pleasure throughout her later years; a reminder and a validation of the fact she'd been exalted and extolled. So long as she retained that tribute, she owned part of Mark himself – his romantic spirit, poetic fire, the white heat of his love. By jettisoning them, she had extinguished her own light and become as drear and lustreless as this funereal December. Now she was condemned to live in darkness; her star eclipsed, burnt out, and – even at this very moment – collapsing into the blackest of black holes.

It was Barbara's star that was firmly in the ascendant.

THICK HAIR

'The trouble with this system, love, it's ancient!'

Like me, thought Connie – malfunctioning and old.

The plumber shook his head, as if despairing of the radiator. She hadn't caught his name – something unpronounceable. He seemed a decent type, though, with a friendly face and kind, brown, trusting eyes.

'You can't get the parts, you see. This gland-valve's had it, so I'll need to find a replacement, but the problem is *where*?'

She already knew that replacements weren't always available. Her two hip-replacements had been reasonably successful, but there was no similar solution, as yet, for her arthritic feet and spine.

'There's just a chance I might have one in the van, but don't hold your breath, love – OK?'

She liked the way he called her 'love'. Love had always been in short supply, so she was storing up these 'loves' in the pantry of her mind. Five, so far.

Following him into the tiny hall, she stood watching at the entrance to her flat, as he went out into the street and wrenched open the door of his battered old white van. Then he disappeared from view – well, all except for the top of his head. His hair was exceptionally thick. She had noticed that the minute he arrived, because it reminded her of a horse's mane, or the thatch on a cottage-roof: close-packed, dense and strong. No one she knew nowadays had hair as thick as that. Most of her friends had passed on, anyway, and the near-strangers at the day centre had either wispy, thistledown hair, similar to hers, or none at all, in the case of the two men. Yes, men were also in short supply: a mere couple, as against at least a dozen ladies, attended the luncheon club.

'You're in luck, love!' The plumber returned with a small metal object, brandishing it as excitedly as if it were a gold doubloon. 'This was sitting at the bottom of my junk-box. I must have kept it from a job I done years and years ago.'

He looked far too young to have been working 'years and years ago'. Twenty-one, she'd guess – Frank's age when he'd died.

Having ushered him back to the bedroom, she returned to keep her vigil by Frank's photograph, which she'd been doing, off and on, all day. She observed the self-same ritual every year, on the day of the anniversary; placing a lighted candle by the photo and a posy of fresh flowers. Today was the sixty-ninth. There was no telling, of course, whether she'd still be around for the seventieth. It already seemed extraordinarily unfair that she should have lived so much longer than Frank, yet, in all those decades, she had never once been tempted even to look at another man. Her name was Constance, after all – and constancy the loveliest of virtues.

'Excuse me, love,' the plumber called, having come to the door of the living-room. 'I'll need to drain the radiator down, so—' He broke off when he saw the candle, casting its gold gleam across the photograph. 'That your son?' he asked.

She shook her head.

'Grandson?'

'No. My ... fiancé. He went down in the *Hood*.'

'Beg your pardon?'

Young people today knew nothing. The two teenage boys in the flat above had never even heard of the Second World War. 'The *Hood* was a battle-cruiser,' she told him, 'and, once, the pride of the Royal Navy.'

'Yipes! So what went wrong?'

This is the BBC Home Service ... The radio announcer's voice seemed to stun the room again; the news slashing across her face, like jagged shards of glass: *HMS Hood has been lost. Shelled by the battleship* Bismarck, *she broke in two and sank.*

Her heart also broke in two – although not at that actual instant, because every fibre of her being was determined to keep hoping. Hope was a need, a duty, a raw, overwhelming instinct. She just had to believe that Frank had escaped:, been transferred to another ship, maybe, before the *Hood* was hit, or rushed to hospital with some serious but non-terminal disease, or – if he *had* been on the fated ship – managed somehow to struggle to safety, through the churning waves and wreckage. But, three days later, his distraught, weeping mother called round at the house and unfolded the dread telegram. She hadn't cried. Tears were for lesser things: a lost job, a stolen purse.

'And your fiancé didn't survive?' The plumber was still gazing at Frank in his uniform, with something approaching awe.

'No.' She was embarrassed by the catch in her voice. Even after sixty-nine years, the pain could still take her unawares; sear and stab, as if she'd put weight on a broken leg. 'Only three men were saved, out of a total of nearly fifteen hundred.' She had never forgotten the names of those fortunate three: Bill Dundas, Bob Tilburn, Ted Briggs. No Frank Frobisher.

'God! I'm sorry, love. That's tough.'

'And it happened terribly fast. Some of the men on the *Prince of Wales* – that was the other British battleship – watched the *Hood* go down, and they said one minute they were sailing alongside a massive iron-and-steel hulk, and the next minute there was nothing left but a gaping hole in the water.'

'But how could a big boat like that be scuppered so damn quick?'

It pleased her that he found the subject interesting, despite its tragic nature. Company and conversation were both luxuries, and rare. Apart from her once-a-month lunch at the day centre and her forays to the corner shop, she rarely saw another living soul. 'It was a chance in a million, actually. A German shell struck the main deck and went right through to the magazine and that set off an explosion, which blew the whole thing apart.' She'd had nightmares for years afterwards, reliving all the details: the pillar of flame shooting upwards like a gigantic blowtorch, followed by the shattering blast, consuming man and ship alike. And she couldn't stop imagining what Frank must have felt in those catastrophic moments as the stern broke away and the bow pivoted helplessly about, and the cold, cruel water closed above his head. Had he been horribly burned, or grotesquely mutilated – her handsome Frank, with his cheery smile and sunshine-coloured hair and his unshakeable belief that things would always turn out for the best?

'Of course, it was a huge triumph for the Germans,' she explained. 'You see, they took it as proof that God was on their side.' Temporarily, that had shaken her belief in the concept of a merciful God. How could such a Being favour Germans, or – worse – destroy her blameless Frank and all his valiant fellow-sailors? Yet, three days later, the *Bismarck* itself was sunk, so she'd been forced to conclude that the Deity must, after all, possess a sense of justice (although she never quite regained her confidence in divine benevolence).

'So where did all this happen?' the plumber asked, adding, with a shrug, 'Geography's not my strong point, so I haven't the foggiest notion what ocean we're talking about – the Atlantic or the Pacific or—?'

'No, the Denmark Strait.'

He was clearly none the wiser; a baffled look on his face, as he slouched against the door-frame. Should she invite him to pull up a chair and join her for a tête-à-tête? It was such a comfort having someone else in the flat, and would be even more agreeable if they could extend this conversation to matters beyond the War. She longed to discuss in detail the one man in her life she had ever loved, which was impossible at the day centre, where no one ever listened, either lost in their own worlds, or in a creeping fog of dementia.

She opened her mouth to say 'Won't you please sit down', only to think better of it. It sounded frightfully forward, as if she were taking liberties. She should be grateful for the fact they were communicating at all. Indeed, if she answered all his questions, he might be encouraged to ask more.

'The Denmark Strait,' she eagerly informed him, relishing this role as teacher, 'is the stretch of water between Greenland and Iceland that connects the Greenland Sea to the north Atlantic. And it's exceptionally cold, because it's fed by a current that carries icebergs in its path.' Horrific for Frank first to scorch and then to freeze. He had always hated extremes, whether of feelings or of climate. Which is why they'd planned to marry in May, when the weather should be balmy and neither too hot nor too cold. They had made provisional arrangements for the May of the following year, depending on Frank's leave, of course.

The wedding would hardly have been a lavish affair, what with clothes coupons and rationing and the whole 'make-do-and-mend' philosophy. Maybe a borrowed dress, a few flowers from someone's garden, and a whip-round among the relatives for flour and eggs and sugar, to make a basic cake. But, in her imagination, the day was invariably sumptuous. The benevolent sun always shone from dawn to dusk – although not too fiercely, to spare Frank's milk-pale skin. And the heady scent of lilacs wafted into the church, and every street for miles around frothed with cherry-blossom; the skittish petals falling in pink-confetti drifts. And, far from being dry and plain, the cake tasted of ambrosia. And her dress was a Parisian creation, guaranteed to turn all heads.

Instead, she had worn mourning-clothes; eaten gall and wormwood.

'Well, if I stand around jabbering like this, the job won't never get done! So could you fetch me a bucket, love, to drain the radiator.'

The disappointment stung. She would gladly endure an eternally leaking radiator just to keep him near. Still hungry for his company, she handed over her old tin pail, then limped after him into the bedroom and stood there, watching him work. Work was a blessing, although few people grasped that crucial fact until it was too late. You could spend half your life looking forward to retirement, but, when it came, 'leisure' and 'free time' turned out to mean endless hours alone.

He was kneeling now, tipping water from the saucepan into the pail. She had put that saucepan under the leak in the early hours this morning, after noticing a damp patch on the carpet. She'd had to wait till eight, though, before she could phone for help. Fortunately, she never threw away the leaflets that popped through her front door and, sorting through them over her morning cup of tea, she had come across a brochure promising the 'speediest response' to any plumbing problem. 'Speediest' she'd doubted, and had thus been pleasantly surprised when this nice young fellow turned up within the hour.

She deliberately kept silent, though, not wanting to disturb him. In any case, her attention was distracted by his tight blue-denim jeans, which were straining at the seams as he bent towards the radiator. The jeans had extra pockets on the sides, which made odd bulges on the outsides of both legs, where he must have stuffed old rags, or small-sized tools, into the handy little pouches. His slim waist was emphasized by a wide, black, leather belt and, beneath that, was a denim strap, buckled like the belt, but part of the actual jeans. Below the strap were two more pockets, their outlines stitched in brown, and with rows of little studs along the bottom.

Until this moment, she had failed to grasp quite how complicated jeans could be. She would never dream of wearing them herself, nor had she ever studied them on anybody else. Yet, these days, half the population seemed to live and die in them, as if blue denim were a uniform, imposed by government decree. As a young woman in the forties, she'd had enough of uniform to last her a whole lifetime. Hers had been fairly casual, of course, compared with her friends in the Wrens and the WAAFs. Land-girls, like her, wore jodhpurs and green sweaters and unflattering felt hats – when they weren't in their coarse brown overalls, ploughing, digging, milking, felling trees. The very first time she'd milked a cow, she had written to Frank in amazement – she, a city girl, who had hardly known one end of a cow from another, now learning how to handle bulging udders, whilst avoiding being lashed by swishing tails. What she hadn't told Frank was how often she was forced to fight off the farmer's advances. Although married, with three children, he'd continually attempted to lure her into the woods, or press her up against a hedge, to steal a kiss – or worse.

'Okey-dokey,' the plumber said, 'let's get the new valve on. Not that it's exactly new,' he laughed.

His cheery guffaw made her smile. Laughter in this flat was as rare as home-made puddings at the luncheon club, where the same semi-melted, white ice-cream appeared each and every month. And the club itself was hardly a place of mirth. Few people there, including the staff, ever managed more than a titter. Indeed, it was so long since she herself had laughed, she doubted if she still knew how. What with the increase in her rent and the constant noise from the two boisterous boys above, there wasn't much to laugh about.

As the plumber reached out to turn on the radiator, she was struck again by his hair. That confident, assertive hair was achingly similar to Frank's, although a completely different shade. Frank's hair had been so golden-blond, people often commented that it was wasted on a man. She could still remember the feel of it when he held her close to kiss her: strong and springy and gleamingly alive. She would cup her hands around his neck and stroke lovingly from the top of his head to the bristles on his neck, then gently up and back again. Of course, he was obliged to wear it very short, but even the no-nonsense navy barber couldn't tame its natural thickness. Her own hair had been baby-fine, even as a girl. She and Frank had differed in so many ways – part of the attraction, she supposed – he solid and thickset; she willowy and frail; he fair; she dark; he from the wilds of Devon; she a Londoner, born and bred.

'Now I'll need to bleed the radiator, OK, love?'

The 'love'-count was increasing all the time. This one was the tenth and she cradled it contentedly while continuing to observe him, then added it, with all the rest, to her store of emergency rations. Once he'd gone, she would remove them from the larder and allow herself to gloat, as she had done in the War, over cartons of dried egg, or an extra tin of corned beef, or the unique treasure of a single peach. Provisions made you safer.

'I'd better ease this valve, love. Mind you, it hasn't been used for donkey's years, so I'm not surprised it's stiff.'

She watched admiringly as he rocked back on his heels, wishing he could ease her joints and muscles with the same expertise he used on valves. His movements were so lithe, in comparison with hers. Her own body was protesting, as she lowered it, with difficulty, onto the dressing-table stool; sharp pains stabbing through her back and hip. Terrible what time could do, to bodies, corpses, battle-cruisers. Parts of the once-famous *Hood* must lie barnacled and rusting now beneath the heedless waves. And its courageous crew would have been devoured by fish, long since; reduced to gleaming bones....

She shivered, suddenly, pulling her old cardigan tight across her chest. She could no longer fasten the buttons – her fingers were too stiff. But she still needed all her woollies, despite it being late in May. It was chilly in the flat – colder still outside – one of the most inclement Mays on record, with bad-tempered winds, squally showers and a grudging sun, too sullen to show its face.

The plumber whistled softly as he worked; the sound harmonizing strangely with the hissing of the radiator. In a few minutes, he'd be gone; off to another job, another street; she just another entry on his work-sheet. Then, time would slow to its former snail-like pace; each sluggish minute dragging like an hour. She'd begun going to bed much earlier, in an attempt to shorten the days, but it was impossible to sleep with the two tearaways thumping overhead.

'All done!' Springing to his feet, again with enviable agility, he seized the old tin pail. 'I'll just empty this down the toilet, if you could show me where it is.'

Her flat was so small, the bathroom was only a step or two away. As she pointed it out, she peered at the dirty water in the pail. Her tears must look like that: brackish, grey and scummy. Sometimes, these days, she cried for no particular reason, whereas in her youth she'd been resolutely brave. Frank disliked excessive emotion, so she'd felt duty-bound to temper her grief and match his own restrained and silent heroism. Besides, bravery was obligatory in wartime, when so many other people had lost beloved husbands, brothers, sons. Indeed, the hundreds of men who'd perished with Frank must all have had grieving relatives. She often thought of those sailors – a struggling mass of helpless, hapless men; choked by smoke, scorched by fire, going down, down, down to the dark, uncaring depths. At the time that it had happened, she'd been part of a large family, with parents and four elder sisters and several uncles and aunts, so she'd felt far less isolated. But, now, nobody was left. Her mother, father, siblings, friends, were all clamped by heavy gravestones; invaded by insolent weeds.

'OK, that's it!' Having returned the empty pail to her, he strode back into the bedroom. 'I'll just clear up here, then I'll be out your way.'

She studied his movements as he replaced his wrench and spanner in his toolbox and stuffed the rags on top; determined to get her fill of him, especially his luxuriant hair. Its sheer bounteousness seemed to symbolize his youth and strength, as if it were a life-force in itself.

'No – maybe I'll just wash me hands....'

'Of course.' She had already thought to put out a fresh towel and open a new bar of soap. If only he'd stay longer, it would give her pleasure to wait on him. But he had refused the cup of tea she'd suggested when he first arrived, so if she offered him a snack now, he was bound to say no again. Besides, she hadn't much in the larder to suit a man-sized appetite.

Already he was emerging from the bathroom, so it was clear he had no wish to hang about. He hadn't even used her pretty, rose-sprigged towel, but was wiping his still-wet hands on the fronts of his old jeans.

'Do you need an invoice, love?' he asked. 'Or, if you can pay in cash, I'll make it only forty quid and throw in the valve for free.'

She stared up at his face: the kindly eyes, the generous mouth. £40 seemed quite a substantial sum; double her monthly heating-bill and more even than her council tax. 'I, er, wanted to ask you a favour,' she faltered, easing herself up from the stool. 'It may sound a dreadful cheek, but—'

'If you're hoping to beat me down on price, there's not a chance in hell! If you were a business, I'd charge you double that, so forty quid's dirt-cheap.'

No need to raise your voice, she thought, as she went to fetch her well-worn, shabby purse. She counted out four 10-pound notes and a five, wondering if she ought to add a tip. Were you expected to tip plumbers, or only taxi-drivers, hairdressers and waiters, none of whom featured in her life? She extracted another fiver, just in case. After all, she was still hoping for the favour.

'Thanks a ton,' he breezed, picking up his toolbox, having pocketed the cash. ''Bye, love. Take care.'

'No, wait! Don't go!' she called, aware that he was almost at the door. Twelve 'loves' in total now – a number with significance. Twelve hours in a day; twelve months in a year; twelve disciples; twelve gates of the Heavenly City. And Frank's birthday was the twelfth day of the twelfth month.

'There's ... there's something I need to ask you – a very personal thing. But I'm frightened you'll object, or ...' The words petered to a halt. Never, in her life, had she been so shamefully brazen. Yet this chance would never come again, she knew.

'Get on with it, then,' he urged, releasing his grip on the doorknob and turning back to face her.

Wasn't that an invitation? 'Get on with it' surely meant agreement. Without another word, she moved close to him and stretched her arms up towards his head.

'What the hell d'you think you're doing?' he snapped, dodging back out of reach.

'Sssh!' she cautioned, adopting a stern tone herself. This was a sacred moment and no way must it be spoiled. Again, she stood close and, this time, cupped her hands around his neck.

'Hang on!' He jerked away. 'Are you trying to strangle me or something?'

'Keep still!' she ordered, knowing *she* must be in charge, for once. Closing her eyes, she took up the same position; arms clasped around his neck. It felt so wonderfully right, as if they were two halves of just one person; only complete when standing heart to heart. Then, slowly, softly, she began stroking from the top of his sunshine-coloured hair, down to the bristles on his neck. And, all at once, Frank was kissing her – not a black-bordered, goodbye kiss, before his ship departed, but a devoted husband's kiss.

Already she could hear the organ, thundering out the triumphant wedding-march. She and her adoring spouse were standing side by side in the flower-filled city church, and the heady scent of lilacs was wafting through the open door, and an exultant but temperate sun was streaming through the windows to halo them in light. And cherry-blossom-confetti was blowing in pink, foamy drifts, and her dress was a froth of tulle, and her heart a wild hosanna of delight. And, as his lips met hers, they repeated, heart to heart, the vow they'd just pronounced in front of family and friends: to love each other – for ever.

And, yes, that vow had endured for sixty-nine years, to the day.

HOPE AND ANCHOR

Jodie turned the corner into yet another street of shops – all still doing business, at well past seven o'clock. At home, there weren't any shops, except bog-standard Patterson's, which closed dead on half-past five, and had festooned its smeary window with a few strings of mingy tinsel, not these swanky decorations. Weird, how, each year, Christmas lasted longer. They'd been selling crackers in Patterson's way back in September. By the time she was fifty, it would probably last all year – the Christmas trees and Christmas cards left over from December recycled on 1 January, and the whole pointless process starting up again. Not that she wanted to live to fifty and have wrinkled skin and glasses and false teeth, or dodder around on a Zimmer-frame, boring everyone to death about 'the old days'.

If she was rich when she was fifty, though, it wouldn't be so bad. Stopping to look in another shop window, she imagined having such stacks of cash she could have anything she chose, and began picking out fancy things to buy. She'd read about a pampered bitch in *Cosmo*, who owned ninety-seven pairs of shoes; some costing a cool three grand a pair. Her own battered trainers had set her back £8.99, although admittedly the soles were wearing thin. If you owned ninety-seven pairs of shoes, how did you decide which ones to wear? Did you follow some strict system over ninety-seven days, or single out your favourites and ignore the boring rest? It had been like that at home – the younger kids hogging all the attention, while she was simply surplus to requirements.

The only shoes she wanted at present were a pair of fur-lined boots. Her toes were so numb she had lost all feeling in them, and her feet were murder, because she'd been on them for so long. But, if she didn't keep moving, she'd freeze solid, like an icicle. The weather was the spiteful kind that kept sussing out the gap between her jeans and top, and pouncing on the bare bit at the back of her neck.

She turned up the collar of her denim jacket and mooched on across the lights. This town was unknown territory and, for all she knew, she could be walking round in circles. What had struck her when she first arrived was the volume of the noise: angry drivers hooting; buses rumbling and whining; the deafening din of road-works; cop cars racing past, with shrieking sirens.

God, the cops! If she planned on sleeping rough tonight, she'd better hide herself away in some secret little alley, or even doss down in a churchyard, if she didn't mind the ghosts. She did actually believe in ghosts, because she'd seen her dead grandma, once, coming out of the village church. She never mentioned it to anyone – they'd only call her mad – although the maddest people, in point of fact, were the ones who closed their minds to things they couldn't understand.

Begging was also risky, as far as the cops were concerned. They were bound to move her on, or start asking dodgy questions. Yet she needed food as much as sleep – no, *more*. She'd already tried the litter-bins; found a few mince-pies, mostly reduced to crumbs, and half a mouldy loaf, but that was ages ago and her stomach was growling again. Hunger and fear kept fighting in her head, but, this time, hunger won. At least people should be generous in this season of loving-and-giving – ha ha.

She chose her pitch with care, right outside the flashiest of the shops. Should she remove her jacket and use it as a cushion, or leave it on, for warmth? She left it on. The pavement was reasonably clean; the street-cleaners out in force, even at this hour. Of course, Christmas meant mess and litter as much as peace and good will.

'Spare some change,' she muttered; angry yet embarrassed by the nasty looks she received. Worse to be ignored, though. The two snotty females just swanning into the shop didn't even see her – too busy gossiping. Both of them were weighed down with shopping-bags – not tat from Boots or Superdrug, but glossy, stiffened carriers, with ritzy logos and proper handles, and probably stuffed with yet more killer shoes.

'Spare some change.'

The blokes were just as bad; glared at her, like she was some grotty form of pond-life that crawled along the bottom in the mud.

Her hand was numb from holding it stretched out. It needed a bit of exercise, such as closing round some nice fat dosh. But these people were so tight, it would hurt them to part even with 5p.

Suddenly, an old woman stopped and bent right down, peering into her face. 'You should be ashamed of yourself, young lady, begging for money, like a down-and-out. You ought to be at home, doing your homework or helping your poor mother.'

Her 'poor' mother probably hadn't even noticed that she'd scarpered. With so many other kids in her hair, one less would be a blessing. As for homework, what a laugh!

Once the woman had moved on, without sparing her a penny, she began to feel so empty, she was tempted simply to nick some food from one of the big supermarkets. Except they all had store-detectives and she didn't fancy landing up in a cell. What she really needed was a dog. People couldn't bear animals to starve, whereas humans could die in droves, for all they cared. She'd seen a beggar just outside the station, with the perfect sort of dog: a curly, cuddly one, with a pathetic look in its big, brown, soulful eyes. It gazed at every passer-by with such a mix of pain and longing, they couldn't help but shell out. Let its owner rot in hell, they probably thought, but save the poor precious mutt.

She had never had a dog, or any sort of pet, come to that. Her mother said she couldn't cope with any more mouths to feed. Years ago, she'd tried to argue for a goldfish, pointing out that fish-food wouldn't exactly break the bank. But her mum had changed the subject and begun banging on about the broken washing-machine and the time it took to get anything repaired.

Shivering in her flimsy jacket, she imagined a big, furry dog – for warmth – then tried to think of a name. Maybe Granby, after the

Marquis of Granby pub – the last place she'd seen her father, before he vanished into the Great Unknown. He had taken her there for a beer – or three. She'd been far too young to drink then, but no one seemed that fussed and, anyway, her dad was very matey with the barman.

'Good boy, Granby,' she murmured, already feeling better, knowing she'd have company tonight. And cash was showering in – tenners by the ton-weight. Granby was a pro; knew the trick of combining charm and desperation, so that no one could resist. She'd be a millionairess soon; could buy her own place and tell her mother to get stuffed.

Then, miracle of miracles, a doddery old fellow shuffled to a halt and pressed a real note into her hand – a fiver, not a tenner, but riches nonetheless. She could buy a whole (unmouldy) loaf and several cans of drink and loads of other stuff. She flashed the guy a smile. It hurt to smile. The wind was so raw it set her teeth on edge.

In fact, she ought to make a move. Why risk trouble with the law, when the fiver would see her through the night, and most of tomorrow, too? Besides, the shops would be closing soon, so she shouldn't leave it too late. Her legs were so cramped, it was hard to get up from the pavement, and her bum was almost freezing off. Who cared? She'd look better if she lost a bit of bum.

Sainsbury's was just fifty yards away. The automatic doors slid open and she was sucked into the heat and glare. Never before had she seen a shop so busy and so big – whole families out in force: harassed mums, bawling kids, even loads of single blokes – all jostling, pushing, grabbing. You didn't get many single men in Patterson's; only the odd old git, coming in for company, or trying to warm himself up.

She stopped, baffled, by the bread counter, counting all the different types of loaf. Not just white or brown, as in Patterson's, but organic, stone-ground, seeded, crustless, high-fibre, Danish, calorie-reduced and dozens more. It was price that mattered most, though, and the cheapest by a long chalk was a large white loaf from the 'Basics' range, at a mere 47p. Next, she found her way to the drinks section, again dizzied by the choice: Sprite, Tango, Fanta,

Red Bull, Dr Pepper, ginger beer and lots she'd never heard of, like dandelion-and-burdock. Best to focus simply on the Cokes, or else she'd go boss-eyed. There was a bottle of 'Basics' cola at only 17p for two litres, which was almost unbelievable, since proper branded Coke cost £1.59. She dithered for a while – didn't fancy lugging a great, heavy bottle – but most of the cans seemed to come in six-packs and cost twenty times as much, so she eventually plonked the 'Basics' in her basket.

She was doing fine, so far, except she needed something hot, so she headed for the cooked-food counter. Sausage rolls were the best – cheaper than the chicken legs and more filling than the onion bhajis. Once the guy had handed over the package, she couldn't resist unwrapping it and taking a huge bite. The warm, greasy pastry was bliss, flaking on her tongue, and followed by the spicy tang of sausage-meat. She tossed a piece to Granby; heard his grateful bark.

Right – that would have to do. She must keep some money in reserve, for emergencies or maybe fares. She hadn't worked out what to do yet, or where the hell to go. She'd intended drawing up a plan, but cold and fear and hunger had stopped her thinking about anything except how long she could keep going without losing heart entirely. Now she came to think of it, cold and fear and hunger were also 'basics', in a way. In fact, her whole existence at the moment could be described as pretty basic. She'd left everything behind, at home, except her mobile, and her bag, and the clothes she happened to be wearing when she'd marched out after the bust-up. And even the battery in her phone had died, so she was cut off from her friends. Normally, she and Kat and Jessica spoke twenty times a day. Without those conversations, she was beginning to feel horribly alone, like that movie she and Kat had seen, where the whole earth had been destroyed, and one lone survivor went stumbling around the charred remains, eating rotting corpses, just to keep alive.

For God's *sake*, she thought, glancing up at the shelves and shelves of food, she wasn't quite reduced yet to eating human flesh. She'd manage – 'course she would. Stray dogs got nothing and they usually survived. Perhaps she'd turn Granby into a stray; a fearless little mongrel wandering the streets, and homeless – same as her.

As she waited at the check-out, she stared in shock at other people's trolleys. Were they catering for whole tribes? No one in the village ever bought such loads of stuff – some of it way out. What the hell was quinoa flour, or Sharon fruit, or gravadlax?

'Granby, d'you fancy some gravadlax dog-biscuits? Or quinoa-flavoured Pedigree Chum? Sorry – can't afford them.'

Bored with inspecting people's shopping, she inspected the blokes, instead – older blokes, of course. Her dad might turn up anywhere, so she had to keep a constant look-out. Dads were always on her mind – dads like Natalie's, who bought his kids anything they wanted and told them they were brilliant; dads like Kat's, who laughed a lot, instead of throwing things; dads who didn't drink; dads who stayed around. At least she'd *had* a dad – off and on – for nearly eleven years, although more off than on when she'd been a tiny sprog. He hated babies, so her mum said. How weird was that – hating babies and having seven? Perhaps he wasn't her real father. How would you ever know?

'Hello, there! Can I help?'

Jodie jumped. She hadn't even realized she'd reached the head of the queue and that the check-out guy was waiting – polite, maybe, but frowning. He frowned still more when she dropped the change he gave her and had to root around on the floor to pick up every coin. The old bag behind her began tutting and complaining; saying she didn't have all day to waste. Too bad. Even the 2ps were precious, so she couldn't simply walk away. She had only £3.60 left, so how was she going to eat next week – or next month, come to that? Maybe she could find some sort of job, except they were bound to want references and stuff. But, first, she had to get some food inside her, so, even before she left the shop, she wolfed the rest of the sausage roll and washed it down with cola.

The cold slapped her face as she stepped out of Sainsbury's and trudged, head down, along the street, now looking for somewhere to sleep, or at least some sort of bolt-hole. The crowds were thinning out, although every time she passed a pub or café, she envied those inside: people with families and friends, who were warm and safe and snug and had jobs and plans and futures.

'*Heel*, Granby!' she instructed, stopping at the kerb and waiting for the lights to change. If you could train a dog, why not a dad? 'Stay!' she ordered her dad – a bit late in the day, of course. She often wondered if her mother had tried to make him stay. They'd never talked about it. Her mum clammed up if she so much as mentioned him.

Soon, she had left the shops behind, but the main street was still quite busy, so she turned off into a side-road and began walking up the hill. The further she went from the town-centre, the safer she would be. It wasn't just the cops she feared, but weirdoes, gangs with knives. She broke into a run, just to warm herself up. She should have bought some woolly gloves in Sainsbury's, but they would have cost as much as half-a-dozen 'Basic' loaves, and it was a question of priorities. The whole of life was a question of priorities. Was school more important than work, or love than independence? She had never been in love – although, judging by her mother's example, love never lasted long, so probably best, on balance, to live without a bloke.

By the time she'd jogged another mile, she was out of breath and knackered. Running with a bag of shopping and a bottle banging against your side wasn't exactly a breeze. She panted to a halt, just yards from a boarded-up pub. Its sign, the Hope and Anchor, was hanging loose and swinging in the wind. Hope and Anchor – how ironic was that? – just what she *didn't* have. It might be a place to hide, though. Warily, she glanced around, but there was nobody in sight. The whole street seemed derelict: a few run-down shops, all permanently closed, by the looks of it. Maybe the area was due for demolition, which suited her just fine, since it meant no one much would come here.

She sneaked round the side of the building. The rear wasn't boarded up, but the two back doors were locked and barred; their paint blistering and peeling. In the grudging light, she could make out a stretch of wasteland – the pub garden, once, maybe, but now overgrown and tangled. It would be far too manky to sleep on, not to mention perishing cold. She peered up at the sky. The clouds looked bruised and ragged; the moon was just a sliver, so thin and sharp it could cut. Continuing round the other side, she stumbled upon a lean-to: a small wooden structure, with a corrugated roof. It didn't have a door, but at least she'd be protected from the wind there.

She stepped in very gingerly, scared of rats, or bats, or worse. She should have bought a torch – more use than gloves or Coke – but there were no rustlings or scrabblings, thank God. The floor was squelchy underfoot, littered with old dead leaves, but the advantage was she'd have the place to herself, apart from Granby, of course. Dogs could protect you: growl in warning if anyone came near; pin down an attacker; bite a chunk out of his leg if he was spoiling for a fight.

Fumbling in the darkness, she emptied out the Sainsbury's bag and put it on the ground, so she could sit on a piece of plastic, rather than on grunge and grot. She felt a sudden longing for her bedroom – those things she took for granted: the rug, the radiator, the big, thick, cosy duvet, the amazing fact you could press a switch and immediately the lights came on. She wondered if her mother had started worrying about her. Unlikely. Lucy's mother worried if Lucy was even *seconds* late. And Kat's parents drove her everywhere, to make sure that she was safe. Great to have a car. The minute she was old enough, she'd learn to drive and buy one. Except a car cost thousands, didn't it?

'Granby, what sort of car shall we have? A Porsche? A BMW?'

How pathetic was that – talking to a dog that didn't exist? But since she had always gone in for imaginary things, she was clearly mega-pathetic. When her mother put her foot down about one piddling goldfish, she'd imagined a whole tropical aquarium; then a Persian cat, followed by a horse – thoroughbred, of course. And she'd had imaginary dads by the score. A pity people couldn't pick out their own parents, instead of making do with the ones laid on by Fate. She knew what sort of mum she'd choose: someone who didn't smoke or shout; had no other kids but her, and who'd let her have any pet she wanted – rabbits, budgies, hamsters, a whole tribe of cats and dogs – and a mother who could cook.

Sitting cross-legged on the Sainsbury's bag, she breathed in the smell of baking. Her mum was in the kitchen, making fairy-cakes. She was allowed to scrape out the mixing-bowl; allowed to eat as many as she chose. No – first they had to be iced. She wasn't sure exactly how you iced cakes, so she ditched that stage and just admired the finished results. There were loads of different colours – pink, white, yellow, lilac, blue – and every sort of topping. The lilac ones had Smarties on top, and the pink ones had whole strawberries, and the yellow ones had sugar stars, and the blue ones sugar hearts and kisses. She bit into a heart; felt it explode in a sugar-rush of love and, suddenly, her mum was kissing her – a real, adoring kiss.

'Fucking hell!' she muttered to herself. 'That's *way* over the top.' Her mother could no more cook than run the marathon, and to imagine her kissing her kids really was a fantasy too far. Even Granby was pretty useless – not warm at all and, actually, no help.

She jumped up, to stamp her feet and swing her arms, just to keep the blood moving. Maybe she should go back into town and buy herself a hot drink. Except being cold was preferable to being nabbed – or knifed – so she stayed put where she was. Perhaps some food would warm her up, so she reached out in the murky dark to find the loaf of bread; removed a slice and chewed it, dry. It tasted limp and flabby, but she added butter and jam, then a bit of cheese and pickle. Easier to imagine cheese and pickle than to imagine a kiss from her mother.

'Was she always undemonstrative?' the counsellor had asked.

'She was always bloody angry,' she'd retorted, and the counsellor had smiled. Mary, she was called – the Blessed Virgin's name. And she had the same sweet, motherly face as the statue of the Blessed Virgin that stood outside the Catholic church; the same gentle, kind-blue eyes. She was small and sort of fragile, like she might blow away in a puff of wind, and her voice was soft and whispery; a voice you'd use in church. She had never shouted; not in all five sessions. They'd promised her *ten* sessions, but, smack-bang in the middle, Mary had moved house and begun working somewhere else.

The news had been so gut-wrenching, she'd locked herself in her bedroom and refused to budge, for days. But then Christopher took over and he was just as nice. His voice was like warm custard: velvety and smooth. He was older, though, much older, and had a wrinkled, jowly face that didn't seem to fit his hair, which was weirdly thick and dark. But, when she saw him for her second session, the hair had disappeared and he was completely shiny bald. It was such a shock, she just stood and stared, however rude it seemed. But he sat her down in her usual chair and explained that he'd lost his hair after cancer treatment and no longer wished to wear his wig, because it was uncomfortable and hot. After that, she simply couldn't concentrate – not once in the whole hour. She'd kept worrying about him having cancer and maybe actually *dying* before they'd completed all the sessions.

But he hadn't died, and he'd continued being nice and talking in his custard-voice, and, once, he had even held her hand. She'd been bawling her head off – about her mother, probably, but he didn't ask his usual questions, just reached out for her hand and clasped it very firm and tight, like he was her anchor.

Hope and Anchor – it had never even struck her before, but that was exactly how things were then: Mary her hope; Christopher her anchor.

Her real mum had been against it from the start, though. 'I'd no more trot off to a trick-cyclist than swallow a mouthful of wasps. I don't believe in poking things with a stick. And I've had far more crap to deal with in my time than *you've* ever had, my girl! Your life's a bed of roses, however much you bellyache. When *I* was your age, my dad thought nothing of giving me a damned good wallop, just because it was Tuesday, or some other damn-fool reason.'

It was always worse for her, of course. So why hadn't she simply topped herself, instead of having seven kids and making *their* lives hell?

She'd soon learned to avoid all mention of Mary or Christopher. Her mum would only jump down her throat, and even her friends thought it weird being sent for counselling, like she was completely off her head. And, if they ever found out about Christopher's wig, they'd all take the piss and die laughing.

She still missed the sessions horribly – you were allowed only ten on the NHS, and you'd need to win the Lottery if you wanted to go private. But at least Christopher and Mary were real, unlike Granby and the fairy cakes. And, in fact, it wasn't totally impossible for them to come and find her here. Her mum might even have rung them; begun to worry big-time when she saw how late it was. No, that was crap – her mother didn't worry even small-time. But Christopher and Mary might have had a deep gut-feeling that she was in some sort of trouble and needed sorting out. After all, they knew each other well, so it wasn't out of the question they could join forces, just for once. In any case, peculiar things did happen – things no one could explain, like ghosts and UFOs and miracles.

It *was* a sort of miracle to have them sitting with her now – and have them both together, which never happened at the clinic. And they'd brought all the things she needed: blankets and an oil-stove; a powerful torch; a Thermos of hot chocolate; butter for the bread and strawberry jam; even cheese and pickle. They weren't flustered in the least. That was the point of counsellors: they were trained to be calm, whatever clients did or said. You could swear, or shout, or go berserk – all of which she'd done – but they still had to keep their cool. Sometimes, she'd been a total pain on purpose, to see how much they'd take. But they'd never shouted back, or told her to get lost, or stalked off in a huff.

And, this time, she wouldn't need to lose them after just ten measly sessions, or want to *kill* their other clients, so she could have them back, and have them to herself. She was no longer even a client now, but living with them permanently – their child, their only child. Mary was spreading the blankets over her and slipping a pillow under her head, while Christopher lit the oil-stove and started buttering the bread. He made tiny, dainty sandwiches, with all the crusts cut off, and fed her like a baby. Then he gave her the hot chocolate, tipping up the Thermos and trickling the warm, foamy liquid gently into her mouth. And, when she was full up, Mary tucked her in and began reading her a bedtime story. '*Once upon a time….*'

While the two of them kept guard, she was safe from everything. The police would never find her, and no drunks or freaks would dare come near, because Christopher and Mary had a special knack of changing stuff, like your screw-ups or your past, and of making bad things good. And, for the first time since she'd walked out, she was beginning to feel almost human. In fact, her eyes were actually closing and she was not that far off sleep, as Mary's voice continued with the story: a story with a happy ending. Yes, her father had come back: brave, bald, kindly Christopher – there, beside her bed; promising to stay; to watch over her, for ever. And her mother, Mary, was just kissing her goodnight, a real, adoring kiss....

No – hold on; slow down. Bedtime stories came later, when she was a kid of five or six. Better to start at the beginning, inside Mary's womb. Her real mother's womb had been cold and hard and grudging, and so cramped she couldn't move an inch, let alone turn round. Most people couldn't remember being in the womb, but her own vile nine months still bugged her to this day: that gruesome feeling of being caged up in a woman who didn't want a baby in the first place and kept her starved of food. All she'd had to eat was pills and cigarette-smoke and, each time she tried to rest, the bang-bang-bang of her mother's manic heartbeat jolted her awake. *Mary's* womb would be different altogether: soft and safe and welcoming, with room to stretch her limbs, and a quietly throbbing heartbeat lulling her to sleep. And there'd be constant streams of healthy food to help her grow, cell by cell by cell, and constant streams of love, right from the time she was a blob. In fact, Mary would probably care enough to read bedtime stories even to a blob. A blob might not understand the words, but it would know that having stories read meant it was special from the start.

She curled into a blobby ball and listen to the dreamy voice whispering through her snug cocoon: '*Once upon a time* ...' Another story with a happy ending – her father in the delivery-room, instead of in the pub, waiting for her birth, in a state of high excitement. Yes, at this very moment, he was reaching out his arms to take her from the midwife, so proud it was like his team had won the Cup. And now he was announcing to the whole wide world that his little girl was the most amazing, gorgeous creature any dad had ever—

'Hey, miss, wake up! What are you doing here at this time of night?'

The loud, stern voice cut right across the story. She squinted through her lids, but the murky gloom had vanished and a glaring torch-beam shone right into her eyes. Peering up, she saw four black legs looming over her; two unfriendly faces, each topped by a black helmet, stooping down towards her. Bloody hell – the cops!

'Is anything wrong?' the taller one asked, although she could hardly hear for the crackling of the radios, which were spitting out traffic news and emergency reports.

'Are you all right?' the second bloke repeated.

She didn't answer. Their fluorescent jackets were a shiny, blinding yellow. She hated violent colours. Christopher's jacket was a soft, peaceful shade of brown; Mary wore quiet blues and greys.

'You look very young. How old are you?'

A new-born baby, she couldn't say – babies didn't speak. Someone small and weak, she mouthed, who had to be fed and kissed good-night; tucked up; watched over; protected from all harm.

'Why aren't you answering our questions? You're obviously trying to hide something. We've asked you, twice, is anything wrong?'

'No,' she muttered. 'Everything was perfect, until you ruined it.'

The radios drowned her voice; both of them at once – a sort of snorting shorthand, all accidents and horrors.

'Pile-up at the junction of ...' 'Serious assault ...' 'Urgent assistance required ...' 'A stabbing in the High Street. Two young men with blades....'

The taller cop squatted down beside her. She could see his muscly hands; the dark hairs on the thumbs.

'This is not the sort of place a young girl like you should hide in, let alone so late. We'd better take you along with us and find out more about you.'

She wouldn't go; not anywhere. New-born babies had to stay safe with their mothers.

'Yeah,' the other guy chipped in. 'Come down to the station and we'll sort this out, OK?'

No, it wasn't OK – not at all. She needed help, and desperately. 'Mum ...' she whimpered. 'Dad....'

But nobody was there – no one except the two big, burly men. They pulled her up to her feet; stood one on either side of her, each holding on to her arm, so she couldn't make a run for it. She tried to struggle free, but it was like a floppy rabbit had dared pit its strength against two fierce old foxes. Already, they were marching her along the path; their grip so hurting-tight, it felt like handcuffs.

She glanced up at the pub, rearing, dark, above her. Even its name was a lie. There wasn't any anchor; wasn't any hope. And the only happy ending was a night in a police-cell.

BOUQUET OF LIES

'I'm here to visit my sister – Marion McCall. Can you tell me where I can find her, please.'

'Hang on a sec.' The nurse spoke with a distracted air.

Eileen glanced at the crumpled uniform; the strands of greasy hair escaping from the ponytail. Did the girl have no professional pride? 'Hang on a sec' was hardly an appropriate response, especially as she'd been waiting at the nurses' station a good five minutes already, with no choice but to eavesdrop on a whispered conversation. The nurse was confiding in her colleague about some disastrous romance; none of the steamy details spared.

'Sorry. *Who* did you say?' she asked, at last, presumably remembering she was paid to work.

'Marion McCall. I'm her sister.'

The nurse consulted the whiteboard on the wall beside the desk, 'Yeah, this is the right ward. Last bed in the last bay on the right.' With a casual wave, to indicate the general direction, she returned to her discussion of Mr Hopelessly Wrong.

Eileen made her way into the ward. There was no sign of her sister from this first bay, all of whose occupants appeared to be in the final stage of life – or perhaps *non*-life would be more apt a phrase. Most were hooked up to a daunting array of drips and tubes and oxygen-masks; three lay completely comatose, and one poor wrinkled crone seemed to be coughing up her lungs. How come Marion, at fifty-six, had landed up amongst these geriatric no-hopers? Her sister's garbled phone-call had been distinctly short on facts, but it was clear she was in no danger. A hysterectomy, however painful or upsetting, was hardly terminal.

She was aware of eyes following her as she traversed the second bay; her mere presence attracting notice because no one else had visitors. Her natural inclination was to pause by every hapless patient's bed and give each one some portion of her time. For all she knew, they might be mostly family-less and friendless, and just mouldering here until released by merciful death. But having realized, on reflection, that the approach of a total stranger might be less a source of solace than of disquiet or even alarm, she made herself walk on. Fortunately, there were more signs of life in the last bay: one patient actually mobile and another even packing to go home, although a third was sobbing piteously, with no one on hand to help. Those nurses at the desk were obviously too busy discussing the vagaries of their love-life to provide comfort, Kleenex or even a listening ear.

She stopped in shock at the sight of her sister, who lay asleep and ashen-pale; her head askew on the pillow and one arm stretched across the counterpane, as if in supplication. Her once-dark, bouncy hair was now sparse and greying; her face haggard, deeply lined. How in God's name could she have aged so much in the five years since they'd last met?

With as little noise as possible, she eased herself into the chair beside the bed. The exotic lilies and hothouse roses she had purchased at the hospital shop seemed to cringe at their surroundings – pampered aristocrats forced to slum it in this shabby NHS ward. Positioning the bouquet across her lap, she gave silent thanks for her own robust health. Her only operation in her entire sixty-two years – a minor hernia repair – had been carried out at St Winifred's, a private cottage-hospital, where she'd had her own luxurious room, fully air-conditioned and with a view of landscaped gardens. Here, the air was stuffy, if not smelly, and the vista from the window was of dismal concrete wasteland. But then Marion had only herself to blame. All her life, she had refused to take a regular job or establish a settled home, and thus had not the slightest chance of affording medical insurance – or even other kinds of insurance. Many times, she, as elder sister, had offered financial assistance, only to see the money squandered on some damn-fool project, such as the ill-fated trip to Mexico, or the attempt to found a commune with a group of equally feckless folk.

She closed her eyes, exhausted by her early start and the long drive from Harrogate. When she'd set out this morning, the temperature had been minus five – the coldest day of January, so far – and the icy roads and flurries of snow had only added to the strain. However, it was impossible to doze in this milieu, with all the noise and disturbance. The sobbing hadn't abated; the patient who'd been packing was now clattering things around, and another had started wailing and complaining. Two nurses had, in fact, appeared, but seemed only to be contributing to the hubbub; one bawling at the weeping woman, who was clearly very deaf, and the other manoeuvring a patient into a wheelchair; managing, in the process, to knock a glass off the bedside-table and spill water all over the floor. If she had her way, she would send these staff straight back to nursing school, to learn manners and appropriate patient-care, not to mention a little TLC.

Although she had to admit that she, too, was somewhat lacking in the TLC department when it came to displays of distress. She herself would never dream of giving way to such public exhibitions, and thus found them hard to tolerate in others. Even at the funeral, she had remained resolutely dry-eyed, despite the appalling shock of her busy, lively mother, with her many friends and interests, and her firm intention of not dying until she passed the hundred mark, suddenly keeling over in a heart-attack. There had been no warning; no prior illness. On Thursday, she'd been an energetic, healthy octogenarian; on Friday, a waxen corpse.

The patient's sobs were setting off unwelcome memories, of other people crying at the funeral; her mother's best friend, in particular, becoming near-hysterical with grief. What a relentless day that had been; grinding on much longer than any normal day. Yet, despite her private heartache, she had never faltered in her role as hostess: greeting mourners; joining in the prayers and hymns, then presiding at the reception. But, notwithstanding the condolences she had received on every side, there *was* no consolation. And, now, all she had left of her mother was a jar of ashes on the mantelpiece.

Moving the bouquet to the floor, she opened her handbag and withdrew the crisp white envelope containing Marion's small portion of those ashes; laying them on the bedside locker, to remind her to hand them over. Whether her sister would actually want them or not was a different matter altogether.

Marion's locker was pitifully bare: no get-well cards; no bowl of fruit or bottle of Lucozade. After her own operation, her hospital room had resembled a cross between a flower-shop and a branch of Clinton Cards – and she'd been in a mere two days! Did Marion have no friends; no one to visit except a sister who was now an almost-stranger? But that, too, was Marion's fault. Her knack of alienating people was legendary, including her own family, of course.

She tried to block her ears, as sounds of moaning and retching arose from the far corner of the bay and a raucous nurse kept urging, 'Spit, dear. Spit some more!' Repulsive spitting noises followed in their turn and, only when they'd subsided, did Eileen shut her eyes again, longing to sink into oblivion. She had barely slept at all this last raw and aching fortnight, yet determinedly, she switched her thoughts from the funeral; from hearses, wreaths and ashes, and that horrendous, final moment when the blue-velvet curtains closed around the coffin. Instead, she pictured her mother in her prime: the resourceful and courageous widow, bringing up two girls alone; never indulging in self-pity, or even in recrimination, despite endless provocation from the rebellious younger child. Exasperation with the black sheep of the family had drawn them close from a very early stage, and, as the years went by and Marion's defiance increased in scale and volume, the bond had deepened further. Frankly, it had been a relief for them both when the black sheep moved down South, although the transgressions had, of course, continued; necessitating frequent trips to bail her out yet again.

'Eileen!'

At the sound of her name, she hastily opened her eyes. It seemed wrong to be caught napping when Marion was in this vulnerable state. But her sister was now wide awake and staring at her in obvious surprise.

'I thought you'd decided not to come.'

'Why on earth should you think that? I told them loud and clear this morning that I was on my way and would they please inform you.'

'Well, no one said a dicky-bird. And it's a good week since I rang you.'

'I'm sorry,' she said, defensively. 'I couldn't just drop everything and head straight for the door. I mean, there's Harold to consider and I had to make arrangements for ...' Her voice tailed off. She could hardly admit that she hadn't been exactly keen to make yet another mercy-trip. It was a good five-hour drive to this unappealing part of London, the weather was atrocious and the only hotel she'd managed to find in the hospital's vicinity was distinctly second-rate. 'Besides,' she added, feeling she had to make a stronger case for her own apparent negligence. 'I had to take the car in for a service. It was almost due, in fact, and I didn't want to risk a breakdown.'

'Sorry to put you to so much trouble.'

She bristled at her sister's sarcastic tone. 'It wasn't any trouble,' she snapped. 'These things take time, that's all. Anyway, I blame the hospital. What sort of hopeless place is it, if they can't be bothered to pass on important messages from relatives?'

Marion shrugged. 'Calm down. No harm done. You're here; I'm here. What's the problem?'

Her sister's unexpected smile only added to her guilt. She was uncomfortably aware that, after a five-year absence, she should have been more affectionate; not sounded off about the hospital's deficiencies. Hastily, she laid the bouquet on the bed, in an attempt to make amends. 'These are for you,' she said, returning Marion's smile.

'You shouldn't have bothered. You know I hate flowers.'

The smile froze on her face. How perverse was that? No one hated flowers.

'And the nurses aren't keen either. They're an infection-risk, apparently – you know, lethal germs breeding in the flower-water. Although they'd be lucky to get any water here, let alone a proper vase. The nurses are rushed off their feet.'

'So I noticed,' she said, sarcastic now herself, yet hating the fact they were already bickering. How did other sisters manage to be companionable and close, while she and Marion had fought for almost sixty years?

'Eileen, I can't believe I actually dozed off! I've barely slept a wink all the time I've been here, then, when *you* turn up, after years and years of deliberately avoiding me, I'm bloody dead to the world!'

Eileen bit back a retort. 'Deliberately avoiding' was really rather rich. Marion had brought her isolation on herself. Fortunately, they were interrupted by the appearance of a nurse, wheeling some machine or other, which she parked beside the bed. Without a word to either of them, she proceeded to take Marion's blood-pressure and temperature; scrawled some figures on the chart, then trundled off as quickly as she'd come.

Eileen raised her eyebrows. 'They're not exactly chatty here.'

'You should see the consultant! Even if he actually deigns to speak, I can't understand a word he says. I've nothing against foreigners. I'd just like them to learn English, as well as medicine.'

'Anyway, how *are* you?' Eileen asked, ashamed to realize she hadn't yet enquired.

'Lousy. Either in pain, or all woozy from the drugs. But the worst thing is the lack of sleep. There's so much racket, day and night – cleaners banging about, or patients crying out for help, or doctors rushing in to deal with some emergency. The minute I close my eyes, somebody or something wakes me up. It's driving me insane!'

'I'm sorry, honestly.'

Another shrug. 'Who cares?'

'*I* do.' It wasn't a lie. She did care – always had – but she'd learned through painful experience that *no* one could help Marion – not she, or Harold, or their two now grown-up daughters; not even her mother, despite their combined, heroic efforts to improve the situation. After decades of contention, they had all been forced to conclude that there was nothing else any of them could do.

She made herself reach down and clasp her sister's hand. It, too, looked distressingly old, with distended veins and brown patches of discolouration. Was Marion hiding something – something sinister that would explain this accelerated ageing? Could the surgeon have found cancer in her womb – cancer that had already spread? The prospect of another funeral filled her with the deepest dread.

Marion seemed uneasy with her hand held and, having wriggled it free, picked up the bouquet, instead, and thrust her nose against the roses. They were scentless, in fact, being out-of-season and forced. Nonetheless, Eileen thought resentfully, a word of thanks would surely be in order, but then gratitude had never been Marion's strong point.

'It was the infection that really loused things up. I mean, I was due to leave this dump two days ago, but that very morning, my temperature shot up. They found the wound was oozing – suppurating, they call it – so that put the bloody kibosh on any chance of going home.'

Was Marion lying, she wondered; inventing an infection to conceal a cancerous tumour? But what would be the point? Besides, she had never spared her family any details of her earlier traumas: the abortion; the disastrous overdose; the near-fatal accident. (Only Marion would be so reckless as to borrow some madcap's Harley-Davidson and do a ton down the motorway, just for the sheer hell of it.) On the other hand, her sister was a practised liar, as if in deliberate contravention of their mother's firm belief that even the whitest of white lies was wrong. Indeed, she herself adhered to the same strict standards and never lied, on principle.

'So when are they thinking of discharging you?' She had to raise her voice above the disturbance from the adjoining bed. An entire medical team had just breezed in and, although they had drawn the floral curtains round the bed, their remarks and observations were clearly audible – not to mention disconcerting.

Marion shrugged. 'Dunno.'

'Do you live nearby?' Shaming that she didn't know her only sibling's address. But then Marion changed her whereabouts as often as most people changed their clothes.

'Not far. I found this crummy bedsit, about six months ago, above a shop in Sydenham. There's barely room for me, let alone for visitors. Which is why I didn't invite you to stay.'

Eileen was hard pressed to reply. She and Harold owned a detached, four-bedroomed house in an attractive part of Harrogate, with extensive gardens back and front. And their daughters, too, lived in salubrious surroundings, having found themselves good jobs and solvent spouses. Marion, however, had never succeeded in meeting what their mother called 'good husband material'. Instead, she had shacked up with a succession of highly unsuitable men, who either dumped her, or betrayed her, or took advantage of her. As for having children, she had never shown the slightest maternal instinct and, anyway, none of the ne'er-do-wells she seemed to attract possessed even rudimentary parenting skills.

'I feel really gutted about the hysterectomy,' Marion remarked, as if tuning in to her thoughts. 'I've never used my fucking womb and now it's been ripped out. I might as well as have never had it in the first place – *or* all those painful periods every sodding month.'

Eileen winced at the swear-words. Swearing was like lying: unnecessary, objectionable and wrong. 'But I thought you didn't want children?' she said, a shade impatiently.

'Eileen, you haven't a clue! Of course I wanted kids, but it didn't happen, did it? Oh, I know I had an abortion, but very much against my will.'

'That wasn't the impression you gave.'

'Look, I *had* to get rid of it – there wasn't any choice. But that doesn't mean I didn't find the whole thing really harrowing. In fact, I had these ghastly nightmares for ages afterwards. I'd be holding a mangled foetus in my arms, but wrapped in a proper baby's shawl and even wearing bootees, would you believe!'

Eileen grimaced in distaste. She and Harold were vehemently pro-life. Would she ever know if her sister really wanted that child, or whether she was lying again?

'It's OK for *you*, with Chloe and Samantha, not to mention a live-in husband to support them. And your pampered little darlings now have kids and husbands of their own, yet Harold still waits on you hand and foot!'

'He doesn't. Don't be silly.'

'He pays all the bills, though, doesn't he? You haven't worked for bloody years. I *have* to work, to pay the rent. And the only job I could find at my age is waitressing in a seedy caff.'

Eileen bit her lip. Whatever irritation Marion had caused, no one could deny that the cards had been stacked against her, right from birth. A sickly, plain and backward child, she had only seemed to emphasize the contrast with the elder sister's blooming health, pretty face and creditable school performance. And, of course, *she* had been the favourite; not only with her mother, but with all the other relatives. But hadn't she earned that position by being always caring and responsible; supporting her widowed mother; following the path of duty and conformity, while Marion ran riot? Indeed, once she'd reached her early teens, she had acted almost like her mother's husband; the pair of them trying – and failing lamentably – to control their obstreperous child, and never giving up until Marion was middle-aged and, by then, clearly hell-bent on self-destruction.

She glanced up at the noise of the tea-trolley being trundled along the ward. The obese black orderly in charge of it was all but bursting the seams of her uniform, but at least she had a radiant smile. Smiles seemed rare among the staff here.

'Tea, dear?' she asked Marion, beaming at them both.

'Yes, please. Two sugars. And could you wangle a cup for my sister?'

'Sorry, dear, I'd love to, but only patients get the tea.'

At St Winifred's, each and every visitor had been offered a tray of tea, with a proper teapot and milk jug and decent floral china. Marion's plain white cup was stained and didn't even match its saucer.

'Anyway,' Marion said, taking a tentative sip, as if expecting the tea to poison her, 'that's enough about me. I didn't drag you all this way to talk about my fucking womb. I want to discuss Deidre.'

Eileen felt the usual surge of irritation at that disrespectful 'Deidre'. From the age of twelve, Marion had refused to call their mother 'Mummy', yet for a child to use its parent's Christian name seemed deplorably casual, not to say bizarre.

'I'm sorry I missed the funeral.'

'Well, that was hardly your fault. Didn't you say you had your operation the very day she died?'

'Yeah. Bad timing!'

Would you have come anyway, Eileen refrained from asking. Privately, she suspected that had Marion been in the rudest of health, she would still have failed to show up. As for her helping with the arrangements, that would require a miracle. *She* was the one who always dealt with the deaths, whether uncles, aunts, grandparents or elderly family friends, while Marion remained conspicuous by her absence. In fact, she had every right to feel aggrieved. Now officially a pensioner, it was sometimes hard to summon up her former energy and organizational powers.

'I did go to the hospital chapel, though, just before my op, to say a prayer for her.'

Eileen looked up in surprise. 'I didn't know you were religious.'

'Praying's nothing to do with religion.'

'What's it to do with, then?'

'As far as I'm concerned, it's a form of energy that you can beam towards a person you want to help.'

'Well, you couldn't do much to help Mummy – not when she was already dead.'

'How can you be so sure? It might have eased her passage to another life.'

'So you believe in eternal life now, do you?' This was getting more and more absurd. Marion had long ago rebelled against religion; refused to go to church; refused even to attend her and Harold's wedding; claiming the marriage service was a sham and the vicar a self-serving ponce. But, of course, if she'd just been told she had terminal cancer, she might have changed her tune and be clutching at the only form of salvation now on offer.

'Look, it may sound weird to you, Eileen, but I feel quite cut up about Deidre – you know, not saying goodbye or anything.'

Well, you had plenty of chances these last few years. Again, Eileen didn't speak her mind, partly because her sister looked so ill: dark purplish circles etched beneath her eyes and a worryingly grey tinge to her complexion.

'She never *knew* me – that was the trouble. And, actually, she didn't want to. I think she was almost scared.'

'Scared?'

'Yes, of what I might reveal. The last time we met, which I remember clearly was in April 2005, she was already eighty-two and I felt this desperate need to tell her who I *was* – you know – what makes me tick, all that sort of stuff, before she was dead and gone. "Deidre," I said, "I might as well be a total stranger for all you know about my life. So why don't we sit down together and I'll give you some idea of how I see things?" And, can you believe, she refused point blank? I think she was terrified of discovering I was a hardened heroin addict, or worked in a brothel, or something!'

'Marion, that's crazy! Mummy would never even have *heard* of heroin addicts.'

'Yes, she only felt at ease among her own kind – that's the very point I'm trying to make. She deliberately confined herself to a narrow segment of society – straitlaced and conservative and all upholding the same bourgeois standards. Even the films and plays she chose to see had to be safe and sanitized – no drugs, no sex, no sink estates, nothing the slightest bit subversive. If anyone put forward an even mildly radical view, she'd feel threatened and run a mile. She didn't just lack soul; she lacked any curiosity about how other people live, even her own flesh and blood. I can't understand that, Eileen – condemning nine-tenths of the human race because they don't sign up to monogamy and safe mortgages, or save for Saga cruises or go to flower-arrangement classes.'

Eileen flushed. She and Harold had thoroughly enjoyed last year's Saga cruise and what, in heaven's name, was wrong with flower-arrangement? In fact, she longed to find a decent vase and get to work on the bouquet.

'OK, *she* can live like that, if she wants, but why inflict those things on me?'

'She didn't, Marion. That's totally unfair.'

'Look, when I refused to toe the line, she more or less disowned me. Take the way she used to condemn me as "promiscuous", if I shagged a bloke I didn't know that well. She couldn't see that sex is actually quite a useful way to find out more about someone – what they're really like beneath the mask.'

Eileen glanced nervously around. Marion's voice could carry and the Indian patient opposite was already glancing in their direction.

'I mean, I've slept with guys I later realized I didn't even *like*. And it was the sex itself that showed me they were bloody selfish, or plain violent, or whatever. And several didn't have a clue about how women's bodies work. But I don't regret it in the slightest because.... Hell! You don't want to hear all this. Let's get back to Deidre. I suppose what I'm trying to say is that I always hoped she'd come to see things differently and stop judging me so harshly as a dropout and a slut. I wanted her to understand that I was genuinely adrift and most of the mistakes I made were just attempts to sort out my life. I was stupid enough to think that, sooner or later, she'd agree to forgive and forget, and we could wipe the slate clean and even get close, at last. And then she has to go and die when I'm lying on the operating table, two-hundred miles away! So now it's too fucking late. Everything's too late – a husband, kids, a decent job ... I've missed the boat all round, Sis.'

Sis! A word Marion hadn't used since they were little, and surely a term of affection. But, as she opened her mouth to say something more amenable herself, she was interrupted by the medicos, who were just leaving the neighbouring bed and making their rackety way back along the ward.

It was Marion who spoke, in fact, as she watched the troupe disappear. 'It's even too late for sex. Look at that little lot – testosterone on legs! But none of them would touch me with a bargepole, not even the old buffer of a consultant. I'm way past my sell-by date.'

Eileen reflected on the fact that, despite being five years older than Marion, and with a husband in his seventies, she and Harold still had sex – gentle, tepid, unexciting sex, although latterly he'd been having trouble maintaining an erection. Had *he* ever really known how women's bodies worked, she couldn't help but wonder, aware that such a speculation was disloyal and probably dangerous? Yet, sometimes, deep, deep down, she had envied Marion all those different men; the tempestuous one-night stands; even just her sister's vast experience. What did she mean by 'plain violent', for instance? Had she been tied up, whipped or – God forbid – semi-raped? Her mind refused to go there. The imaginative leap was too great, since she herself had slept with one man only, in her entire adult life: her lawful, wedded husband. Normally, she saw that as a virtue, yet occasionally and secretly, she had allowed herself to fantasize about the sort of men Marion described, only to feel immediate guilt.

It was time to change the subject, though, if only for the other patients' sake. Now that the doctors had left, the woman in the adjoining bed could easily listen in, while the patient opposite seemed to have nothing better to do than watch them with a disapproving air. 'Look, Marion, is there anything you need? The hospital shop is really rather good, so I can easily pop down there and buy you some fruit, or orange juice, or a few magazines to read.'

'I loathe magazines – women's mags especially. They're so trivial they make me puke, as if all us women care about is clothes and make-up and orgasms. What about our sodding minds? But I keep going off the point. Listen, Eileen – this is really important. Deidre hasn't spoken to me for five and three-quarter years, but surely she must have thought about me sometimes?'

'Of course.' No mother could forget her child. Besides, she and Deidre had never failed to discuss the burden they'd shared for decades: the intractable problem of Marion.

'OK, prove it! What I need to know is did she actually mention me in the twenty-four hours between her heart attack and her death?'

Eileen cast her mind back. Their mother *had* been conscious, and surprisingly *compos mentis*, and they *had* spoken, quite extensively. But, no, Marion hadn't featured in any of the conversations. As she opened her mouth to say so, she noticed the expression on her sister's face: anguished, almost pleading; a prisoner begging for reprieve.

'Er, let me think,' she prevaricated. 'Of course, we didn't have much time together and—'

'But you told me on the phone that the two of you had a really good long chat. And you were amazed how lucid she was, despite all the drugs and stuff.'

Eileen cursed herself for having mentioned that communication. But then it had never crossed her mind that Marion would care a jot whether their mother had remembered her or not. She was relieved to see a nurse approaching. Perhaps her sister would be wheeled away for some scan or test or procedure, allowing them to evade the issue.

'How's the pain?' the girl asked – an Asiatic, this time, pretty and petite.

'Awful! Can I have more painkillers?'

The nurse consulted the chart at the foot of Marion's bed. 'Sorry, it's only three hours since the last lot, so you're not due for any more yet. But I'll come back in an hour, OK?'

With a shrug of resignation, Marion returned to the thorny subject. 'For Christ's sake, Eileen, she only had us two kids, not a bloody tribe. You were there at the end; I, unfortunately, wasn't. And, since you say she hadn't lost her marbles, how could she have forgotten me entirely?'

Eileen shifted uneasily on her seat. Would it hurt to lie, just this once; just the smallest, most innocuous white lie? Her stern inner voice immediately told her that it *would* hurt; began issuing dire warnings about slippery slopes.

'I mean, to think of my own mother dying without sparing me one single thought. It's as if I don't exist, as if she'd never had me. But that's the point, isn't it? She probably wished she hadn't.'

'How could you even consider such a thing?' Eileen all but shouted.

'Easily. If I caused her so much trouble – as you never stopped pointing out – it would be completely natural for her to conclude she'd have been better off with just her elder daughter: the adored and perfect one. You can't deny you were her favourite.'

Eileen opened her bag, rummaged for her handkerchief and pretended to blow her nose. Easier than having to reply.

'So that's it, is it? The two of you spent ages prattling, but it never even occurred to you to mention *me*, or—'

'It wasn't "prattling",' Eileen cut in. 'She was near death, for heaven's sake!'

'But you said she talked about Chloe and Samantha, so why not me, as well?'

'Hold on ...' Eileen kept the handkerchief half across her face, as if to hide from that accusing inner voice. 'I ... I remember now. She ... she did actually say how sorry she was you couldn't be with her at the end.'

'*Really*?'

That one word was crammed with such a Niagara of relief, Eileen suppressed all the strict, unyielding principles she had spent her life upholding. Perhaps white lies didn't count. 'Yes, and she seemed ... worried about you generally. She even talked about that awful time when your flat-share with Patricia broke up and you were more or less forced out onto the street. She realized how upset you must have—'

'But that was years ago! You mean, she actually remembered?'

Was a nod a lie? Before the reproving voice could snap an uncompromising 'yes', she nodded, vigorously.

'Honestly?'

Another shameful nod. 'Honestly' made it ten times worse.

'You're not having me on?'

'No.'

'Oh, *Sis*!' Marion's whole face had relaxed. She even looked less gravely ill.

How extraordinary, Eileen thought, that lies could be compassionate – kind, humane, almost like mental painkillers. She suddenly realized, with a sense of shock, that her sister had never felt loved – not by anyone. The fact was so blindingly obvious she could hardly believe her own obtuseness in failing to acknowledge it before. While *she* had basked in their mother's love, and a husband's love, and the love of their two daughters and two sons-in-law and, more recently, her three granddaughters' love, Marion had been forced to make do with odd scraps and shreds of affection, thrown at her by unsuitable men or by fickle, faithless friends. There had been no one central person in her life to provide any source of support. In fact, all those wild affairs might simply have been compensatory; the regrettable transgressions just a bid for attention. Perhaps, in the absence of love, attention might seem the next best thing.

And, of course, both she and Marion had been deprived of a father – Marion from the age of eighteenth months. She herself had eventually found a substitute in the form of marriage to a responsible, reliable, conscientious, older man. But all the father-figures her poor sister had pursued had proved reprobates or conmen. For the first time in her life, she was able to see Marion's life not as reprehensible but as achingly unfulfilled. And thus wouldn't it be an act of mercy to grant her some small comfort before it was too late?

She cleared her throat. 'Because Mummy couldn't say goodbye herself, she ... she asked me to say it for her.' All at once, she was struck by another thought: perhaps Marion *knew* she was lying, yet was so desperate for their mother's blessing, she was willing to believe a gross distortion of the truth. But did it really matter? Lies weren't only kind; they could also be necessities; more valuable, maybe, than even financial handouts.

Marion was actually smiling; her whole face animated. 'Oh, Sis, I just can't tell you how relieved I feel.'

'Sis' three times now. The expensive flowers she had scorned; this bouquet of lies was clearly a more precious gift.

'Sis ...' she dared reciprocate, although the word felt strange on her lips: a rusty, unfamiliar word, long since consigned to the toy cupboard, along with other abandoned childish things. 'Yes, Sis,' she repeated, looking directly into Marion's eyes. Harold always claimed that liars never looked you in the face, but, for this one crucial moment, Harold could go hang. 'Not only did she say goodbye, she particularly wanted you to know that she ... she always loved you very deeply.'

Eileen let out a long breath. How peculiar that lies could feel so freeing! And she was groping towards a still more singular fact: that even if they were both aware that this whole thing was a lie (and a flagrant black lie; not a pardonable white one), they could somehow *make* it true. Here, now, in this substandard, inefficient ward, a new truth was being established – and, for all she knew, a life-saving and redeeming truth – that Marion, the recalcitrant younger sister, had been genuinely loved.

'Thank you, Sis,' Marion said, in a quiet, contented tone of voice; joltingly different from her usual peevish bark.

Then, lying back against the pillows, she shut her eyes, as if to sleep. Eileen stared in surprise. Surely no one in such obvious pain and assailed by all this noise could expect simply to switch off? A nurse in heavy brogues was now clumping up and down, and a group of boisterous kids had arrived to see their grandma; ignoring the old lady, whilst they fought amongst themselves. Yet, despite the hubbub, her sister's breathing had already slowed; her mouth was slack; her fingers now unclenched.

Eileen drew her chair in close. Always conscious of her duty – and happy now to do it – she knew she must keep watch beside the bed, to ensure Marion was not disturbed. This sleep would be restorative and deep, because, incongruous as it might seem, love itself had provided the narcotic.

MICHAEL

'Fancy a drink, Carole? We thought we'd try that new wine-bar down the road.'

'I'm ... I'm sorry. 'Fraid I can't.'

'Why should she join *us*,' Ruth taunted, peering over her spectacles from where she sat slumped at the adjoining desk, 'when her precious Mike is waiting for his beloved to get home?'

Carole bit back a retort. Mike was history – as of yesterday – but, were she to admit that, Ruth's look of gloating triumph would be more than she could bear. Ruth had met him on the sole occasion he had showed up at the office, but, since that time, her pointless, poisonous jealousy had expressed itself in constant jibes.

'Oh, come on, Carole,' Libby urged. 'It is Friday, after all!'

She fiddled with a strand of her hair, twisting it round and round her fingers. Even at the best of times, she often felt distinctly spare when they all got together after work. As the youngest and by far the least experienced, she would sit very nearly tongue-tied amidst the raucous jollity – and today she might disgrace herself by actually bursting into tears. 'No, honestly, I must get back.'

'OK, please yourself.'

As Libby shrugged and turned away, Carole took her chance to escape, snatching up her jacket and sidling towards the door. It was already almost seven and they were meant to leave early on a Friday.

'Have a good weekend!' John called, as she scurried past his work-station.

'Will do!' Her breezy voice sounded false, even to her own ears. No weekend could ever be good, now that Mike had walked out.

'And make sure you're in on time on Monday,' Averil barked, suddenly appearing from her office.

'Of course,' she muttered, again stifling her resentment. She had been late only once since she started in the job, yet Averil never let her forget it, nor the fact she was strictly here on trial. There was no certainty about promotion for *any* general assistant – or dogsbody, to use Ruth's snide term. The girl prior to her had failed to make the grade and been unceremoniously given the boot, after a mere six months, as Averil enjoyed reminding her with depressing regularity. The intention, presumably, was to keep her up to the mark, although in point of fact it only increased her nervousness and made her more likely to fail, in her turn.

It was a relief to be out in the dark and shadowy street, surrounded by anonymous people who would neither nag her nor attack. But, as she trudged towards the tube, her footsteps slowed, until she finally stood indecisive outside the station entrance. The sleepless night, followed by a long, tough day at work, had left her tired and jittery at once, and in no mood for the journey home on a crowded rush-hour train. Anyway, it was only home if Mike was there. The sofa would seem unwelcoming without him sprawled beside her, sharing a pizza or a takeaway, and their large, lumpy double bed would mock a lonely singleton. And how could she leave for work in the morning without his coffee-flavoured kisses to speed her on her way?

Impulsively, she walked on past the tube and continued striding along the street, blindly turning left and left and left, just to give herself an action-plan. Action dulled the pain; provided tiny distractions, such as dodging passers-by, or squeezing past the crowds of drinkers gathered outside the pubs. Even non-smokers had flowed out onto the street, despite the November chill. She and Mike had signed the lease on their flat in March – a hopeful month, with everything in bud. Now, the leaves were falling, or lying brown and waterlogged. How could just one evening have kyboshed their nine months together? Enough time to make a baby....

No, she mustn't think about kids – or about Mike, or marriage, or anything – or she'd spend another seven hours just staring out of the window at the dark, indifferent sky, as she'd already done last night. She was in need of more distraction, but her plan of turning left meant she kept going round in circles, so now she just walked blindly on, focusing instead on counting bars and cafés. Two, five, six, eight, eleven ... Every other building appeared to offer food and drink, although she had lost her own appetite entirely. Each breath she took set off the pain – a pain spreading from the purple bruise branding her whole stomach. In any case, the bars and restaurants all reminded her of Mike: his weakness for a pint (or three) of Stella; his love of red-hot curry; his dislike of salad in any shape or form; the way he always ate chips with his fingers, cramming his mouth with three or four at a time....

Despite the weight of memories, her brisk walking-pace was helping, in that it acted like a drug and helped to calm her mind. So she decided to go further: across Waterloo Bridge and down Kennington Road – a road she knew, because Libby lived there and had once invited her to supper, after work. Libby was a decent type, but had always lived on her own, so she wouldn't have the faintest idea how much a break-up hurt. She had even once remarked that she much preferred her single state to having to share her life with some useless, boring bloke; clearly unaware that men could be super-charged and super-skilled, like Mike.

The crowds were thinning as she turned into Lancaster Place and she began to feel horribly alone, especially when she crossed the river, with its dark expanse of water stretching on each side. Despite the lights reflected in its surface, it looked menacingly black and she imagined all the corpses rotting on the river-bed – girls like her, so desperate, they had plunged into its depths. Well, at least Mike would be consumed with guilt when he was forced to identify her bloated body, yanked out from the mud. Shit! Her mind was back on him again. But, now she had cut down Baylis Road, there were no more bars and cafés to count, so, instead, she tried to keep her concentration solely on her feet.

That proved easier in Kennington Road, which, being very long and straight, meant she could stride along, full-pelt. She had lost all track of time and, once she'd passed Libby's flat, had no notion where she was. Not that she cared a toss. She was willing to walk anywhere – or nowhere – just so long as it stopped her brooding. She veered off to the right and went blundering on along a nondescript and treeless street, only panting to a sudden halt outside a yellow-brick church.

What had stopped her in her tracks was the sight of a small, elderly man actually kneeling on the pavement, in front of a large crucifix positioned outside the church. She watched, riveted, as he made the Sign of the Cross; his lips moving as he gazed with reverence at the naked, thorn-crowned figure. He must be praying – praying in public, despite the cold, and regardless of what passers-by might think. He looked genuinely holy: his hands joined; his eyes intent; his lips forming silent words. Light from the adjacent lampposts merged his shadow and the Cross's into one elongated, spooky shape. Then, finally, he eased up to his feet – the action stiff and slow and clearly causing pain – and, having brushed dirt from his trousers, he made a second Sign of the Cross and slowly shambled off.

Hardly thinking what she was doing, she darted in pursuit, overtook him and stood blocking his path. 'Are you a priest?' she demanded.

He looked startled at her question; grunted an emphatic 'No!'

'But you were ... praying just then.'

'Well, yes, I was, but that happens to be my church and I like to pay my respects to the crucified Christ.'

Her knowledge of prayer or churches was sketchy in the extreme. Her parents had no time for either, but, from what she'd gathered, prayer could be a force; might even work a miracle, so some believers said. 'Could you pray for me?' she blurted out, aghast at her own request. Had she gone insane? This guy was a total stranger – could be a perv, for all she knew.

He looked her up and down, as if harbouring similar doubts about her own credentials. 'But ... I don't know who you are. All this is rather sudden, don't you see? It's hard to pray in a vacuum, so I'd need to know something about you – your name and—'

'Carole,' she interrupted. 'Carole Gibbs. I need help.'

They were still standing in the middle of the pavement, causing an obstruction to people trying to get past. He steered her towards a doorway; continued gazing at her quizzically. 'Are you a Catholic, Carole?'

'Yes,' she said, on impulse. If she said no, he might refuse.

'Well, in that case, you really ought to see your parish priest. He could help you far better than I can.'

'I ... haven't got a priest. I've not been in London that long.' At least both of those were true.

'Do you live round here?' he asked. 'If so, I could have a word with our own priest, Father Patrick, and see if he might....'

'No, I don't.' Should she have said 'yes' again? Yes's seemed more hopeful.

'Well, where?' he persisted.

'I'm ... not sure. I mean, I'm going to have to move soon. I can't afford the flat I'm in at present.' Without Mike's contribution, it would be impossible to pay the rent. Indeed, if it hadn't been for Mike, she would never have come to London in the first place. Her own measly salary would barely cover the cost of even a small bedsit. So where would she go? What ever would she do? All at once, the full horror of her plight struck home with hideous force: she was completely on her own. Her parents hated Mike. If she turned up on their doorstep, they would only say, 'I told you so!' and might even send her packing. Her only sister lived in New Zealand, busy with her own life, and was miles older anyway. And, as for all her old friends back in Norwich, she'd been so absorbed with Mike, she had shamefully neglected them. Desperate now, she clutched the old guy's arm. 'You have to help,' she sobbed. 'There's no one else.'

He seemed embarrassed by her tears and stood, shoulders hunched, shifting from foot to foot. 'Look, you'd better come home,' he said, at last, 'and have a word with my wife. She's better at these things than me.'

In uneasy silence, they walked on, side by side; she slowing her pace to his uneven, halting gait. What in God's name was she *doing*, craving help from some weirdo in the street? Was she so dependent on Mike that, without him, she was lost?

Yes, was the pathetic truth. She had never been alone before; had gone straight from living at home to living with him in the flat. Without someone else around, she felt like tissue paper: flimsy, insubstantial, easily crumpled up.

'I'm Arthur, by the way,' he said, as he led her round the corner into a narrow road of shabby terraced houses. 'And this is where I live.'

She muttered something inaudible, more concerned with scrubbing at her face before she met his wife. She must look a total fright; eyes red; mascara streaked.

Halfway down the street, he stopped and stood fumbling for his key outside a battered black front door. Old people were so *slow*, she thought, as, having found the key, he then struggled to insert it in the lock.

'Eunice!' he called, ushering her into a narrow, dim-lit hall. 'We have a visitor.'

A small, dumpy woman emerged from the back room, bundled up in a capacious home-knit cardigan, the colour of mushy peas. Her straggly hair was scooped up on top; her eyes faded-blue but kind.

'Carole's new to London,' Arthur explained. 'She's a Catholic, so she needs to find a church. And she's in need of help in general, so maybe you could sort her out.'

With obvious relief, he escaped upstairs, while his wife showed her into the sitting-room – a stuffy, uncongenial place. The three-piece suite was so big and bulky, it seemed to push against the confines of the walls, while the scrum of knick-knacks, amassed on every surface, only added to the overcrowded effect. Things should be bare, uncluttered – Mike had taught her that.

Eunice, clearly flustered, was letting out a stream of words, without pausing for any answers. 'Nice to meet you, dear, but do excuse the mess. If I'd known I was having company, I'd have had a thorough clear-up. Would you like a cup of tea, to warm you up? You look frozen in that jacket. It barely comes down to your waist! When *I* was young, people wore good, thick, winter coats, but now it's all these lightweight things. Do you take milk and sugar in your tea? And how about a sandwich? I could make you....'

'Nothing, honestly.'

'Well, do sit down. No – not that chair. It's Arthur's. Take this one, near the fire.'

Mike would dump the gas-fire – a hideous thing in a sickly shade of yellow, with an ugly metal grille. She hadn't realized till this moment that he had turned her into a snob. Even her parents' home seemed embarrassingly out-dated, seen through his appraising eyes. But, as far as Eunice was concerned, she should be grateful, for heaven's sake, not criticizing every smallest thing. At least she was in the warm and not alone. Without this refuge, she might have walked the streets all night.

The woman was still fussing – clearly ill at ease, or perhaps unused to visitors. 'Are you comfy there, or would you like a cushion behind you?'

'I'm fine, thanks.'

With a worried sigh, Eunice arranged a cushion behind her own grey head. Then she smoothed her skirt, adjusted her glasses and sat rubbing at her chin, before finally she asked. 'Well, what's the trouble, dear?'

The popping of the gas-fire filled the silence. Where did she begin?

'Have you run away from home?'

'*No*.'

'Well, what about your parents? Can't they help?'

'No.'

Eunice shifted her bulk on the sagging, chintzy chair. There was a second, unsettling pause, before she spoke again in her breathy tone. 'Forgive me, dear, for suggesting such an indelicate thing, but you're not ... expecting, are you?'

If only. If she'd fallen pregnant, Mike might have stayed, simply for the kid's sake. 'No,' she said, third time.

Eunice gave another sigh. The sighs seemed nervous, rather than impatient, as if she were running out of suggestions. 'But Arthur said you needed help, so there must be *something* wrong.'

Carole clasped her arms across her chest; conscious of the pain in her ribs every time she moved. 'It's my boyfriend – Mike – he's left. We share a flat, you see, but last night we had this really awful bust-up. He actually punched me in the stomach and....'

Eunice took in a sharp intake of breath.

'Oh, he didn't mean to. It was *my* fault, actually. You see, he'd sent this text to a girl called Kath and I happened to see it and got insanely jealous. He'd never mentioned a Kath to me, and I just couldn't bear the thought of him having secrets or seeing someone else. So I went on and on about it, even though he kept warning me to cool it. But I refused to listen, and every time he tried to change the subject, I'd hark back to Kath and insist he told me who she was. And, in the end, he went berserk – said he didn't want to live with someone so suspicious and unreasonable, quizzing him on every little thing. And, in any case, he hated the way I was so insecure and clingy and couldn't stand on my own two feet, and, frankly, he'd had enough of me – full-stop. And then I lost it, too, and started screaming and shouting and went – you know – hysterical and that was when he hit me.'

'But, Carole' – Eunice sounded deeply shocked – 'surely you're much better off without a man like that?'

'I'm not. I'm not! You don't understand. I'm useless on my own. And, anyway, he's never hit me before.'

'I should jolly well think not!'

'I drove him to it – don't you see? He told me that himself.'

Eunice scooped up a stray wisp of hair and pushed it back into her bun. Neither of them spoke. In the silence, every sound seemed magnified: the snort of a car reverberating down the street; the insistent pop-pop-pop explosions of the gas-fire.

'Have you tried to *pray* about this?' Eunice asked, at last. 'Called on the Blessed Virgin for help?'

'I don't know how to pray. I'm not religious.'

'But Arthur said—'

'I know. That's my fault, too. I didn't like to tell him that I've never been to church in my life – well, except for my sister's wedding. My parents are atheists.'

'Well, obviously, we must pray for them, as well, in the hope they see the error of their ways. God loves all His creation, Carole, whether they're Catholics or not. And the Blessed Virgin Mary has a special concern for every single woman in the world, especially women in trouble, like yourself.'

Carole looked up impatiently. 'But I know almost nothing about her, so how ever could she help?'

'Because she has powers far greater than ours. She sits at the right hand of God.'

'Maybe,' Carole countered, with growing irritation, 'but I'm no expert on God, either. I never learnt those things. We did a bit at school about all the world's religions, but I never took much interest, to be honest.'

'In that case, we'd better start with your Guardian Angel.'

'My what?'

'Your Guardian Angel. Angels are the link between our human world here below and the heavenly world above, so they're very useful go-betweens. They bridge the gap between us poor sinners and the perfection of—'

'I don't *have* a Guardian Angel,' she cut in.

'Well, there you're mistaken, Carole. Everybody has one, whether they're aware of it or not. Your Guardian Angel was with you from the moment you were born and he'll stay by your side until the very moment you die, when he'll help you on your journey to the next life. He's like your closest friend – always there for you and on your side, looking after you and protecting you from danger.'

The idea sounded blissful, but totally unlikely. No one was always there for you – not parents, sisters, workmates, boyfriends. 'But how do you know all this?' she demanded. 'I mean, can you prove that angels exist?'

'Of course I can! It's part of the Church's teaching and our Blessed Lord Himself often spoke about angels. An angel even came to comfort Him when He was suffering His terrible agony in the garden. So if someone as great as Christ was in need of an angel, how much more do we poor humans need one?'

'Just because you need something doesn't mean you get it,' she muttered to herself.

Eunice didn't appear to have heard and continued in her soft, wheezy voice. 'Have you ever heard of St Gemma Galgani?'

Carole shook her head. She'd never heard of half these things.

'She died of TB when she was only twenty-five, but all through her short life she was constantly talking to her Guardian Angel. She said he was her teacher and guide, and sometimes he even gave her special secret messages about politics and suchlike.'

'Why do you say "he"? I thought angels were meant to be female?'

'Well, actually, they're spirits, so they're not strictly male or female. But, when you see them in pictures, they're usually shown as men and they also have male names. Take Michael – your boyfriend's name. Michael was an archangel and—'

'What's an archangel?'

'They're angels of the highest rank. The name Michael means "He who is like God".'

Well, that was true. Mike *was* like a god – tall and powerful and brilliant in every way. She knew he would go far in life; make loads of money, maybe even be famous....

'If you'll excuse me for a minute, dear, I'll show you a picture of him.'

Eunice rose to her feet, with difficulty, and made her slow way to the door. While she was gone, Carole pulled up her jacket and sweater and studied the bruise again. It wasn't as bad as she'd thought. OK, her parents would go mental, but only to get at Mike. They'd met him a mere twice, yet they were convinced he was a nasty piece of work, but that was just their prejudice.

Hastily, she pulled down her clothes as Eunice reappeared, carrying a small black book, which she opened at the very first page.

'That's the Archangel Michael,' she explained, pointing to a picture of a tall, winged figure in a breastplate.

'But he's wearing armour.'

Eunice nodded. 'Yes, he's a great warrior – the commander-in-chief of the whole heavenly host, which, of course, means he's extremely powerful. It's unusual to have pictures in a missal, but this is a very old Italian one, which a dear aunt of mine – now sadly passed away – brought for me in Rome, when I was just a little girl.'

'What's a missal?' Carole asked. Another word she didn't know.

'It's our Catholic Mass-book, with all the different Masses for every day of the year.'

Although none the wiser, she gazed at the figure with interest. Michael was impressive – there was no denying that – with his athletic build and the huge feathered wings springing from his shoulders and rearing up behind him, like a shield. The expression on his face was determined and intense, and he was poised, as if for action, carrying a long, gleaming spear. The picture was in black and white, but, as she studied it, she could almost see the armour shining silver and Michael's skin tanned a healthy bronze; his hair like burnished gold; his wings a dazzling white.

'Carole, I'd like to make you a present of this missal. I never use it and it's only gathering dust in a drawer.'

'Oh, I couldn't take it! It's precious.'

But Eunice put the book firmly into her hands and plumped back on her chair, even managing a smile now.

Carole ran her fingers over the stiff black leather cover; tracing the gold-tooled letters on the spine: *Missale Romano*. The pages were all edged with gold and so gossamer-thin she was scared her nails might tear them. Certain pages were marked with coloured ribbons – five in all, in faded red, blue, yellow, green and purple. The typeface was a fancy one, set out in double columns on each page, although she couldn't read a word of it, of course. 'What language is that?' she asked, pointing to the text.

'Latin on the left of the page, and Italian on the right. And in an *English* missal, it would be—'

She broke off as the door opened and Arthur put his head round. 'All finished now?' he asked.

'Not quite, dear. Could you give us a bit longer?'

'Eunice, we need an early night. We have to be up at six tomorrow, don't forget.'

Carole half-rose from her seat. 'Look, I'm sorry, I'm in your way.'

'Not at all.' Eunice silenced her husband with a look. 'Arthur, dear, you go on up. There are just one or two more things I need to say to Carole. I shan't be long, I promise.'

With a compliant nod, Arthur disappeared again.

'Now listen, dear,' Eunice said, leaning forward in her chair. 'Before you leave, I need to make sure that you're going to be all right – you know, on your own, in the flat. So I want you to take this missal with you and sleep with it beside you, to remind you that you're *not* alone, because your Guardian Angel is with you. He always has been and he always will be, so you'll never feel lonely again. His job in life is to look after you and help you on life's journey. And, I assure you, Carole, these things are not just a matter of belief, but a matter of experience, as well. In fact, you may have felt your Guardian Angel's presence in the past, but just not realized who he was. Have you ever had the sense of a guiding hand on your shoulder, someone whispering to you, pointing out what's right?'

Yes, she thought, intrigued. She'd had exactly that sense the first time she met Mike. She knew the very instant she laid eyes on him that he was completely and utterly right for her, which she'd never felt about the odd bods she had dated prior to him. 'But what shall I do about Mike?' she asked, suddenly realizing she had forgotten all about him for at least the last five minutes.

'Arthur and I will need to pray about him. I must admit I'm not very happy about you being with a violent man.'

'He's not violent, I swear! It was just that one occasion and I more or less asked for it. He kept warning me to stop obsessing about Kath, and I didn't take the slightest notice, so you can't really blame him, can you? Besides, he doesn't know his own strength, so I doubt he meant to hurt me in the first place. I'm the kind of person who bruises very easily, you see. With anybody else, it wouldn't even have left a mark.'

Eunice frowned deeply, as if far from being convinced. 'Well,' she said, at last, 'perhaps you can bring yourself to forgive him – give him one more chance, maybe. But I suggest you let him cool off first – say, for a couple of weeks, and only then get back in touch and see how you feel about things. Certainly, forgiveness is important. Our Blessed Lord taught us to forgive our enemies.'

'Mike's not my *enemy*! He's the most fantastic person I've ever met.'

'Well, that's as may be, but it sounds to me as if he could do with some direction in his life. But, look you'd better set off home now. It's getting late and I don't like the thought of you travelling at this hour. Do you know your way back from here?'

'Not really.'

'At the end of our road, turn right and a hundred yards further down, you'll see Stockwell Tube.'

'Oh, Stockwell. So *that's* where we are!' Somehow, she'd imagined she was miles further out, as if she had walked to the ends of the earth. Yet Stockwell was only two stops on from Libby's tube at Kennington.

Moving very stiffly, Eunice stood up again. 'It's on the Victoria Line and the Northern Line. Are either of those any good for you?'

'The Northern Line is perfect.' She wouldn't even have to change. Was her Guardian Angel already looking after her?

'And, once you get in, I'd like you to give me a ring, then I'll know you're safe.' Eunice ushered her into the hall, took a Biro from the drawer of the small, rickety hall-table and wrote the number on a slip of paper.

'But your husband said he wanted an early night.'

'Don't worry – you won't disturb us. It takes us a while to get ready for bed and, anyway, Arthur always reads for a while, before he settles down.' Eunice rummaged further in the drawer and withdrew a pair of gloves. 'It's probably really cold now and that coat of yours wouldn't keep a sparrow warm, so why don't you take these?'

'No, honestly … I never wear gloves.' Least of all such gruesome ones: woolly green and huge.

'Well, I'm surprised you don't get chilblains, then. But, look, take them anyway, in case you change your mind. And do that coat up properly!'

Carole moved towards the door, obediently buttoning her jacket and about to say goodbye, when Eunice called her back.

'No – wait a minute, dear. I know Arthur would like to say

goodbye, as well. Arthur!' she shouted, moving to the foot of the stairs. 'Carole's on her way.'

The elderly pair stood side by side on the step, watching anxiously as she set off down the street. Every time she looked back, they were still there, waving and smiling, as if she were bound for Sydney Harbour, rather than Archway Tube. She felt protected and important. Her parents would never see her off with such concern about her safety, or fret about her getting cold. In fact, in all the years she had lived at home, her mother barely seemed to notice whether she was there or not.

She took the gloves from her pocket, where she had stuffed them, out of sight, turned round again, and began putting them on in a slow, elaborate dumb-show, so Eunice could see what she was doing. The gloves were surprisingly cosy and her hands felt protected, too, now.

With a final wave, she rounded the corner, slinging her bag across her shoulder, and feeling for the hard outline of the missal. It was the best present she had ever had, because it meant that Michael was with her – an archangel, no less – and, just as Eunice had promised, she no longer felt alone, or lost, or scared.

'You're late!' Averil snapped, bearing down towards the door, as Carole rushed into the office.

Catching her breath, Carole stifled the apology that was almost second nature now, when speaking to her boss. Instead, she adopted a no-nonsense tone – one she had never dared to use before. 'I'm only late with good reason,' she said, coolly. 'There was a broken-down train at Camden that delayed us for a good half-hour. I left home at eight o'clock sharp, so, in the ordinary way, I'd have been here in loads of time.'

'Well, in that case....'

As Averil's voice tailed off, Carole realized this was a first: her boss had actually accepted a legitimate excuse, without querying its honesty, or rudely interrupting with some venomous attack – all Michael's doing, of course. Having an archangel in tow had hugely boosted her confidence. She wasn't sure if archangels *did* act as

Guardian Angels, but, since she needed a protector of the very highest rank, she'd simply opted for the best – exactly as she'd done with Mike.

In truth, her mind was reeling with angels, having spent much of the weekend Googling angel-sites. Extraordinary how many people believed in them: almost sixty-five per cent of the entire British population, which only went to show how out of touch her parents were – as in so many *other* ways. She herself was now part of that sixty-five per cent. It was a matter of experience, as Eunice had explained – something she had only really understood when she reached the end of their road and turned the corner to the tube. And, at the very moment she lost sight of the old pair, she was suddenly aware of some other sort of presence beside her. The effect was so empowering, she had lost all her usual fear of being accosted by a mugger in the dark, and made her way down the unfamiliar street without the slightest qualm. And, once she was in the carriage, she hadn't started panicking about the only other passenger: a suspicious-looking bloke with a scar across his face. She was safe from any stranger or attacker – Michael would see to that. And even when she let herself into the flat and was confronted by Mike's possessions – his favourite mug, still full of scummy tea; his blue toothbrush in the bathroom; his trainers lying tongue-to-tongue, as if chatting to each other – she hadn't collapsed in a pathetic heap, but simply trusted he'd be back. His namesake had assured her of the fact and angels didn't tell untruths. And, instead of having to face the void of an empty, lonely, boyfriend-less weekend, she'd had company and comfort, in the shape of her Guardian Angel. Indeed, with every hour that passed, he seemed to become more solid and substantial, until—

John's voice cut across her thoughts. 'Had a good weekend?' he asked, as she hung her jacket on the coat-stand. All the other staff were busy on the phone, including Ruth – thank God.

'Fantastic!' She had spent Sunday afternoon venturing into churches, hesitant at first, but gradually growing bolder as she discovered angels everywhere – in windows, statues, paintings and stained glass. How could she have ignored them all her life? It was like Mike and motorbikes. Before she met him, motorbikes were just noisy nuisances, but, slowly, under his guidance, she had begun to learn the subtleties; the vital difference between one machine and another – just as now she knew the difference between an angel and an archangel, a Dominion and a Throne.

Humming to herself, she sauntered into the kitchen, to check the supplies of tea and coffee and ensure the cups were clean. She had washed most of them on Friday, just before she left, but more had been dumped into the sink since then. She scoured them thoroughly, wiped down all the surfaces, then made a shopping list. Coffee-creamer, biscuits, sugar, were all in short supply, so she would buy those when she went out for lunch. She was used to running errands in her lunch-hour, because the other staff were often too busy to leave their desks and just grabbed a quick sandwich between interviews. In any case, why should they want to hobnob with the 'dogsbody'?

Once she'd finished in the kitchen, she darted out to the office, to check that the consultants had everything they needed: time-sheets, notebooks, terms-of-business forms. Libby's phone was ringing, unanswered on the desk, so she picked it up, smiling as she spoke, as John had taught her when she first arrived. ('You can *hear* a smile,' he'd said.)

'Alangate Agency. How can I help?' Usually, her voice went shrill with nerves, but with Michael's sheltering wings behind her, she managed to speak assertively. Indeed, Michael's power was so great, she felt ready to deal with anyone, even the grouchy area-manager.

'I'm sorry, Mr Tucker, she's away from her desk just at present. I'll ask her to ring you as soon as – no, hold on, she's here.'

As Libby emerged from the toilet, Carole handed her the phone. 'It's Rory Tucker – it's urgent, he says.'

A moment later, she was summoned by Sandra. "Carole, get a cup of tea for Mrs Preston. Milk and two sugars, please.'

She scurried back to the kitchen, Michael in attendance, of course. Only now did she realize – and only because of Michael – that her role was vital here. Without her, the others would be lost. They relied on her to keep things running smoothly; to cover for them when they were on the phone or otherwise engaged; to buy their lunchtime sandwiches, and – most important – to greet the clients and the applicants, if no one else happened to be free. All that was crucial work, so they should treat her with respect. From this moment on, she intended to defend herself. If Averil was vicious, Ruth sarcastic, or Sandra patronizing, she would make it very clear that she didn't intend to be insulted or exploited.

Her archangel wouldn't stand for it, for one thing.

She sat back on the bench, gazing up at the stained-glass window, which showed a plumpish angel with a shock of yellow curls, weird blue wings and beseeching, big, brown eyes. He wasn't in the same class as Michael, but she liked him, nonetheless. She also enjoyed this new experience of sitting quietly in a church, which she now did every lunch-hour, if only for five minutes. What it made her realize was how starved she'd been of peace – something completely lacking in her chaotic childhood home, and impossible in a busy office, with four consultants on the phone at once, and applicants coming and going all day long. But here in the church, she was cut off from both people-noise and traffic-noise and, because she had the place to herself, she could pretend it was her own new home – somewhere worthy of Michael, who was standing beside her, of course. (Angels never sat, she'd found.) He must feel in his element in such an awesome setting, with its brilliant windows glowing in the dim, dramatic gloom, and the stone arches soaring up so high, and those fancy golden candlesticks gleaming on the altar.

To her surprise, she'd discovered quite a number of churches, all within easy reach of work. Her favourite was St Cecilia and St Anselm, partly on account of its name. No one she knew was called Cecilia or Anselm – nor, for that matter, Rafael, Gabriel, or Uriel: the names of the other archangels. She wished her mother had called *her* Cecilia, instead of boring Carole, or even Uriel, which was definitely exotic.

She glanced at her watch – 1.30 – which meant she still had half an hour before she needed to be back. She'd completed all her errands – taken in Ruth's dry-cleaning; collected Sandra's theatre tickets; bought the Scotch for Averil's VIP client – so there was just one thing left to do: make the call to Mike.

The very thought of speaking to him made her jerk up from the bench and start pacing along the aisle in an agitated state. He hadn't called or texted her even once, which meant he might be mad still – or even have shacked up with the hateful Kath.

No, she *couldn't* ring. Such devastating news would be almost like he'd died.

'Take courage, Carole. I'm with you now, so you can rest assured that things will turn out well.'

Michael's solemn voice seemed to be sounding in her ears and she could almost feel his protective wings brushing against her cheek. Had she forgotten he was there to fight her battles; lift her mood when she lost heart? And, in any case, she couldn't break her word to Eunice. They had discussed Mike on the phone, last night, and she'd promised to get in touch with him – today, if possible. Nearly a fortnight had passed since the bust-up, so the old lady thought it was time to make a move. It still seemed quite extraordinary that a couple she had met through a chance encounter in the street should have become so involved in her life. Eunice was almost like a grandmother; someone who truly cared about her and was always on her side; someone who even prayed for her each day. She herself still hadn't learned to pray. Frankly, she found it embarrassing – so much so, she gave a nervous glance behind her before falling to her knees in front of the statue of the Virgin. Ruth and Averil were safely in the office, so there was no way they could see her, yet she imagined their derisive laughter, as she clasped her hands, like Arthur had, and moved her lips in prayer.

'Please, God,' she began, uncertainly, but, as Michael nodded his approval, she continued with more confidence. Not only did he stop her feeling self-conscious, he even helped her find the words. And, once she'd said 'Amen', he led her from the church to a secluded spot behind it, where she could make the call in private. Best to try now, in the lunch-hour, rather than leave it till the evening, when Mike would probably be out drinking with his mates.

She slung her bag firmly over her shoulder, so that no one would nick the Scotch – not that there was anyone about; just her dazzling archangel, giving her the strength to dial. He even preventing her from losing her cool when she actually heard Mike's voice, the first time in thirteen days. Those days had seemed like thirteen years and, without Michael's constant presence, she doubted if she could have coped.

'Hi, Mike,' she said, impressed by her casual tone of voice – belied, in actuality, by the pounding of her heart. 'It's Carole.'

Even in the awkward pause that followed, she refused to be deterred. 'I was wondering how you are.'

'Er, fine.'

'I've had time to think about what you said and, yes, you do have a point. I *have* been too clingy and I can see now how it might annoy you. On the other hand ...' She faltered. It was much harder to reprove him than admit to her own faults.

'Don't stop,' Michael urged. She felt him move still closer; his wings a feathered firewall, shielding her whole body.

Before she spoke, she took in a deep breath, pausing, so that the words would come out calmly and not in a feverish rush. 'On the other hand,' she repeated, determined to make her point, 'what *you* did was loads worse. Hitting me like that was—' She was about to say 'unforgivable', but quickly changed it into 'downright disgraceful'. Eunice claimed that nothing was unforgivable and had also supplied the phrase 'downright disgraceful' – one she would never have used herself because it sounded so extreme. Mike always resented criticism and might well explode with rage.

In the silence, she almost lost her nerve. Should she backtrack; tell him it hadn't hurt that much?

But Michael shook his head in warning, so she waited, cowering, for the expected furious outburst. None came.

'I ... I'm sorry, darling,' Mike muttered, at last, sounding genuinely ashamed.

Her relief was like a tidal wave. Both words were clearly Michael's doing. 'Darling' meant the relationship was on still; 'sorry' meant that Mike admitted blame.

'It *was* wrong,' he grunted, 'yes. And, to be honest, I feel rotten about it. Look, why don't we meet, so I can make it up to you.'

Even more fantastic. But before she could shout, '*Yes*!' Michael put a restraining hand on her shoulder. 'Keep your composure,' he advised.

So, when Mike said, 'How about tonight?', she bit back her instinctive 'Great!' and replied, with deliberate reserve, 'Next week would suit me better.'

'Monday, then?'

'Wednesday.'

'Brilliant! Wednesday. I'll come round to the flat.'

Again, she took her cue from Michael, who was frowning at the suggestion. 'No, I'd rather go out for a meal. How about that Italian place in Camden – you know, where we went for our first date? Shall we say eight o'clock?'

It felt extraordinary to be taking the lead, instead of letting Mike make the decisions, regardless of whether they suited her or not. But, when she'd admitted to Eunice that he rarely took her out to eat these days, as he'd done when they first met, the old lady seemed indignant.

'Why should you settle for TV dinners every night, or a pizza on your lap? You say he spends hours in the pub – well, he ought to devote at least some of that time to spoiling you a bit. Arthur and I still go out several times a month, and we've been married nearly fifty years, so I reckon your Mike needs to buck up his ideas a bit.'

'OK, darling,' he was saying. 'I'll book a table at Antonio's.'

She all but hugged herself in glee. Not only a second 'darling', but no objection to the expense. Antonio's wasn't cheap. And, when she glanced up at her angel, she was gratified to see that his normal grave expression had softened into a smile.

She slipped off her grubby office clothes and flung them on the bed, barely able to contain her excitement. Mike would be back tonight – back in this very bed. And, once he saw how self-reliant she was, their relationship would go from strength to strength. It wasn't just in character she'd changed – she was in better shape, as well. Studying her reflection in the mirror, she was relieved to see that she could now fit into her skinny jeans, having lost a good half-stone. And they would go perfectly with the new sparkly top she'd bought yesterday at Top Shop. Michael had even helped her there. She'd had no idea that Guardian Angels would concern themselves with trivial things like clothes, until she had slowly come to understand that nothing which involved their charges could be classed as trivial. If it mattered to her, then it mattered to Michael, too; be it her body-shape, a new brand of blusher, or the latest bargain in the shops. Nor did she have to be shamefaced – as she had been at the outset – at the thought of him seeing her naked. Angels didn't do embarrassment.

Indeed, Michael accompanied her to the bathroom while she showered and washed her hair; instinctively aware that she needed a non-stop confidence-boost this evening. He could pick up on her mood, even when she hadn't said a word, so she didn't need to tell him that, without his steadying presence, excitement might spill over into panic. He'd already had to persuade her to stop dashing around like a dervish, as there was plenty of time to get ready. He had planned that from the start, of course; insisting she made it clear to Averil that she wished to leave the office dead on six. And, miracle of miracles, Averil just said 'Fine', without the usual argument, or even the slightest objection. Since the advent of Michael, they all treated her with new respect. Sandra had actually paid her a compliment this morning, and even Ruth was less sarcastic and sharp-tongued.

Darting from the bathroom as she heard her mobile ringing, she picked it up with a sudden sense of dread. Suppose it was Mike, about to cancel? The very thought was—

'Eunice here. I just wanted to wish you luck, dear. I know how much this evening means, so Arthur and I will both be praying for you.'

As she thanked her new 'grandma', she wondered how she had ever managed without the kindly pair. This coming Sunday, they had invited her to accompany them to Mass and then go back with them for lunch. It would be her very first Mass – the first of many, she hoped – and would also give her a chance to tell them, in person, all about tonight. And Sunday was perfect timing, since Mike was going to Tottenham to watch the match with Fulham.

'Hey, Eunice, listen – Averil said I'm definitely in line for a pay-rise, after my yearly review. Apparently, they all think I'm doing well ... No, it won't be a fortune, but every little helps. In fact, I'd like to buy you a present, so can you think of something you'd like? ... No, sorry – I insist. But, look, I'd better go. I've just stepped out of the shower and my hair's dripping down my back!'

Once she'd dried it and removed any hint of frizz, she rifled through her drawer to find some sexy underwear. She had to admit she did feel distinctly awkward putting on her black-lace knickers and matching Wonder-bra, with Michael only yards away. But, with his usual tact and good breeding, he simply glided to the window, only turning back to face her again, once she was sitting at the mirror, about to do her make-up.

Even her complexion had improved since his arrival, and he'd undoubtedly made her worry less about the tiny hairline scar above her eyebrow. Friends had been assuring her for years that it didn't really show, but only now did she believe them. In fact, she felt more attractive in general, as well as loads more confident. After all, if she was important enough to have the highest rank of angel as her personal attendant, she must be special, surely. Nor had it failed to impress her that a commander-in-chief like Michael was willing to ignore his warrior duties, in order to devote himself solely to her – an even greater sacrifice than when Mike gave up his ticket for the Tottenham/Man United match, to come shopping with her in Oxford Street, the first Saturday they'd met. Admittedly, it hadn't happened since, but it would again – she knew. Michael had taught her two really vital things: first, you had to believe you were worthy of good fortune, and then trust that life would provide it.

She applied her blusher with careful concentration, glad she'd invested in a decent brand, since her healthy glow looked natural now, not falsely pink, like the Tesco one. Lipstick, next, which she blotted several times, to prevent it coming off on Mike. She still missed him terribly: his wild, insistent kisses; the way he gripped her body so tightly, his nails left deep red marks – marks she prized, as a reminder of their love-making.

Angels didn't make love, she'd now found out; nor did they eat or drink and, if they needed to move from one country to another, on some angelic mission, or streak up to heaven and back, they could cover such vast distances in micro-seconds. Not only had she learned much more about them, she had also come to realize that it was extremely common for ordinary folk to experience their intervention, just as *she* was doing. Some of the stories were incredible: one woman, weighing a scant seven stone, had overturned a car with her bare hands, to free the child trapped underneath – all with the help of an angel. And a lonely old man, in the last stage of prostate cancer, had been comforted by an angel in the form of his long-dead mother, who sat holding his hand in the hospice. And angels didn't balk at doing much more mundane things, such as finding their charges a parking-space, or a free seat on a crowded train.

What she *didn't* like were the commercial angel-sites, which sold such low-grade tat, they seemed an offence to Michael. Why should she want an angel fridge-magnet when she had a real-life angel – an angel who was part best friend, part an older, English version of Zac Efron, and almost a god in his own right.

Shit – her mobile again! Each time it rang, she was terrified it might be Mike: he'd gone down with some bug; had a ghastly motor-cycle accident; or been knifed by a drunken yob.

'Hi, Carole! It's Tracy. Sorry to ring you out of the blue, but—'

'Tracy! Great to hear you! It's ages since we spoke.'

This call was Michael's doing. He must have realized, instinctively, that, however mad she was for Mike, she did truly miss her old Norwich life: the girly talk, the shopping expeditions, the sense of female solidarity. And now here was Tracy on the phone!

'Why I'm ringing, Carole, is to let you know that me and Sue have decided to follow your example.'

'What do you mean?' she asked, lolling back on the bed.

'We're moving to London … Yes, honestly, it's true! We've found this flat-share in East Finchley that needs two extra girls.'

'Brilliant! We'll be neighbours, more or less. East Finchley's on the same tube-line as me, just a couple of stops further out. So when do you plan on coming?'

'Quite soon, with any luck. We have to wait for Sue to find a job, but that shouldn't take too long. *I'm* OK, because I can just transfer to the London office, which they've been wanting me to do for yonks. Anyway, it would be great to meet and everything, and we're hoping you might fill us in on the best shops and bars and night-spots and all that sort of stuff.'

'Yeah. 'Course. No problem. And we could even have a party, once you've settled in – maybe persuade a few of the others to come down for it, as well, if only for a night. But, listen, Tracy, I'm a bit pushed for time right now. I'm dying for a chat, so I'll give you a ring tomorrow and we can gossip for hours, OK?'

As she snapped the mobile shut, she wondered how Tracy would react to the idea of an angel sharing her flat. As yet, she hadn't told a soul, mainly because the crowd at work were such total cynics, they would regard her as insane. Yet, in point of fact, they were in the minority, by far. An online poll showed eighty-two per cent of respondents believed they had a Guardian Angel, while only a mere one per cent thought no such things existed.

She rose slowly to her feet, feeling rather apprehensive about having to give her friends the lowdown on trendy night-spots. As yet, she hadn't been out clubbing even once and, as for bars, the only ones she knew were those she went to after work with John and Ruth and co, and Mike's favourite pub, The Antelope.

The whooshing sound of Michael's wings roused her from her thoughts. 'It's time to finish dressing,' he prompted, moving from the mirror to the wardrobe. 'We ought to leave in fifteen minutes.'

She didn't need an alarm clock. Michael got her up in the morning; reminded her of every engagement and gently intervened if she happened to be running late – and all without owning a watch. (Angels didn't have possessions, despite the pictures showing them with harps and spears or whatever, which were simply artist's licence.) It was undoubtedly convenient to have an in-house time-keeper, but that was a minor matter compared with the overwhelming fact that Michael had transformed her world entirely. She was no longer forced to cling to other people, because she believed she wasn't good enough in and by herself. And all her usual dread about things going horribly wrong had been banished at a stroke.

Indeed, when she finally left the flat – looking as good as she had ever done – she had total faith that the evening would be an unqualified success. And, as she set off down the street, with all-powerful Michael shadowing her steps, she knew, deep down, that she was worthy of all the good fortune in the world.

'My boyfriend booked a table – name of Cartwright.'

The waiter checked his list. 'Ah, yes. Come this way.'

He led her to a table in the corner – an empty table.

'Don't worry,' Michael soothed, folding down his wings to fit the crowded restaurant. 'He's probably been delayed.'

Having drawn out her chair with a flourish, the waiter offered her a drink. Her first instinct was to wait for Mike and let *him* choose the wine, but, with Michael's blessing, she went right ahead and ordered a glass of Chardonnay. Normally, she drank Diet-Coke, but Chardonnay was Averil's favourite tipple, so presumably it must be cool.

While she waited for the wine to come, she surveyed her fellow diners, most of them in couples, of course. In the ordinary way, she would feel distinctly awkward sitting on her own, or even imagine people pitied her because they assumed she had no friends. Tonight, it didn't bother her at all. If they only had the eyes to see, they would realize that a superior Being was hovering in attendance.

When the waiter brought her wine, she was tempted to offer Michael a sip, or at least pass him the bowl of olives, or a piece of crusty bread. It still seemed rather strange to her that he should have no appetites; had never experienced a sexual urge, or enjoyed the smell of garlicky prawns – now wafting in her nostrils as a waiter scurried past – or the taste of hot buttered toast. But perhaps her own enjoyment of such things only proved how far she was from being spiritual. She hoped, with the old couple's help, to remedy that lack, and she was certainly looking forward to seeing their local church. All her life, she had regarded churches as dreary, even dismal places, but now she was keen to add some new ones to those she'd already discovered near the office.

Despite Michael's presence, it required an effort not to keep glancing at her watch. Her glass was already half-empty, yet there was still no sign of Mike. Instantly, however, Michael tuned in to her thoughts.

'Remember that broken-down train at Camden? Well, it's probably something similar. Just trust that all will be well.'

'Trust' was a word she distrusted, mainly because of her mother, who was always saying 'Trust me, Carole', only to betray that trust. Her childhood would have been easier altogether had she been aware of her Guardian Angel from the moment she was born – as Eunice and Arthur had. But at least now she had her beloved Michael for the whole of her adult life, and angels, unlike parents, were free of all human frailties. Dishonesty, unkindness, selfishness and unreliability were simply foreign to their nature. So, if her angel told her to trust, then trust she would, despite the fact that Mike was now eighteen minutes late.

She stretched out her legs, glancing down at her knee-length, mock-croc boots. They pinched at the toes and the heels were crazily high, but Mike adored high heels and that alone made them worth the pain.

'Try to relax,' Michael advised, aware how fidgety she was. So she leaned back in her chair and made a deliberate effort to stop fretting; focusing instead on the thrill of her first date. They had sat at a corner table and she'd noticed several women eyeing Mike with interest. They envied her – that was obvious – and the waiters had all treated her with incredible respect, because they could tell he was somebody exceptional. Every detail of the restaurant had remained imprinted on her mind since then: the terracotta floor-tiles and rustic glass carafes; the posters on the walls depicting fabulous places like Venice and Verona; the romantic music and air of happy bustle; the blackboard with the daily specials chalked up in looping script. And, this evening, it was just as lively; a buzz of conversation competing with the Italian crooner pouring out his heart and soul on the sound-system; wild bursts of laughter exploding from the customers, and waiters darting to and fro, with trays of steaming pasta and exotic coloured ice-creams. Maybe she and Mike could come here once or twice a month, as Eunice had advised. After all, he earned a lot – far more than she did, anyway – and, once she got her pay-rise, she could even treat him, sometimes, if she saved up long enough. She could see their future stretching ahead in a glorious golden glow – the only problem being that he hadn't actually arrived. Had something hideous happened? A fatal stabbing? A terrorist attack?

Just as she began to panic, Michael bent his majestic frame a little closer to her ear. 'Turn round towards the door,' he whispered.

Swivelling round obediently, she gave a cry of delight to see Mike hurtling into the restaurant, out of breath and clearly in a state – a very different Mike from the one who'd kept her waiting in the past and usually sauntered blithely in, without a twinge of guilt.

'I'm terribly sorry,' he panted, rushing up to the table and all but colliding with a waiter. 'There was a signal-failure at Moorgate and it buggered up all the bloody trains.'

'Don't worry,' Carole said, registering Michael's impassive face. Angels never said 'I told you so!', but hers had every right to do so. How could she have doubted that her boyfriend would turn up, when Michael had assured her of the fact? But, mixed with the relief, was a sense of almost ... shock. His changed behaviour was a blessing, but not the change in his appearance. However weird it sounded, he just didn't seem the same – not as tall and nothing like as gorgeous. And he'd obviously shaved in a rush, because there were tiny spots of blood on his face and even a few stubbly bits he'd missed. Angels didn't need to shave, which meant Michael's chin was as soft as a fluffy summer cloud and, of course, he wouldn't dream of swearing, whereas Mike was still ranting on about 'the sodding underground'. His voice struck her as almost coarse, to be frank, compared with Michael's hushed, celestial tones, which resembled the sweet pluckings of a harp. And she was so used to her angel's lustrous eyes, with their piercing, otherworldly gaze, Mike's eyes seemed plain insipid – blue, maybe, but the blue of faded denim, not the blue of heaven.

'You look fantastic, darling!' He stooped to kiss her – a full-on tongue-kiss that lasted so embarrassedly long, she tried to pull away. People at the adjoining tables might be offended by such public snogging and, anyway, she was distinctly worried about how Michael would react.

'What's wrong?'

'Nothing.'

'Can't I kiss you, for God's sake?'

'Later, Mike, OK?'

He pulled out a chair and plonked himself down. 'Christ! I could murder for a drink!'

She frowned in disapproval. Eunice had taught her not to say 'Christ' or 'God', unless she was actually talking about the Deity. Using such words in ordinary conversation was called 'taking the Lord's name in vain', and was blasphemous, apparently. Even 'bloody' was wrong, so Eunice said, because it literally meant 'By Our Lady' and thus was just as disrespectful.

Mike snapped his fingers at the waiter and, again, she was tempted to protest. The staff were rushed off their feet. Couldn't he show a bit of patience; copy Michael's graciousness and forbearance? Besides, he hadn't even asked her how she was, but was still complaining about his 'fucking awful journey'.

'Mike,' she said, more sharply than she intended, 'let's change the subject, shall we? You're here now and that's the important thing.'

'OK, keep your hair on. I need a drink, that's all.'

'Fine. Shall we have that wine we had before?' She knew nothing about wine, so she couldn't remember its name, but what she did remember was how gloriously fizzy and bubbly it had been – a true celebration drink.

'Which one do you mean?'

'You know – the one we had on our first date. The waiter brought it in an ice-bucket and—'

'No way!' he interrupted. 'That was a sparkling white and it won't go well with steak.'

'Who said we were eating steak?'

'*I* did. I fancy a nice, thick sirloin.'

She stole a glance at Michael, needing guidance in this matter – and immediately received it.

'You can let the small things go, Carole, so long as you don't compromise on more important matters.'

'OK,' she smiled, 'red's fine, Mike. But, before we order anything, I think we need to talk. It's ages since we've seen each other and, on that last occasion, you behaved extremely badly.'

He had the grace to look shame-faced; even reached across to grip her hand. 'Yeah, as I've said already, darling, I feel gutted about that. I lost my rag – I admit it. But can't we – you know – start again? I've missed you terribly – missed our shags especially.'

Did he have to use words like 'shags', which must seem dreadfully vulgar to an angel? Besides, she hated the thought that it was just the sex he had missed.

His hand strayed down her thigh; moved lower, to her crotch. 'In fact, why don't we skip dinner and go back to the flat right now? I'm *dying* for you, Carole, so let's not waste precious time.'

'No,' she said, firmly pushing off his hand. 'We need to discuss things first.'

'What things?'

'Our whole relationship – is it going to work or not?'

''Course it is. Don't be stupid! We've always hit it off in bed. You're the best lay I've ever had.'

'I'm *not* stupid, and I'm *not* a lay. And, in any case, sex isn't the only thing that counts.' How had she ever found the courage to take so bold a line? That question didn't need an answer – not with Michael standing by.

'Oh, come on, darling, you know what I mean. Don't be difficult.'

'You keep accusing me of being this or that, when all I want is to get a few things straight.'

He raked an impatient hand through his hair. 'I don't know what's got into you. You never used to be so bossy.'

'It's not a matter of being bossy. What I've come to realize—' She broke off as she saw a waiter making for their table.

'Can I get you a drink, sir?'

'Yeah. A beer – a large one.'

'Mike, I thought we were drinking wine.'

'*You* can, if you want.' He gestured to her glass. 'Fancy another of those?'

Again, she looked to Michael for advice.

'As I said,' her angel whispered, 'let the small things go. If a man prefers beer to wine, that's hardly cause for a quarrel.'

'Thanks,' she murmured, gratefully, then thanked Mike, as well, telling him that, yes, she'd love a top-up.

'And let's order, shall we? I'm famished. Hold on!' he yelled at the waiter's departing back. 'I'll have a sirloin steak – medium-rare, with chips.'

'And what for the *signorina*?'

Shouldn't he have asked the '*signorina*' what she wanted, before putting in his own order? And said 'please' to the waiter, rather than sounded so high-handed? 'I haven't looked at the menu yet,' she pointed out, tight-lipped.

'Well, buck up! I'm ravenous.'

'I thought this was meant to be a nice, romantic dinner. Do we have to rush?'

'Stop jumping down my throat, will you? Frankly, it's beginning to piss me off.'

'I'll come back in a few minutes,' the waiter said, making a tactful getaway as Mike's voice rose in irritation.

Once he was out of earshot, she said with deliberate calmness, imitating Michael's tranquil tones, 'Well, if you're so pissed off, as you call it, why don't we ditch dinner altogether?'

'For Christ's sake, Carole, *you're* the one who wanted to go out. I said all along it would be best to meet in the flat.'

'Best for you, maybe, but not for me.'

'And what's *that* supposed to mean?'

'Well, to be honest, I'm not sure I want you in the flat.'

'Bloody cheek! It's *my* pad, more or less.'

'In actual fact, we share it.'

'In which case, I'm perfectly entitled to return to my own place.'

'Fair enough. But I'm not coming with you.'

Kicking back his chair, he slammed his fist on the table. 'What the hell are you talking about?'

'If you listened for a moment, you might find out.'

He sprang to his feet, all but knocking into Michael. 'You've met someone else, I bet! That's the reason for all this shit! I don't see you for two fucking weeks and you sneak off behind my back and shack up with some other bloke!'

She was in desperate need of Michael, to help her keep control. And, as always, he was there for her; his soft, melodious voice reminding her that any sort of altercation would demean her and gain nothing and that, whatever happened, she must refrain from shouting abuse. Yet her silence seemed to rile Mike even more; clearly increasing his suspicions.

'So I'm right! You can't deny it. You've been lying all this time, you two-faced cow! You soft-talk me into coming here; persuade me to wine and dine you on completely false pretences, because all you plan to do is give me the push.'

It would be so easy to retaliate; call him names, in turn; tell him he was wrong – had always been wrong, in fact. But recrimination was pointless and undignified. Instead, she kept her gaze on Michael; breathing in his majesty and power. Only in an archangel would such sublime authority be combined with such true gentleness and grace. How refined he seemed; how distinguished; how effortlessly superior to all mere mortal men.

'Go on – admit it!' Mike was standing over her, fists clenched; his whole stance threatening. But beyond him there was Michael – Michael with his peaceable expression, his shimmering gold halo and luminous white wings; Michael in all his supernatural splendour.

'Yes,' she said, shifting her gaze reluctantly to Mike's flushed and furious face. 'There *is* someone else in my life – someone truly awesome who'll be with me for ever.'

BRIEF ETERNITY

'Supper's ready, Ian!' she called.

No answer.

Well, what did she expect – with Tiger Woods playing in the Masters? She should have planned the meal for earlier, but then, whatever time she served it, her husband would have been too absorbed to eat. The entire evening, he'd been cemented to the sofa; first watching some interminable documentary, about baboons in Tanzania, and now, of course, the golf. She should really have dispensed with the formalities – years ago, as so many people had – and resorted to simply eating on their laps. But sirloin-steak-and-snooker, ravioli-and-rugby, fried-fish-and-football, didn't exactly appeal. In any case, she liked sitting at a table, properly laid up, as she had done throughout her childhood. Her mother had insisted on maintaining decent standards; deploring those undisciplined women who allowed their families to eat in different rooms, at different times, or even graze on the hoof.

Did she *have* to be so rigid, though, this evening? She and her mother were completely different people, after all. In fact, she had rebelled against her, fiercely, from the start, and been forced to knuckle under only by a bitter twist of fate. Best to put Ian's meal on a tray, for once, and take it in to him, rather than keep it warm in the oven, where the vegetables would spoil and the meat soon shrivel up.

'Thanks,' he murmured, once she had placed the tray on his lap. His eyes, however, never wavered from the screen.

She lingered by the sofa. 'Who's in the lead?' she asked. Having been alone all day, while – needless to say – he was playing golf, she was as hungry as much for company as food.

'Sssh! Angel Cabrera's just taking a putt for a birdie.'

'Sorry I spoke.' She flounced back to the dining-table, where a glaze of grease had formed on her lamb chops. She cut into them with venom, as if attacking Ian. It was *his* fault they'd never had children – for her a cause of deep distress. Admittedly, it was hardly fair to blame a man for defective sperm but, if he had only agreed to adopt, or even foster, she might be surrounded now by a brood of four or five.

'More peas, Suzanne?'

'Good boy, Edward! You've finished all your carrots.'

'James, don't kick your brother, dear.'

Despite the fact she was talking out loud and had left the door ajar, Ian wouldn't hear a word. For him, no one else existed except Tiger Woods, Angel Cabrera, Shingo Katayama and the rest. What bizarre names they seemed to have.

'Angel, it's rude to talk with your mouth full.'

'Tiger, I've told you before, we don't shovel in our food like that.'

'Elbows off the table, Shingo!'

Extraordinary how her mother's strictures remained jangling in her head, even ten years after her death; those maternal admonitions lodged in her mind as permanently as an inscription engraved in stone. But then, as an only child, the attention of both her parents' had been focused on her exclusively: her deportment, manners, attitude, appearance, all matters of the gravest concern. If they didn't curb, control and constrain her, she might end up 'going to the bad' – one of her mother's favourite phrases.

Spearing a carrot onto her fork, she snapped its head off, viciously. She had been born a free, wild creature and they had turned her into a lap-dog. They had even chosen her husband, more or less; picked a nice, domesticated Labrador, whom, they felt, would guard her, and the house, and not harbour treacherous longings to run wild with the pack. Left to her own devices, she might simply have eloped, and selected a cheetah as mate, someone fast and fierce and dangerous.

Still chewing her carrot, she mooched into the sitting-room again. 'Good match?' she asked, noticing his untouched meal. He had offloaded the tray to the coffee-table, as if food were a complete irrelevance, in face of this life-and-death event. Sitting bolt upright, with fists clenched and furrowed brow, he might have been watching the fall of the Twin Towers, rather than a mere two-foot putt.

'Christ, yes! It's incredibly dramatic. Phil Mickelson's just lost his ball in Rae's Creek!'

Three sentences. She should be deeply grateful for such bounty, although it was clear she wasn't wanted. Wives, comments, conversation, were invariably distractions when any kind of sport was in progress.

Drifting back to the table, she found herself counting peas, as if needing some sort of mantra to calm her jumpy state. Eight, nine, ten, twelve.... A million-and-twelve, if she totted up all the peas she had ever cooked for Ian. And why not add the Brussels sprouts and broccoli florets, the carrots, leeks and runner beans – all the things she bought to keep him healthy. Yet *she* was the one with the illness – the cause of her sell-out, in fact; that compromise she'd been forced to make with life, adventure, love – and at the age of just nineteen. A red-blooded cheetah would hardly want a mate with diabetes. While *he* was out on the prowl, she'd be tied down to her insulin injections; fussing about her blood-sugar levels; swallowing a whole cache of drugs to prevent those complications threatened by the specialist: kidney failure, eye-disease, heart attack and stroke. But, of course, her mother had been crucial then, as nurse, adviser, comforter. Indeed, she had clung to her, in gratitude; willing to lose her 'self' in the process, simply as the price she had to pay.

All at once, she snatched up her plate, strode into the kitchen and tipped the contents into the bin. She was sick of eating healthily; sick of drugs, injections and the strict, restrictive diet. All the pies and puddings she made for Ian were, for her, forbidden fruits.

'Are you ready for your apple pie?' she asked, venturing in to see him again. Pointless question, when he hadn't eaten so much as a mouthful of his main course. Nonetheless, he gave a distracted nod.

She dolloped almost half the pie onto the biggest plate she could find and put it on the coffee-table, next to the congealing chops. The pie, too, would soon go cold, and a clammy skin would have formed across the custard, by the time he got round to eating it – at midnight, more than likely.

Wouldn't it be better to go out somewhere and leave him to his golf? True, it was blowing a gale – last week's blustery showers having given way to more tempestuous weather – but at least that would be in keeping with her mood. On-screen, all was calm; the Augusta sky serenely blue and cloudless, with not a breath of wind. And, of course, it was daylight there, not dark.

Back in the kitchen, she ate a tiny piece of pie, guiltily and standing up, then slurped some custard from the jug, envisaging her mother's face – aghast with horror and distaste at so sluttish a departure from the rules. Neither pie nor custard satisfied. She craved more – and yet still more.

Wandering over to the window, she peered out at the windswept garden: the branches of the apple trees bending and protesting in the murky, curdled darkness, and the gypsophila quivering, as if it had an ague. She tried to imagine being the wind – untrammelled, unconfined; free to rage and roar, blast, explore, instead of cowering safe indoors. Sundays were always tedious; days sacrosanct to hearth and home, when most of her friends were involved with their children, or entertaining relatives. Sadly, she didn't have those options – with both her parents dead, no siblings and no offspring, and her only aunt miles away in Wales.

Annoyed by her own restlessness, she debated whether to watch the match with Ian. So long as she kept silent and didn't interrupt the game, her presence would be tolerated.

'Bloody golf!' she said, aloud.

Not that she was anti-sport in general. A rugger scrum never failed to excite her: all those muddy, muscly bodies grappling with each other, high on testosterone. Boxing, too, had a definite appeal; the deft footwork, lunging blows, the genuine risk of injury. But golf was so well-mannered in comparison; lacking pace, attack and risk, and determinedly middle-class – as she and Ian were, of course.

Class had mattered profoundly to her parents, who'd built their lives around tennis parties, bridge evenings and membership of the Rotary Club and, when at home, were slaves to the whole rigmarole of tea-strainers and butter-knives, immaculately ironed tablecloths, even sugar-tongs, for God's sake. She suddenly pictured her fastidious mother handling her father's penis with a pair of sugar-tongs – if he *had* a penis, that is. Such a lustful appendage seemed totally inappropriate for a timid civil servant who had emerged from the womb already clad in pinstripes and carrying a briefcase.

All at once, a blood-curdling shriek pierced the silence of the kitchen. Alarmed, she rushed in to Ian. Had he suffered some sort of seizure, precipitated by the tension of the game?

No. He was still alive, still upright. 'What on earth's the matter, darling?' she enquired, forced to raise her voice above the din on-screen: roars of approval, rapturous applause.

'Sssh! Don't speak. Cabrera's just chipped in from a hundred yards!'

Although relieved he was unharmed, that shriek was still resounding in her head – a shriek of such intensity and passion, she wondered if she'd imagined it. In all his years of watching sport, her undemonstrative husband had mustered little more than an appreciative smile or sigh, however huge the triumph or appalling the disaster. Yet the noise had been so deafening, it must have reached to Augusta itself. She was all the more surprised, because chipping in from a hundred yards wasn't *that* astounding – almost as rare as a hole-in-one, maybe, but hardly a cause for hysteria. As she stared at him, incredulous, a second yell issued from his throat; even louder and more dramatic than the first; the very walls seeming to reel in shock.

Abruptly, she left the room and slumped down at the dining table, still neatly laid for two. *How*, she thought, with rising indignation, could Cabrera prompt so blatant a reaction, when she herself could not? Ian was a silent lover. Even at the point of climax, not a sound escaped him. Good manners again, no doubt. Noise would disturb the neighbours; might even make him look debauched. Such a lack of self-control was excessive and over-the-top, and certainly wouldn't go down well in the Rotary Club.

Suddenly, she was back with Stefano, her unruly Sicilian lover; flushed and naked in his rumpled bed. He was letting out a torrent of Italian – expletives, curses, love-talk, all jumbled and mixed up. Although she couldn't grasp the words, her body understood – and more so, when he switched to gasps and moans. She, too, was yelping and growling – above him, underneath him; out of her own skin and inhabiting some new, wild world where Stefano was both beast and god. She was high – on *him* – all the colours brighter; every part of her opening in response: her mouth, her body, her infinitely voracious cunt. All boundaries were disappearing, between beast and human, him and her. There was only *now*; this extreme, excessive moment; everything tumbling and tumultuous and brutally ecstatic.

As she came, she bit his shoulder – a ferocious love-bite, drawing blood, since she was solely flesh and blood now. That was only fitting. She had left her spoilsport intellect behind; her whole rationed and restricted side engulfed.

Impetuously, she sprang up from the table, raced upstairs and stripped off all her clothes. Then, rifling through her wardrobe, she grabbed a black-lace négligé she hadn't worn in years – see-through lace, with side-slits. Her feet barely touched the stair-carpet as, now clad in the diaphanous lace, she darted down again.

'Fuck me!' she demanded, charging in to Ian.

He stared at her, as if she had gone insane. 'What in God's name are you up to, Fay?'

Stefano had never called her Fay; always *Fiammetta*: 'little flame'. With him, she *was* a flame; on fire for him; ablaze with every sensation he aroused. 'Fuck me,' she repeated.

'Don't use that word! You know I find it gross.'

'Screw me, then; make love to me – call it what you like.'

'Fay, what the hell's got into you? I've never known you in such a crazy mood. But I'm afraid you've got your timing badly wrong. This is the most riveting match I've seen in twenty years, so if you imagine I'd miss the end of it, to gratify some whim of yours, then you're very much mistaken.'

'Fine,' she said. 'I understand.'

Quietly, she left the room; closed the door carefully, considerately. Why shouldn't he enjoy his game? She knew the rules – not just of golf; of marriage. That wild Sicilian interlude had been an aberration, before the outrage of her mother summoned her back to duty and decorum; to butter-knives, net curtains, sterility, suppression. She could hardly blame her mother, though. The diabetes diagnosis had been the deciding factor; casting a dark shadow on her life – making it a *half*-life, as it doused all spontaneity, all sense of being free to seize the day. Fine for her contemporaries to be heedless and happy-go-lucky, but *she* was required to maintain a constant vigilance. Monitoring became a daily ritual, and everywhere she went she had to lug her test-kits, needles, glucose – unwanted and resented baggage. Once, love had kept her alive; now it was insulin. Of course, those short six months with Stefano had seemed all the more precious in comparison; a kind of brief eternity, when – despite her restrictive parents – romance, adventure, passion, had all been possible, all real.

Suddenly, on impulse, she hitched up her lace négligé, threw her thickest coat on top, fetched her shoes, and keys, and stampeded out of the house. To hell with syringes and test-kits! However reckless it might be to venture out without them, she didn't give a toss. Who cared about dangers to her health? All that mattered at this moment was to be living at full flame again, if only for a day, a night.

The wind embraced her; a brazen and unbridled wind; running fevered fingers through her hair; tugging at her coat, as if to pluck it off and grope her naked skin; a violent force, tormenting the cowed clouds and tearing them to tatters; ripping branches off the trees, breaking them to bits. She was one with it; unruly, headstrong, subject to no law, throwing off the shackles of her constraining, lifelong illness. She broke into a run, revelling in the gale – its insolence, its zest; the way it slapped her face; thrust cold and lustful fingers down between her legs.

Soon, she had left the streets behind and began climbing the steep hill on the outskirts of the town – not climbing – soaring, like a creature of the sky. All boundaries were lost in the moonless, starless night; light and darkness fused; she and the wind intermingled, merging, as, fuelled by its explosive power, she *flew*.

At the summit, she surrendered; let it pummel and possess her; heard its orgasmic moan. She, too, was crying out; had escaped her skin, her universe; returned to youth and joy.

Somewhere, faint and far away, she heard Ian's shriek re-echoing. Perhaps he had dared another shout, at some eagle, birdie, hole-in-one. She would never know; never discover who had won the match.

Because she wasn't going back to him; refused to settle for a half-life.

Danger was her drug now.

BEGGARS

'Talk about shopping till you drop....' Sophie grabbed the last two seats and, having collapsed into the first, guarded the second for Laura. 'I'm so completely knackered, I couldn't even crawl to Selfridges if they offered me all the freebies I could grab!'

She was talking to empty air. Laura, hampered by her purchases, was still trying to fight her way into the carriage. The largest of the carrier-bags had caught in the wheels of a pushchair – to the annoyance of the harassed mother struggling to get out.

'Kids!' Sophie muttered, once her friend had disentangled herself and slumped, breathless, into the adjoining seat.

'*We* were kids once,' Laura retorted, anxiously checking the contents of the bag. Each item had been swathed in layers of tissue, so no damage had been done, thank heavens. She unwrapped just one of the tops: the Marc Jacobs cardigan. 'Do you think I went overboard – I mean, buying this and all the other stuff?'

''Course you did – you always do – but what the hell? Considering what you're paid, you can afford to splash out a bit.'

Laura heard the note of envy in the comment. True, advertising creatives earned twice as much as beauticians, but Sophie might eventually catch up, were she to open her own salon. And the King's Road would be the ideal spot, to attract the ideal clients. Having just spent most of the day there, in and out of the shops, they had both been struck, as always, by the number of well-heeled Sloanes, constantly whipping out their credit cards for yet another 'must-have'.

As the train rattled into South Kensington, a crowd of people pushed into the carriage, including a pathetic-looking girl, with a thin, pinched face and long, greasy, unkempt hair. Despite it being unseasonably cold for April, the poor creature was bare-legged and clad only in a skimpy skirt and a distinctly threadbare blouse. Struck by her air of abject misery, Laura studied her, with sympathy. Her head drooped; her shoulders sagged; her whole posture was one of defeat. Perhaps someone really close to her had died, or she'd been uprooted from her home or—

Sophie snapped her fingers. 'Wake up, Laura! You're miles away! I asked if you'd like to join us in Giovanni's. Jake said he'd love to see you, and he's bringing all his friends along, so it should be a fun evening.'

'I'd rather get back, if you don't mind. I've loads of stuff to do.'

'Like what? Trying on all that gear and admiring yourself in the mirror?'

Laura flushed. 'No. Other stuff.' In truth she wasn't overly keen on Jake – or his friends, for that matter. Admittedly, she could do with a new man, having just broken up with Alex, but she didn't yet feel ready to put herself about. Why risk another rejection?

Her gaze returned to the girl, now positioned directly in front of her and holding on to the handrail, as the train lurched and jolted along. As she watched, the poor thing raised her head and spoke to the older woman standing beside her. The latter's well-coiffed curls and smart camel coat only emphasized the girl's bedraggled state. As the two began to talk, Laura strained her ears to hear. The girl was obviously upset and seemed to be pouring out her life-story; kneading her hands together and looking close to tears, although the words themselves were impossible to catch.

'Mind you, Jake's in a bit of a sulk. He's had another run-in with his boss and—'

'Sssh!' Laura interrupted.

'What do you mean, "Sssh"?'

'That girl's in quite a state,' she whispered, 'and I'm trying to hear what's going on.'

'Which girl?'

As Laura pointed upwards, she saw the older woman open her handbag, rummage for her purse and extract a twenty-pound note.

'Oh, Lord!' Laura hissed. 'She's touting for cash.' She watched, amazed, as the woman pressed the note into the outstretched small, grubby hand. £20 was a hell of a lot to give a total stranger.

'I hate these beggars,' Sophie muttered, 'especially on the tube, where we're all just sitting targets.'

Laura barely heard; too absorbed in watching the girl, who appeared completely overwhelmed by her unknown benefactor's kindness and was thanking her repeatedly; each heartfelt thank-you accompanied by a subservient little bow.

'There was this weird guy only yesterday, going from carriage to carriage, telling everyone his hard-luck story – not that I believed a word. All they want are hand-outs to splurge on drink and drugs.'

Sophie's voice was drowned by the rattling of the train as it pulled into Gloucester Road. The minute the doors shuddered open, the girl darted out of the carriage and dashed full-pelt along the platform.

'See!' Sophie jeered. 'She can't wait for her next fix.'

'She did look truly skint, though. She wasn't even wearing tights, let alone a jacket.'

'Oh, that's just a ploy. They deliberately dress in rags, or even borrow dogs or babies, in order to tug at your heartstrings. I saw a woman the other week, sitting on the pavement, with *three* babies, would you believe – and so close in age, they couldn't all be hers. Yet a few suckers were tossing her coins and even five-pound notes. But, you know, it's actually wrong to encourage them. Any cash you hand over simply feeds their habit.'

'We don't *know* they've got a habit, Soph. I mean, it's equally wrong just assuming they're all addicts.'

'Why don't they find themselves a job, then – slave all hours, like *we* do?'

'You can hardly go out to work with three babies to look after.'

'Come off it, Laura! Those babies were just part of the act.'

'OK, take that girl just now – she might be too ill to work. She looked like death, you must admit, with her ghastly, greyish skin.

She might even have TB. Apparently, it's on the increase in London. Or maybe she's homeless, or a refugee.'

'Laura, the trouble with you is you're way too soft.'

And you're too tough, Laura refrained from pointing out. She and Sophie might have known each other since primary school, but that didn't make them soul-mates. OK, they shared the same taste in clothes and music, and liked to go shopping together, but that was as far as it went.

'It's kinder to be cruel,' Sophie persisted. 'Giving her money could *kill* her, if the cash ends up in a drug-dealer's pocket and she dies of an overdose. We're talking serious drugs here – heroin and crack – and those can cost your typical addict not far short of a grand a week. So don't imagine for a moment that any hand-out, however well intentioned, will be spent on food or clothes.'

Laura opened her mouth to reply, but Sophie cut her off.

'In any case, the longer people like her manage to keep going by scrounging off the rest of us, the less chance there is of them ever making something of their lives. In fact, they're more *likely* to catch TB sitting around in the cold for hours, rather than being indoors at work.'

'Yeah, I suppose that's true,' Laura admitted, grudgingly. Her attention had now strayed to the young couple opposite, who were gazing at each other with enviable devotion; hands entwined, noses almost touching. Once, Alex used to look at her like that.

'You mustn't think I'm callous,' Sophie added, nudging her in the ribs. 'I'm just as sorry as you are for those genuinely on the breadline. But, for some, it's just a scam – like people already on benefits, simply pretending they're destitute.'

Laura gave a shrug. Frankly, she'd had enough of the subject, although Sophie seemed determined to flog it to death.

'I mean, I read not long ago that a beggar in central London can expect to make three hundred pounds a day – which is far more than you or me earn. And the ones from Eastern Europe are organized in gangs by these unregulated gangmasters, who deliberately pack them off to all the best pitches in London, like outside Harrods or Harvey Nicks, then claw the money back and keep it for themselves.'

Laura sat silent; uncertain *what* she thought. Was Sophie right, or just rehashing some prejudiced rant from the tabloid press? Being unsure of her own opinion was depressingly familiar. She could never seem to make up her mind – not just on the issue of beggars, but in personal matters, too. Did she want marriage and kids, or a glittering career? Was the split with Alex entirely her own fault, or was he a hopeless visionary who expected her, unreasonably, to live up to his ideals, as Sophie always said? Also, the relationship with her father left her endlessly dithering: should she make a concerted effort to see him, or leave him to stew in his present silent sulk? Even as a teenager, she'd continually been switching between opposing points of view; far too easily swayed by anyone with real conviction.

Someone like Sophie, in fact, who was invariably convinced that she was right; whether about holidays (Biarritz was divine; Paris overrated); organic cosmetics (a con), and her pet-hate, James Blunt (the most insipid, whiney singer on the planet), and now, of course, beggars.

'Another thing about those bums is that they can louse up a residential area – you know, with their piles of disgusting old blankets and syringes and stuff. There's such a stink of puke and piss in the underpass near my flat, you're forced to hold your nose if you cross the road that way.'

Laura had to admit there was a similar stench in the alley near her own flat, which street-people used as a toilet. But, before she could decide where her sympathies lay, Sophie was sounding off again.

'But the most shocking thing, in my opinion, is that, far from being homeless, some so-called beggars actually have mortgages – and well-paid jobs to fund them. Apparently, they come back from their day-jobs, take off their suits or whatever, and dress in rubbish clothes, just to look the part. Then they spend their evenings raking in a second income – all tax-free, of course – by making out they're living from hand to mouth.'

'Oh, Sophie, I can't believe that!' Laura stole another glance at the couple opposite; locked in an intimate embrace. Clearly, they were oblivious of their highly public surroundings and of the matron sitting next to them, frowning in disapproval.

'It's true, I swear. There was this policeman on TV, determined to expose the sham. He said cheats like that often use the extra cash to pay for a new kitchen or bathroom, or even to go on holidays abroad.'

'But how on earth could he prove it? I mean, no one's going to admit ...' Laura jumped up in mid-sentence. More passengers were piling in at High Street Kensington and she felt duty-bound to offer her seat to a doddery old gentleman, struggling to keep his balance. She was getting off at the next stop, anyway, so this unsettling exchange about beggars would have to come to a stop – and about time, too, she thought.

''Bye, Soph!' she called, as the train rumbled to a halt. 'Have fun at Giovanni's!'

''Bye – and thanks for lunch.'

But there was no escaping beggars, because, as she came through the ticket-barrier, the first thing she noticed was a young guy sitting cross-legged on the ground; begging-bowl beside him, bottle of cider and, yes, a mangy dog. In the ordinary way, she would have probably ignored him, but, in light of Sophie's remarks, she paused to scrutinize his general appearance. Unlike the girl on the tube, he seemed in the pink of health, and was warmly dressed in a thick sweater and hooded fleece. Perhaps Sophie had a point and there *were* a lot of people who preferred to scrounge, rather than work for their living – or even do both in succession, which seemed still more reprehensible.

'Spare some change, miss?' he whined, eyeing her cache of upmarket carrier-bags and presumably classing her as easy prey.

Shaking her head, she strode resolutely past and up the steps to the street, relieved to see it free of any down-and-outs. Indeed, it was looking at its best; the trees glazed with glistening green, as new spring leaves burst forth, and the sky a hopeful blue, despite the cold. She loved living in this part of London, with its range of trendy shops, its bustling bars and cafés, and the sense of it being almost a 'village', with its own distinctive atmosphere.

She stopped to peer through the huge glass frontage of the new Japanese restaurant, which had opened here a month ago. There was barely an empty seat at the rotating sushi conveyor-belts; crowds of diners enjoying the funky décor, as well as the delicate food. The whole place was bathed in a purple-tinted glow and the glittering giant disco-ball, suspended from the ceiling, cast dancing shimmers of light across faces, tables, surfaces. On the back wall was a psychedelic mural of rainbow-coloured butterflies, which seemed to flap their wings as she watched. Butterflies were the signature theme and, no doubt, the Butterfly Bar upstairs would be every bit as packed. Alex had taken her there for cocktails, the very last time they'd met; kissed her passionately in a dark corner of the bar. The memory alone seemed to rekindle the zizz of champagne-bubbles tingling in her mouth; the kick of crème de cassis on her tongue, all overlaid with the taste of those wild kisses. That evening, she'd felt like a butterfly herself: ethereal and brilliant, and flying high, high, high.

So how could things have gone so disastrously wrong? And in such a short space of time?

She shivered, suddenly – and not just from the cold, although the bad-tempered April wind had not let up. But, however keen she was to reach her cosy flat, first she had to stop off at the cash-machine, to withdraw money for the coming week. She was annoyed to see a longish queue outside it and, yes, two more beggars, squatting on the pavement, one on either side. This was clearly a good pitch. People moving off from a cash-point, with their stashes of tens and twenties, could hardly plead poverty as a reason for ignoring outstretched hands – which meant Sophie's words about deliberate calculation clearly had some truth. One of the pair was ancient: a foxy little guy, sprawled on a piss-stained mattress – again with a dog, and again with a supply of booze. She was shocked to see him actually puffing on a cigarette. It did seem truly crass that he expected other people to fund his smoking habit. The other one was young: a foreign-looking woman, dressed in a ragged skirt and jacket and clutching a small infant, with a notice pinned to its shawl: 'Feed my baby, please!'

Until today, the morality or otherwise of begging had rarely occupied her mind. She might toss a handful of change to some saddo, down on his luck, but then continue on her way; more concerned with a challenge at work or problem in the flat-share. But now she was beginning to realize that perhaps Sophie was far less heartless than she had judged her at the outset. If that woman's rags were just part of her 'performance' and her child a borrowed 'prop', then the whole thing was a con. And she *did* look East European, which meant she could be controlled by a gangmaster, some brutish thug creaming off the profits. And maybe the bloke with the cigarette could earn £300 a day, on top of a good salary – cash he would use to keep himself in tobacco, or even splash out on an exotic foreign holiday.

Once she had withdrawn her cash, she stalked past the pair with no compunction, indeed, now sharing some of Sophie's indignation. The rent on her flat-share was steep, mainly due to its fashionable location and, to pay that rent, she was forced to work long hours. So why should such a desirable area be spoiled by grungy bedding and empty cans and bottles, littered all over the place?

As soon as she got home, she poured herself a glass of Prosecco, kicked off her shoes and sank down on the sofa, glass in hand; relieved that Amanda was out. Her flatmate's penchant for hard rock, preferably played full-volume, was a frequent bone of contention and, just at present, she wanted peace and quiet.

Only when she had finished her wine – and relished the rare silence – did she saunter into her bedroom, to try on her new clothes: first, the Chloe dress: short and tight and a subtle shade of bluish-grey. She studied herself in the mirror. Yes, it would go well with the vintage jacket she had bought last week in Portobello market, *and* with her new pashmina, so, all in all, it was worth its inflated price. Next, she tried the three tops. One was rather daringly low-cut, but the other two would be perfect for work. Finally, she struggled into the leopard-printed leggings; worried they might make her look too fat. Alex had told her repeatedly that he preferred women with some flesh on their bones to anorexic beanpoles who might as well be boys. He'd always tried to dissuade her from slimming and used to hide her low-fat yogurts and cans of Diet-Coke, and stock up with highly fattening foods instead.

Alex is history now, she reminded herself; annoyed she should still care so much about what he said and did. Having stowed the new gear in the wardrobe and put on her old denim skirt and sweater, she rummaged for her iPod, hoping some upbeat music might help to lift her mood. Then she lay back on the bed, glancing round the room with a sense of almost proprietorship. Although the flat was only rented, and had come part-furnished with a cheapo wardrobe and decidedly shoddy bed, she had succeeded in putting her stamp on it, particularly here in the bedroom. The antique coat-stand and 1940s Vogue prints had also come from Portobello market, as had the two brass bedside lamps. She had disguised the bed itself with piles of stripy cushions, and tacked rows of fine-art postcards on the wardrobe, to cover its faded wood. And there were other decorative touches, added to divert the eye: her collection of perfume bottles on the dressing-table; strings of brightly coloured beads looped around the mirror. Maybe, next weekend, she would have another prowl around the market and snap up a few more trinkets. After all, she earned a decent salary and, sadly, there was no one else in her life, at present, to spend that money on.

Except the beggars, a voice inside her seemed to say.

She countered it immediately. According to Sophie, beggars were frauds and cheats, enslaved to drink and drugs. Yet was that actually true? The girl on the tube, for instance, had given the impression of being someone really genuine. Her unassuming manner and unassertive voice had done nothing to suggest she was an addict or a drunk. And the way she'd poured out her thanks had seemed utterly authentic. Indeed, whatever Sophie might say, she just couldn't believe that so forlorn a female had a mortgage or a salary, or was touting for cash to supplement an already substantial income. She had looked completely poverty-stricken and, despite the warmth of the carriage, had been literally shivering – maybe a sign of some serious illness. Admittedly, she now had £20 in hand, but that wouldn't stretch very far, especially if she was too sick to work and had to buy medicines, or pay for basic heating.

And what about the foreign woman, squatting on the pavement with her kid? She, too, had been pale and haggard, and had gazed up at the people walking past with a truly desperate expression. There was no proof her baby was 'borrowed' or her tattered clothes just a ploy. And, even if she did belong to a gang, that could make things still worse for her. Gangmasters were bound to be callous, and certainly wouldn't give a toss whether a woman had milk for her baby or clothes to keep it warm.

'Laura, you're way too soft – I keep telling you.'

Sophie's voice was now added to the first one, confusing her still further. Wasn't it better to be soft than hard as nails? Yet, if she swallowed every sob-story without knowing the true facts, she could be taken for a ride. On the other hand, such 'facts' were constantly changing, according to which paper you read, or so-called authority you recognized.

She sprang up from the bed, impatient with her own uncertainties. She didn't even know what she thought about the war in Afghanistan, or the situation in Palestine. Almost everyone at work had set-in-stone political convictions, while she dithered on the side-lines; swinging from one view to another, without ever reaching conclusions.

Mooching out to the kitchen, she realized she was hungry, having eaten nothing since their small snack-lunch, at noon. She peered into the fridge, guiltily aware that most bona-fide beggars would envy her its contents: a full bottle of Prosecco, as well as the one she'd opened; a large pack of smoked salmon; a whole Camembert, still wrapped in its waxed paper; a punnet of strawberries, and any number of smoothies and yogurts. And there were further supplies in the freezer and the cupboard – all for just two people, yet enough to sustain a beggar for a month.

Having cut herself a wedge of cheese, she fetched some cranberry relish and the bread, and sat at the tiny table, giving a sigh of deep regret. Alex might never have expressed an opinion as to whether she was soft or tough, but he *had* criticized what he saw as her addiction to shopping. Neither was he keen on her profession, which, in his opinion, sold unnecessary products to gullible people unable to afford them. *He* worked for a charity, so he was bound to take the high line, and she did actually admire him for his altruism and dedication. The trouble was she couldn't give up shopping. It *was* a sort of addiction, although one shared by most of her friends. And, as for resigning from her job, with its high pay and many perks, that was out of the question. Mahler-Knox-McKay was a wildly stylish agency (with its own Martini bar, roof-terrace and even a visiting masseuse), and everyone who worked there was ultra-super-confident – well, everyone but her. In truth, she sometimes felt she didn't quite belong; lacking the others' sophistication and witty cynicism, their ability to quip and joke about even the grimmest subjects.

Which was precisely why Alex had appealed to her, as a sort of counterbalance; a man of true integrity and burning seriousness. So, once again, she was caught between two different ways of being, and had no idea which one was right. Sophie, of course, was completely and utterly certain that Mr Do-Good Alex was a fanatic and a smart-arse, and it had actually been a stroke of luck that he'd decided to break things off.

'Completely and utterly certain' was something *she* had never felt, about anything whatever; least of all about Alex. For Sophie, it was simple. If she would only stop pining for the freak, she could set her sights on one of the Mahler-Knox executives, move in with him and enjoy a cushy life. It was true she could never share Alex's principles and high ideals – didn't even want to, if it meant starving in a garret – and yet....

And yet ... And yet ... And yet ... She'd been 'and-yetting' since her teens; forever wavering, irresolute; forever in two minds.

Suddenly, impulsively, she slammed her knife down on the plate; grabbed her bag and coat from where she'd left them in a heap, and marched out of the flat.

Sprinting to the end of her road, she continued dashing along Ladbroke Grove; not slackening her pace until she was back at the main street. The queue outside the cash-point had now dispersed, thank God – the last thing she wanted was anybody watching. The young beggar who'd been smoking had also disappeared, but the woman with the baby was still there, looking even more dispirited and tired. Dusk was falling and the wind as sharp as ever – no weather for an infant to be out. Indeed, the child was crying frantically – a hopeless sort of sound that seemed to fill the whole of Notting Hill, as it wailed on and on and on.

She stood half-hidden in the shadows, wondering if the kid was sick, or maybe just half-starved. She knew nothing about babies and all she could see of this one was its red, indignant face, screwed up and distorted as it bawled its futile protest.

A gaggle of young football fans came swinging down the street, all laughing and joking and with beer-cans in their hands. Immediately, the beggar-woman tried to attract their attention, calling out in some foreign tongue and pointing to the notice pinned on the baby's shawl. Without a knowledge of English, she obviously couldn't resort to the usual 'Spare some change' – although the baby's shrieks would have drowned it anyway. Yet, despite the noise, none of the group even glanced in her direction – too busy having fun. The minute they'd moved off however, Laura unzipped her purse and extracted the notes she had withdrawn from the cash-point earlier: four twenties and two tens. £100 was a pretty substantial sum, but she had spent triple that in the shops today, and was forever buying herself treats, be it fancy food and wine, expensive face-creams and manicures, or yet another pair of shoes she didn't actually need. Alex was right – she *did* adore possessions; just couldn't have enough of them, and, in that respect, she knew she'd never change.

With a furtive look to left and right, she approached the huddled figure, who seemed unable to calm her baby, or – presumably – to feed it, and looked totally defeated. Stooping down, she pushed the sheaf of notes into her hand, then strode off down the street, not wanting to be thanked. The baby's howls seemed to follow her; sounding even louder now, as if the child itself was reproaching her for giving such a large sum to its mother – a sum that might be handed to a gangmaster or splurged on crack-cocaine.

Pausing in a doorway, she was surprised to feel so downbeat. Alex often used the phrase 'the joy of giving', so she'd expected to be suffused by some sort of virtuous glow, but there wasn't so much as a trace of joy, or even the mildest sense of gratification. Perhaps she had only been generous in an attempt to win Alex back. Had she imagined he'd been watching from his little dive in Shoreditch and roaring his approval?

'Get real!' she muttered, irritably. The relationship was over, doomed, and the sooner she accepted that, the better. He might even have found a new girlfriend by now; some worthy type who worked for Shelter and regarded shopping as a vice.

As she trudged round the corner, in the direction of her flat, she suddenly stopped dead. An amazing thing had just happened, yet it had totally failed to register until this very instant: she actually knew beyond all doubt – and knew for the first and only time in her whole life – that what she'd just done had been completely and utterly right. In giving that money, she had deliberately taken a risk; been willing to trust that the child *would* be fed and clothed, and the woman begin to feel less desolate. Just one act of charity could give a person hope, make them less convinced that life was remorselessly harsh – and that in itself was enough to justify her action. Of course, she hadn't the faintest notion whether the beggar was a fraud, or someone genuinely in need, and had even less idea whether the £100 would be used for evil purposes or good. But that only made it more incredible that she had acted so decisively, because, despite it being such a gamble – despite what Sophie might say, or the police, or the tabloid press, or the world-weary types at Mahler-Knox-McKay – she was still completely and utterly certain that the right place for her money was in that woman's hand, rather than in the till of yet another King's Road boutique.

She gave a whoop of triumph. Certainty felt brilliant – so completely and utterly brilliant, she just had to celebrate. Veering round the other way, she skittered back to the Japanese restaurant, singing to herself, as she took a short-cut through the side-streets, and not bothered who might hear. She raced upstairs to the Butterfly Bar; found a seat on a stylish purple couch, surrounded by kaleidoscopic butterflies, and ordered the same cocktail she'd had a month ago, with Alex. Then, lolling back against the flamboyant purple cushions, she breathed in the buzzy atmosphere; that sense of being high, high up – level with the top branches of the trees. The nightlights on the tables cast a dramatic damson glow, and their gleam and flicker seemed to throb right through her bloodstream, together with the pounding, pulsing music.

'Your drink, madam. Enjoy!'

The frisky pink of the cocktail reflected her mood exactly and she took an appreciative gulp, relishing the zing of crème-de-cassis, the sparkly bubbles fizzing in the glass; the subtle tastes of passion-fruit and peach. This time, she didn't need Alex's kisses to give it a heady tang. It was perfect as it was.

As perfect as conviction.

SURVIVORS

'Good luck!' the driver called, giving her a cheery wave as she alighted from the bus.

Jet-lagged and exhausted, she could do with some good luck – or at least with a more exact idea as to where she actually was. If she had only visited her father before it was too late, she would have got to know the area and not felt so disoriented in this unfamiliar county.

Having crossed the deserted road, she checked her watch, relieved to see that, far from being late, she had two whole hours in hand. In fact, much to her surprise, the entire journey had been hassle-free. The flight from New York had arrived precisely on time; both trains had been punctual and, having seen no sign of a taxi and expected to wait ages for an infrequent country bus, she had found one just about to leave, right outside the station. So, all in all, fate had been benign.

Except 'benign' seemed much too callous a word, with her father so recently dead. Rather than counting her blessings, she should be rending her garments, although, in truth, her emotions were so complex and unsettling, she had, as yet, hardly dared confront them.

As she walked along the narrow lane, she marvelled at the silence – all the more striking after the cacophony of Manhattan. No planes, no traffic; not even any people-noise or birdsong. Perhaps the birds were dozing, since everything else seemed somnolent, swathed in the oppressive August heat. Indeed, she, too, had been lulled into a state of semi-trance as the bus rumbled along the short distance from the station and she'd gazed out at the majestic sweep of hills and fields beneath a cloudless sky. Majestic maybe, but undoubtedly benighted. As a Londoner born and bred, her forays to the countryside were rare in the extreme and she still couldn't wholly understand why her father should have insisted on moving to the wilds of Devon, when he had lived in Wandsworth for his eighty-eight years to date.

Probably just to be cussed, she suspected. The more she had suggested sheltered housing, or at least somewhere closer to her Camden flat, the more he had reiterated his need for solitude and seclusion. And, when she had pointed out that a man approaching ninety might need easy access to help and social services, rather than withdrawal to the back of beyond, he'd retorted peevishly that the last thing he required was interfering busybodies poking their noses into his intimate affairs. Of course, he might have intended the move partly as a test of her devotion: would his wayward daughter deign to make so long a journey to visit her elderly Dad? A test she had failed, although not through any neglect or lack of duty.

With a sigh of mingled frustration and regret, she turned off the road and slipped through the elaborate wrought-iron gates of the crematorium. She found herself in well-kept, spacious gardens, with close-cropped lawns and immaculately neat flowerbeds – a marked contrast to the wilder landscape beyond. Despite the heat, no shrub was wilting, or flower-head drooping, and the grass itself was lushly green, rather than parched and brown, as usual in a heatwave. Yet no gardener was in evidence; no sign of any funeral in progress, nor any casual visitors. In fact, she had the uncanny feeling that she had travelled to the limits of the populated world and would never see another living person. The plane had been jam-packed and the fast train also crowded when she'd boarded it at Paddington, but, having changed to the second, slower train, her carriage had been empty, save for a couple of old ladies. As for the bus, she'd been the one and only passenger, so, the further she travelled, the more isolated she seemed to become, with no fellow human beings left in existence. Even the friendly bus-driver would now be swallowed up in tree-cloistered country lanes.

Impulsively, she rummaged for her phone. As yet, she hadn't spoken to a soul; too ashamed to admit that her father had died alone and – almost as reprehensible – that she hadn't flown straight back the minute she heard the news. But, of all her circle, Kate was the most likely to sympathize, being a singleton, like her, with no strong family ties, and similarly single-minded when it came to her career.

'Kate? Hi! How are you?... No, I'm not in New York.... Yes, the meetings went well, considering, and my job appears to be safe, thank God! But, listen, the very day I arrived, I received the most awful shock – my father had dropped down dead from a heart attack and I wasn't even *there*.'

She registered her friend's gasp of surprise. Although Kate had never met him, she was nonetheless aware that, despite his age, Robert was in robust health and even took a daily constitutional, trekking a mile or more over challenging terrain.

'... No, a neighbour found him and rang the vicar – the Reverend Matthews, a marvellous man. He managed to reach me at my hotel and he's been an absolute saint, Kate. Once he understood my predicament – you know, that I couldn't just drop everything and catch the next plane home – he agreed to register the death for me, take care of the formalities and arrange the funeral. And he's even going to officiate himself. So everything's sorted out, without me having to do a thing except pay the various bills. I feel awful, really, leaving so much to him, but I didn't have any choice.'

Of course she'd had a choice. But her whole career had been at stake and if she had returned to the UK before all the vital business was concluded, it would have given the worst possible impression. So she had made a deliberate decision to stay on in New York for the entire series of important meetings, and then rushed headlong from the boardroom to the airport. Was that irredeemably selfish, or simply prudent in the circumstances?

She stopped wrestling with her conscience to answer Kate's next question. 'Yes, I suppose we could have postponed it, but....' Her voice tailed off. In fact, the vicar's original suggestion had been to leave the body in the morgue until she herself could take charge of the arrangements. But the thought of putting her father in cold storage for longer than was strictly necessary seemed not only grotesque but an affront to his lifelong hatred of delay and procrastination. Kate clearly considered it odd, though, allowing a stranger to carry out what was, frankly, a daughter's duty. In fact, she was beginning to regret ever having phoned her friend; there were too many awkward questions.

'No, I'm not staying at Dad's cottage. The vicar said it was in no fit state for visitors, which, I have to say, made me worry, Kate. He was always incredibly neat and couldn't abide living in a mess, so it means he must have gone downhill – and fast!'

She hoped Kate wouldn't ask her next if she'd booked into a hotel, as she was loth to mention that she was actually going home tonight – however late she might get back and however tired she was of travelling – which she had been doing for the last thirteen hours. It seemed imperative to sleep in her own bed and be surrounded by her own familiar things. Besides, she needed a few days' grace before she made this journey a second time, in order to ratchet up her energy for the series of grim tasks ahead: sorting out her father's affairs; deciding what to do with his possessions; sprucing up his cottage and endeavouring to sell it, despite the vagaries of the housing market. And – a minor point, maybe – she hadn't any overnight things, having deposited her case at Paddington Left Luggage.

'... Oh, I'm sorry, Kate. I'm totally forgetting you're at work ... No, I'm all right, honestly – a bit whacked, of course, but coping.... OK, fine – I'll ring you later.'

As she replaced her mobile in its pouch, she felt still more alone. She might have shared the news with Kate, but not her inner turmoil. Anyway, no friend could really understand that her predominant emotion wasn't grief – or even guilt – but the deep sadness of knowing that it was now too late for her father ever to tell her he loved her. But then what had she expected? A sudden change of heart in his nineties; cosy little cuddles and avowals of affection from a father who had loved one person only, in the whole of his long life: his small, shy, retiring wife. Daughters didn't count, and he never bothered himself with friends; had long since cut all ties with relations and, even in his younger years, preferred to live as a recluse. In fact, she doubted if there would be anyone at the funeral except maybe a few fellow-villagers who felt duty-bound to attend.

Wandering on along the path, she kept looking out for some sign of human activity. Admittedly, the service wasn't scheduled until four, but surely there would be funerals before it? Perhaps the crematorium closed for lunch, which would explain the absence of hearses or mourners, but it still seemed strange that not a single soul appeared to be around. In fact, these extensive gardens, devoid of people and with no sign of any buildings, seemed peculiarly unreal, like the insubstantial landscape of a dream. All the crematoria she had visited before had been decidedly more compact, with the chapel and the offices immediately apparent, and clusters of friends and relatives providing an air of normality.

Much better if the whole thing *were* a dream, then she would wake up in New York, with the prospect of the two days' respite she had planned originally, to sightsee in Manhattan and recover from the shock and stress of the takeover. A hundred questions and anxieties were still swarming through her mind. Would their own far smaller firm be bullied by the American giant who'd swallowed it? And what were her future prospects, with a recession in both countries and an increasing number of managers facing the chop?

But she was thinking of herself and not her father – a spur for yet more guilt – although, in fact, these well-groomed grounds brought to mind his obsessive need for neatness and regularity, in every aspect of existence. She imagined his satisfaction at the sight of the regimented flowerbeds, where the plants were arranged in concentric circles, each one perfectly gradated according to size and colour. He had always detested disorder; spent most of his life attempting to put things back in line and tame anything or anyone unruly – including her, of course. In point of fact, she had never been unruly, or wayward, or recalcitrant, or all the other things he used to called her. It was just that, in his eyes, all children, without exception, were undisciplined and messy creatures and, even when they grew to adulthood, most – including her – failed to reach his exacting standards.

As she continued to walk on, she was aware how hungry she was, having eaten nothing since her sandwich on the train. If only she'd bought a second sandwich, then she could have picnicked here in the grounds, rather than risk a rumbling stomach at the funeral. Except sprawling on the grass would have messed up her smart suit – the same suit she'd worn to yesterday's meeting, conveniently black.

Her father had always hated picnics: part of his general antipathy to slovenliness and disarray. He liked meals with proper tablecloths and cutlery, and thus it was penance on a heroic scale for him to eat with his fingers and ward off wasps and flies; risking indigestion, sunburn and grass-stains on his clothes – a penance endured solely for his wife's sake. She remembered one disastrous time in Worthing, when she had dropped her cheese roll on the beach, retrieved it, wet and gritty with sand, then wolfed it down before anyone could stop her. He had stalked off in disgust and eaten his food on the promenade, alone, but mercifully removed from his clumsy, uncouth daughter. Seaside picnics were, for him, the most intolerable: defiant breezes dishevelling his hair; other people's unruly kids throwing up more sand as they shrieked and skittered past, and the raucous noise of funfairs assaulting his fastidious ears.

In fact, they never went on holiday again. By the following September, her mother was a corpse.

Her gloomy introspection was cut short by the sight of a large, free-standing notice-board, indicating the direction of the chapel, car-park and Garden of Remembrance and, fifty yards beyond, a group of buildings. Although it was a relief to get her bearings, she felt annoyed with the authorities for not erecting a similar notice at the entrance to the site.

It was still only ten past two and, since she had no desire to turn up at the chapel almost two hours early, she wandered into the Garden of Remembrance. It, too, was extremely well-maintained, with not a weed or speck of litter in sight, and thus eminently suitable for her father's final resting-place. She began reading the inscriptions on the various memorials: *Much loved and sorely missed ... Always in our thoughts ... Beloved husband and father....*

In her own father's case, she had better restrict the wording to 'beloved husband' only, since he had never wanted children in the first place. Having married a woman of forty-six, the last thing he'd expected was the arrival of a baby on the scene and, although he'd bowed to the inevitable, he'd always harboured a certain resentment that his blissful coupledom with Ella had become an awkward threesome. Hence Ella's early death was not just tragic for him but highly inconvenient. Father and child had somehow stuck it out together, until she solved the problem for him by leaving home the same week that she left school. Ever afterwards, her visits had been sporadic, yet, in honour of her much-missed mother, she had never failed to ensure that he was in reasonable health and coping on his own.

Until this very week.

At peace, said the adjoining plaque – a reproach to her patent lack of it. And, indeed, peace had been largely absent in her childhood, because of her father's state of mind. He continually blamed himself for Ella's death – when he wasn't blaming *her* – or even blamed the perfectly competent oncologist for 'dereliction of duty'. In fact, one of the phrases from the funeral – *in the midst of life we are in death* – had been all too true of him. He wore mourning clothes for the rest of his days, metaphorically, at least.

As she completed her tour of the garden, she wondered which type of memorial he'd prefer: a bench, a sundial, a plaque? Certainly not a tree, which would shed messy leaves all over him and harbour feckless birds. Nor anything that required a lot of maintenance, because she could hardly nurture a rosebush or a shrub, when she lived such miles away. It was her mother's grave she tended, and with the utmost love and devotion; visiting once or twice each month and—

Oh my God, she thought, blundering to a halt. Shouldn't her father be buried *with* her mother, or at least in the same graveyard? Had she made the wrong decisions, simply under pressure? In point of fact, her father had never left instructions about his funeral, refusing categorically to discuss his death at all, despite his advancing years. Yet all the other alternatives now began stampeding through her mind, in a stream of accusing 'should-haves': should she have transported his body to London and begged the local council to find room in her mother's cemetery, or even in her grave; should she have investigated *other* London cemeteries; should she have gone through all his papers, in case he had, in fact, drawn up some final directive? But doing all those things long-distance would have been more or less impossible, especially when time was of the essence. Besides, if her father wished to be buried with his wife, surely he would have mentioned the fact in the thirty-three years since her death.

She was so deep in speculation, she failed to look where she was going and almost tripped on a loose kerbstone. She was also perspiring in her formal suit and high-necked, long-sleeved blouse. The outfit was fine for New York's air-conditioned offices, but felt uncomfortably sticky in a temperature of close on ninety degrees. And her tight, high-heeled shoes were totally unsuited to a long ramble through a garden. It was clearly time to go inside – cool down, calm down and stop torturing herself. She could always sit in the waiting-room until the service started and, if nothing else, escape the fierce stare of the sun.

As she approached the chapel complex, there was still no one to be seen and even the waiting-room was deserted, so she resigned herself to her own company again. Perching on one of the upright chairs, she glanced around at the pale-blue walls, squiggled, grey-blue carpet and skimpy rayon curtains. There were no pictures on the walls or magazines to read – both presumably too frivolous in this context of death and grief. Neatness reigned supreme once more: the chairs arranged in severely straight rows; the room scrupulously clean. Well, at least her father would approve, as he would of the plastic orchids on the otherwise bare table. Real flowers dropped their petals, or shed a dust of pollen on highly polished furniture, and their water turned green and smelly, especially in hot weather.

She cleared her throat, the noise intrusively loud in the empty room, and her sense of isolation prompting further memories of childhood. After her mother's death, her father used to closet himself in his study, requiring to be alone with his grief, but that, of course, had left her on her own. Since he never welcomed visitors or allowed her friends to come, she often felt like a child in quarantine – infectious not from illness, but from her faults of character.

She fidgeted on her seat, wishing brain-transplants were available, so she could replace the jangling chaos in her mind with serenity and peace. Yet, in the absence of such procedures, her thoughts kept circling back to that same oppressive time, when she and her father had co-existed as separate, silent mourners, sharing nothing but their loss and the same house. Being motherless at the age of twelve had been a test of endurance; having to learn to sleep without her usual goodnight kiss; to live on tins and takeaways, instead of home-cooked food; to go through puberty alone, with no mother to explain things, or help her buy the Tampax.

Rudderless and terrified, she eventually stumbled on a way to survive. She would close her eyes and *imagine* the goodnight kisses; *imagine* her mother's presence; paint vivid pictures in her mind: her mother standing in the kitchen, in her familiar blue-checked pinny, making apple pie, spiced with cloves and cinnamon and awash in velvety custard, or bread-and-butter pudding; its crusted, sugared top contrasting exquisitely with the eggy, creamy softness underneath, or the lemon sponge they always had on Sundays squidgy inside, with little shreds of lemon peel to provide an extra kick.

She was just savouring its taste again, when she was aware of sounds outside: cars pulling up, people talking, even a burst of laughter from a child – signs of life, at last. Opening the door a fraction, she saw a largish crowd, waiting outside the chapel – the three-o'clock booking, presumably – and felt ridiculously relieved to be not the only living person in the world.

Returning to her seat, she closed her eyes and did her best to relax. There was still an hour to wait and she would be ragged by tonight if she continued giving way to all these futile regrets and painful memories. The ponderous clock on the wall ticked out a soothing cadence, which, gradually, began to calm her mood. She was all but drifting off to sleep, when a door opened from the chapel side and an official popped his head round to enquire, 'Are you for the three-o'clock service? If so, please come through immediately, as it's just about to start.'

She stared at him, confused and, scarcely knowing what she was doing, rose from her seat and let him usher her into the chapel. As she slipped into the last pew at the back, she was astonished by the music – not a solemn organ, but some jaunty pop tune, blasting out full volume. And everyone was dressed in bright, eccentric clothes – the only severe black suit was hers. Some of the congregation even had flower-garlands looped around their necks, as if they were partying in Hawaii, rather than attending a funeral. And the coffin itself wasn't the usual mahogany or oak, but a psychedelic affair, painted in flamboyant colours, and looking as out-of-place in this sombre chapel as a hippie in a community of hooded, black-robed monks.

'Hi! I'm Tamsin,' the woman beside her whispered, flashing her a friendly smile.

Debby glanced at the tie-dyed dress, the profusion of beads and bangles, the flowers twisted through the long untidy hair. If Tamsin was the hippie, *she* was the hooded, black-robed monk.

'Here – you'll need one of these,' the woman mouthed, passing her an Order of Service.

Again, it was a shock. On the cover was an elderly man – not far off her father's age – but dressed in leathers and sitting astride a ferocious looking motorbike; his safety-helmet rivalling the coffin in its riot of crazy colours. BOBBIE DUGGAN was printed below the photograph, A CELEBRATION OF LIFE.

Although her father's name was also Robert, no one ever presumed to call him Bobbie. He had abhorred abbreviations and, despite her dislike of her own full and formal name, insisted on calling her Deborah. She was about to study the service-sheet, when a plump and tousled female in a gypsy blouse and full-length crimson skirt got up from the front pew and positioned herself behind the lectern on the altar. Some sort of hippie priest, maybe.

'His daughter,' Tamsin hissed. 'But I expect you know her, don't you?'

'Er, no.'

'Meg – she's fab! And she and Bobbie were always really close. His wife died young, you see, so he brought her up on his own.'

Surprised by the coincidence, she studied the woman with new interest. 'Fab' she might be, but also distinctly unconventional, at least in her appearance. Despite looking about sixtyish, her long, grey hair hung loose and straggly to her waist and on her feet were incongruous pink flip-flops.

'Welcome to you all!' she said, reaching out her arms in an expansive gesture, to include everybody present. 'I know Dad would be thrilled to see you here, at this, his final party. As you know, he loved any sort of celebration, so we're gathered here together to give him a rousing send-off.'

Debby was startled by the burst of applause; the congregation clapping and cheering, as if they were at a gig. Except 'congregation' was hardly the word, with its churchy connotations – these were party guests.

Once the noise subsided, Meg continued. 'We've chosen all his favourite songs and we're going to kick off with his namesake, Bob – Bob Dylan.'

As 'Hey, Mr Tambourine Man' boomed out on the sound-system, two girls in their late teens joined Meg by the altar; clad in pelmet-short skirts and each shaking a tambourine.

'His great-granddaughters,' Tamsin informed her in a whisper, 'Poppy and Isadora.'

Listening to the offbeat words – 'jingle-jangle mornings', 'magic swirlin' ships', 'dancin' spells', 'ragged clowns' – Debby couldn't help comparing the stern, black-bordered hymns that she and the Reverend Matthews had chosen for her father's funeral: 'Day of Wrath, O Day of Mourning'; 'Abide With Me'; 'Fast Sinks the Sun to Rest' – all themes of dust and ashes, darkness, gloom, decline. Admittedly, Dylan had his dark side, too, but she still found it near-incredible that those two sexy-looking girls should be leaping around only inches from the coffin, shaking not just their tambourines but their hips, their hair, their boobs.

'And now,' said Meg, returning to her seat as the girls give a final flounce and twirl, 'a tribute from Bobbie's best mate, Rex.'

A big, bluff man took her place at the lectern. Although eighty, at least, and completely, shiny bald, he was attired in drain-pipe jeans and a lurid purple T-shirt printed with BOBBIE DUGGAN'S FAN CLUB.

Waving an age-spotted hand towards the coffin, he addressed its occupant. 'Bobbie, old pal, I'm going to miss you terribly. I've no one to go to the pub with now, or share a vindaloo.'

Debby found herself gradually warming to this bizarre but upbeat service. Most funeral tributes focused on the virtues of the deceased, not their penchant for beer and curry.

'Bobbie was a one-off,' Rex declared, now turning to his audience. 'Everyone adored him, so I'm sure you're all as gutted as me to lose such a special guy. I'm proud to be his oldest friend. He and I go back more than seventy years. We met at primary school and he was a right little devil even then!'

Everybody laughed, including Debby. Who wanted all those tears and lamentations? As a child of twelve, she had found her mother's funeral unbearably oppressive, with its stress on loss and decay, and the gruesome spiel about people turning into dust or withering like dried-up grass. She had wept for days, imagining her lovely, pretty mother, with her rosy cheeks and curly hair, rotting into a black sludge on the compost heap.

'And when we were young and both out of work,' Rex continued, with a grin, 'we just said "What the hell?" and took ourselves off on his bike, in the hope of something turning up. And it always did, you know. Bobbie was a born survivor! He even survived his widowhood with amazing guts, determined to put his daughter first and—'

Debby found her thoughts returning to her own rather different experience and was roused only by a Jethro Tull song resounding through the chapel: 'Nothing is Easy' – a sentiment her father would most definitely endorse. For him, difficulty and hardship were basic facts of life. Yet the words she was actually hearing seemed to stress the total opposite: relax and take things easy; stop rushing, tearing, agonizing. The lyric was like a private message, directed to her personally, since she had *never* taken things easy; spent her entire life under pressure. And this last week especially had been stressful in the extreme.

As the last chords died away, another elderly man went up to the lectern, armed with a guitar. 'Hi, folks!' he grinned. 'I'm Ricky and this here is Bobbie's guitar. A few years ago, a good friend of his made him a new one, to his own specifications, so he gave me his old trusted Gibson. But what I want to talk about today is not his skill in music, or his sheer generosity, but the way he coped so brilliantly with being a lone dad. To take up Rex's theme, I know Meg would agree that he managed to be a mother to her, as well as a fantastic father....'

Debby barely heard what followed. All at once, she had plunged back into childhood – twelve again and bringing much-missed people back to life. All she had to do was close her eyes and her dead mother would appear; conjured up in such vivid, detailed pictures they were very nearly real. But now it was Bobbie she was resurrecting – Bobbie not as *Meg's* dad but her own. She shut her eyes and, instantly, everything transformed: no more silent solitude; no more need to creep around like a timid little mouse, for fear of disturbing his grief. Instead, the house was full of people – fun, friends, music, laughter, constant cheerful company. But, however many friends might come, he always put her first; spent patient hours teaching her to read, and swim, and how to play the guitar. Yes, she was playing his trusted Gibson and making a quite glorious din and he wasn't complaining about the racket, but praising her new skill. And now she was on his motorbike, riding pillion, as they roared off together to Glastonbury or Brighton or any place she fancied. She was no longer 'clumsy', 'greedy', 'silly', but the best little girl in the world.

Their house had changed completely. The dark green walls had vanished and it was painted from top to bottom in psychedelic colours. And there were flowers in vases everywhere, shedding pollen and petals on all the polished surfaces, but no one cared a fig. And she didn't have to keep her room as tidy as a nun's cell, but could leave her clothes in great, messy piles, and put up posters on the walls, and go to bed whenever she liked, instead of ridiculously early, and even miss whole days at school, if her Dad decided it was time for another motorcycle jaunt.

And then a few years frolicked on, and he was taking her out for a pint in the pub and on to the local tandoori, for a vindaloo and chips. And they were forever throwing impromptu parties, and redecorating the house in new crazy colour-schemes, and she could bring whole groups of friends home from university and play music, really loud, all night.

And now it was her graduation and he was so thrilled by her success he was applauding harder than anyone, and then ordering champagne when she landed her first job; drinking to her future in some trendy little restaurant – and, of course, telling her he loved her: again, again, again. And every birthday he was there, laying on some fantastic celebration; assuring her continually that she was the most important person in his world.

'Beloved', 'precious', 'special' – the words were so bewitching, she rolled them round her tongue, like sweets. But, all at once, she was blasted back to the present by an explosion of sound erupting in the chapel. Opening her eyes, she was utterly astounded to see party-poppers being let off all around her; their scarlet streamers flying everywhere. And the guests were blowing red tin-whistles, making a rumbustious din, whilst a tide of rainbow-hued balloons floated exuberantly up to the ceiling. And then she noticed the curtains slowly closing around the coffin, which meant they must have reached the committal. Normally, she loathed that moment, when the mourners stood silent and the vicar intoned appropriately sepulchral words. But here all was jubilant uproar, as more party-poppers exploded, more tin-whistles were blown, and a roistering swarm of kids skedaddled about the chapel, in pursuit of coloured streamers and balloons. She could hardly believe that any crematorium would allow such pandemonium. Certainly, things had changed dramatically since her mother's joyless funeral.

Suddenly, she gripped the side of the pew, struck not just by the startling sight but by an extraordinary revelation. Having spent her life blaming herself for her mother's death (so clumsy, greedy and idle a child *must* have been the cause), only now did it dawn on her, with a profound sense of consolation, that it had been nothing to do with her and her deficiencies. It was simply a matter of chance – a cruel twist of fate, for which no one was to blame. And, if her widowed dad had been different, she would have grown up to be more serene; not become a workaholic, terrified of marriage and too frightened to have children, in case some tragedy occurred and her offspring were as miserable as *she* had been in childhood.

How could she have reached middle age without perceiving such an obvious truth before? But at least she had grasped it now and the relief was so overpowering, she grabbed the tin-whistle Tamsin was holding out to her and blew it in raucous tribute. She must give Bobbie a rousing send-off, but, after that, another, more important task awaited and this incongruous elation must give place to due solemnity. While the revellers were swarming out of the chapel, to congregate in the courtyard just beyond, she turned the other way, slipped out through the main chapel doors and back into the waiting-room. The staff would need some time to clear the debris from the chapel; make it neat and tidy for the funeral to follow.

And *she* needed time, as well, to compose herself and banish the last traces of those disconcerting, but captivating, fantasies of being Bobbie's daughter. That little girl – safe, secure, protected, but also lively, rowdy, boisterous – was still cavorting in some region of her mind; troublingly at variance with the tense, temperate, adult businesswoman. In just the last half-hour, she seemed to have been storm-tossed by emotion, but now it was required of her to be calm and in control. Leaning back in her chair, she focused on the carpet; its drab grey-blue gradually replacing Bobbie's rainbow brilliance; its timid squiggles taming his exuberance; its very ordinariness slowly returning her to the task in hand.

'Ah!' said a deep, kindly voice, breaking into the silence, 'you must be Debby. I'm Gavin Matthews, the vicar. How good to meet you, my dear – although I feel I know you already after all our conversations on the phone.'

She rose to greet him, immediately reassured by his appearance: the immaculate white surplice, worn above a long black cassock; the well-polished shoes and freshly starched clerical collar; the neatly cut grey hair. He was male, mature and eminently presentable

– all the things her father would expect. And an obviously warm-hearted person, who could give her moral support.

Having ushered her outside, they stood together, waiting for the hearse. No one else had turned up, but that was how it should be. Her father had always valued privacy and seclusion, so it was only fitting that at this, his final stage, there were no villagers to tittle-tattle, or nosy neighbours to pry.

She heard the noise of wheels and bowed her head respectfully as the hearse drew up and the coffin was unloaded – a traditional model in darkest oak, with the expensive wreath she'd ordered positioned sombrely on top. No riotous, unreliable flowers to fling their petals over him or droop in disarray. And the funeral director was a model of decorum, in his sleek black morning-coat, pinstriped trousers and matching waistcoat, and even an elegant top hat and silver-topped black cane.

With a suitably grave expression, he supervised the bearers as they hoisted the coffin on their shoulders and began their solemn procession into the chapel. Deliberately, she walked alongside, her hand also on the coffin; needing to be part of this last rite. Indeed, if she had only possessed the strength, she would gladly have carried his full weight – without any bearers helping – to make some tiny recompense for the long disharmony between them. The fact that her father was so entirely different from a genial, easy-going type like Bobbie was a question of genes and temperament and therefore simply due to chance again. And, having lost the one great treasure of his life, was it any wonder that he had become distant and detached, and unable to be close to anybody else? At least, now he was beyond distress; released by death from death.

Once the coffin was placed on the catafalque, the vicar stood at the lectern; his neat, dark, slender figure a total contrast to Meg's tousled, bright voluptuousness. He began reciting the same words as at her mother's funeral, yet, strangely, they had changed their tenor: consoling and serene now, instead of cruel and harsh.

After the opening prayers and readings, he gave a brief address. There was no one but her to listen; no one but her to join in the responses, but her father would undoubtedly be gratified that all the due formalities were being so punctiliously observed. Indeed, when it came to the hymns, both she and the vicar sang with power and resonance, to compensate for the lack of other voices. And, once again she noticed that, instead of sounding wrathful and morose, they seemed solemn and majestic and thus appropriate.

'May our brother rest in peace,' the vicar concluded and, as he bowed towards the coffin, she realized, with a jolt of mingled solace and surprise, that guilt and grief, uncertainty and worry, had all disappeared entirely. Now there was only peace – peace soothing like a balm; peace unforeseen, unprecedented; peace restorative and rare – peace not simply for her dear departed father, but for her, as well – at last.